The Go.........Us Gifts:

An Anthology of African Short Stories

Sefi Atta

The Gods Who Send Us Gifts:

An Anthology of African Short Stories

Forewords
by
Wole Soyinka
&
Baroness Valerie Amos

Edited by Ivor Agyeman-Duah

ayebia

An Adinkra symbol
meaning *Ntesie matemasie*
A symbol of knowledge
and wisdom

Design Copyright © 2017 Ayebia Clarke Publishing Limited
Text © Editor Ivor Agyeman-Duah 2017 *The Gods Who Send Us Gifts:*
An Anthology of African Short Stories
All rights reserved

First published in the UK in 2017 by Ayebia Clarke Publishing Limited
7 Syringa Walk
Banbury
OX16 1FR
Oxfordshire
UK
www.ayebia.co.uk

ISBN 978-0-9928436-9-4

Distributed in North America by Casemate-IPM
www.casemateipm.com
Distributed in the UK and Europe by TURNAROUND Publisher Services
at www.turnaround-uk.com

British Library Cataloguing-in-Publication Data

Cover Design by Workhaus, Abingdon-on-Thames, UK
Cover photo image reproduced with kind permission from
Chimurenga Chronic, South Africa www.chimurenga.co.za
Typeset by Avocet Typeset, Somerton, Somerset, TA11 6RT, UK
Printed and bound by CPI Group (UK) Ltd, Croydon, CR0 4YY

Available from www.ayebia.co.uk or email info@ayebia.co.uk
Distributed in Africa, Europe, UK by TURNAROUND
at www.turnaround-uk.com
Distributed in Southern Africa by Book Promotions
a subsidiary of Jonathan Ball Publishers in South Africa.
For orders contact: order@jonathanball.co.za

Dedication

This book and the stories herein by contemporary African writers, is in memory of the participants – the departed and survivors of the 1962 Makerere Conference of African Literature which took place in Uganda fifty-five years ago. History remembers it as an impactful gathering of progressives. This volume comes as a collective gratitude to the elders of modern African Literature by generations after.

Contents

Contents

About the Book

This anthology of African short stories by some of the continent's prominent writers is dedicated to the immediate post-colonial African literary forebears. A good number of that earlier generation attended the Makerere Conference of African Literature in Uganda in 1962 where they behaved as though they were ordained interpreters of Africa to the rest of the world. Those who gathered included poets, novelists, playwrights, literary critics, historians and journalists: Chinua Achebe, Wole Soyinka, Christopher Okigbo, JP Clark, Kofi Awoonor, Frances Ademola, Cameron Duodu and others from West Africa as well as the following writers from South Africa: Dennis Brutus, Lewis Nkosi, Ezekiel Mphahlele, Bloke Modisane and African American writers including Langston Hughes and the Africanist Indian Ugandan, Rajat Neogy.

Fifty-five years on, many of them including Awoonor have joined the ancestors, as he wrote in the immortality of his poetic prologue, "Those Gone Ahead." There are a few octogenarian survivors. The editor of this anthology who is also a literary historian, has brought together "some of our most eloquent and able voices" as they, through their individual stories from across the continent, pay their respects to those before them. The efforts of the past inspired confidence in a new generation of Africans capable of telling their own stories whether in English, French, Portuguese, Twi, Gikuyu, Swahili, Shona, Yoruba or Igbo.

These are multi-thematic stories of love and humanity whether set in Ghana about a happy relationship between a Ghanaian woman and a Rwandan future economist she met in Missouri, or in Nigeria – of the consequence of a Catholic father's paedophile love, or in Senegal – of an issue of complex matricide in an ancient city, by one of its leading writers, Boubacar Boris Diop, or in the Democratic Republic of Congo – of a rape story. Other stories include a mother-daughter relationship in Botswana, Monica Arac de Nyeko's "Grasshopper Redness" in Uganda, Zukiswa Wanner's historical piece of fiction in the context of the second Anglo-Boer War in South Africa – "Upon This Handful of Soil" as well as a magical realism story set in the Sensela village in Zambia.

Finally, it is fitting that this anthology is published by Ayebia Clarke Publishing Limited, an Anglo-Ghanaian publishing specialist, a publishing imprint of Nana Ayebia Clarke MBE and her British husband David. Nana Ayebia is a Ghanaian-born Publisher based in Oxfordshire and a former Editor and the first African woman Editor of the Heinemann African Writers Series at Oxford. Nana Ayebia has been my Publisher since 2006 when I first published President Kufuor's biography *Between Faith and History: A Biography of JA Kufuor* in hardback and we have continued to collaborate on publishing African-centred books to international audiences.

About the Editor

Ivor Agyeman-Duah, Director of the Centre for Intellectual Renewal in Ghana, was a Special Advisor from 2009 to 2014 to President John Kufuor of Ghana, on international development cooperation including work with the World Food Programme in Kenya and Ethiopia and also with the Geneva-based Interpeace. He had previously worked in the diplomatic service as Head of Public Affairs at Ghana's Embassy in Washington DC and later as Culture and Communication Advisor at the Ghana High Commission in London. He is co-author of two appraisal and advocacy anthologies, *Assessing George W. Bush's Africa Policy* (2009) and *Assessing Barack Obama's Africa Policy* (2014) for the Washington DC-based African Studies and Research Forum. He is also editor and co-author of *Pilgrims of the Night*: *Development Challenges and Opportunities in Africa* (2010), *Africa*: *A Miner's Canary Into the Twenty-First Century – Essays on Economic Governance* (2013) and *An Economic History of Ghana* (2007).

He currently serves as Development Policy Advisor to The Lumina Foundation in Lagos, which awards *The Wole Soyinka Prize for Literature in Africa* and was the 2014–15 Chair of the Literature Jury of the Millennium Excellence Foundation. Agyeman-Duah was part of the production team for the BBC and PBS – *Into Africa* and *Wonders of the African World* presented by Henry Louis Gates, Jnr. He wrote and produced the acclaimed television documentary, *Yaa Asantewaa*: *The Heroism of an African Queen* and its sequel, *The Return of a King to Seychelles*. He co-edited, with Peggy Appiah and Kwame Anthony Appiah, *Bu Me Be: Proverbs of the Akans* (2007);

with Ogochukwu Promise, *Essays in Honour of Wole Soyinka at 80* (2014) and edited the well-received, *All the Good Things Around Us: An Anthology of African Short Stories* (2016). In addition, he co-edited *May Their Shadows Never Shrink: Wole Soyinka and the Oxford Professorship of Poetry* (2016) with Lucy Newlyn, Professor Emeritus of Oxford. Agyeman-Duah has received fifteen awards, fellowships and grants from around the world including: Distinguished Friend of Oxford Award from the University of Oxford, Member of the Order of the Volta, Republic of Ghana, Fellow of the Phi Beta Delta International Society of the College of Arts and Letters, California State University, Pomona, US State Department International Visitor, the Commonwealth's Thomson Foundation Award, among others.

Agyeman-Duah has held fellowships at the WEB Du Bois Institute for African and African American Research at Harvard University and been a Hilary and Trinity resident scholar at Exeter College, Oxford. From 2014–2015 he was a research associate at the African Studies Centre, Oxford. He holds graduate degrees from the London School of Economics and Political Science, the School of Oriental and African Studies, London and the University of Wales.

Foreword I

I

The Editor of this anthology's request for me to reminisce on the 1962 Makerere Conference on African Literature in the form of a Foreword, takes me back to 1998 when we re-visited Makerere.

So there we were again, an all-Nigerian delegation, thirty-five years after the conference of African writers that first brought me to Uganda. We had serious business, but I had an agenda of my own, consisting of two parts. One was to track down the birthplace of *Transition*. I did not intend to put a plaque on the wall, but I was, after all, visiting Uganda for the first time in some thirty eventful years of Africa's endless transitions: post-Idi Amin; post-Julius Nyerere's *Ujaama*; post-apartheid; post-mortem Christopher Okigbo, who fell in Biafra; post-mortem Robert Serumaga, who "disappeared" in Moi's Kenya; but, most poignantly; post-modern Rajat Neogy, who gave us Africa's first forum of intellectual and artistic eclecticism. He was an inescapable presence at the writers' conference. So there was nostalgia, yes: a remembrance of friends gone, things done, battles lost and won.

My second project was the very antithesis of nostalgia. When we set out from Nigeria in 1962, we had been on an excursion of creative buoyancy and high optimism. Now we were returning in a season of despondency, of which the most gruesome manifestation was the massacre in Rwanda in 1994. I needed to visit Rwanda to confront the realization of my direst predictions. Had I not cautioned that the fashionable incantation of a humanistic African past might prove a romantic illusion in *A Dance of the Forests*, the play I composed for Nigeria's independence and read at the writers' conference in 1962?

Perhaps it was fitting, then, that our mission this time was purely political: to press African governments in the Commonwealth Ministerial Action Group for sanctions against Sani Abacha's Nigeria (The Politician of 1998 confronts the artist of 1962?). Our earlier incursion into Kampala had focused almost entirely on culture: we went to join a convocation of writers and intellectuals from every corner of the continent. In 1962, we were a motley group: poet, novelist, dramatist, critic, scholar, painter, broadcaster, producer and architect. We were on a safari on African soil: the signs along the way all showed the same slogan: Destination, Kampala! We were young, self-assured, and pregnant with projects. We had just launched the *Mbari Writers and Artists Club* in Ibadan; an allied group was forming in the city of Kampala. Above all, we were consciously crashing the colonial boundaries of nation and language. What were other writers up to? Why were the Francophone writers so *French?* What was this Negritude? Not that politics was completely absent: Was Ghana heading for dictatorship? Would apartheid crumble within our lifetime? Did the Portuguese colonials really want their independence? Wars of Liberation were woefully ill-reported within our Anglophone colonial laager!

In 1962, we were invulnerable, too: so confident in our community that we took on a group of Congolese soldiers as we changed planes in Leopoldville. Frances Ademola, the editor of *Reflections* – the first anthology of post-colonial Nigerian writing, was passing through Customs when a Congolese soldier barked an order at her, in French, of course, but French so thickly accented that no one could possibly understand him. When she continued on her way, the soldier pushed her, roughly. What followed was a minor fracas, but look, *you don't just shove a member of the Nigerian delegation, and a woman at that!*

We had known, then, that the Congo was tense: Katanga Province was exploding, and the killing of Patrice Lumumba had filled the continent with foreboding. But this was no excuse.

The Congolese also had a mean reputation; perhaps that fuelled our indignation. *So, you think you're tough? Well, let us tell you, we are Nigerians!* Christopher Okigbo, JP Clark, and I got physical... But it is all very confused from this distance. Were we briefly detained? Threatened with being shot? So many scenes of violence later, I cannot recall the untidy details. Good counsel intervened and we left unscathed, scowling at the miscreant as he silently cursed, most likely in French. We made sure that we did not pass through Leopoldville on our return journey.

Our host had been Makerere College (University); the Congress for Cultural Freedom was the main sponsor of the conference. Langston Hughes was there, lecturing on the history of Negro poetry. Ulli Beier, Dennis Duerden, Robert Cook and a handful of others formed the expatriate contingent. We had heard of another semi-expatriate, an Indian called Rajat Neogy. We would soon make his acquaintance in *Transition's* makeshift editorial office – the veranda of his residence – snipping away at the gallery and laying dummies. The conference was fractious and intoxicating: this was the meeting where Christopher enraged the school of commitment by declaring, "I only write my poetry for other poets." I was not innocent in the commotion: it was here that I first observed, apropos Negritude, that the tiger does not proclaim its "tigritude"...

Night-time was clubbing time; it relieved the heat of the daytime debates, where, despite our best intentions, lines were drawn between Francophone and Anglophone, between those who required that African Literature be written in African languages and the rest of us. In 1962, Kampala rivalled Lagos for its nightlife; there were live bands and lively music. *Shall we show these people how to dance?* We did! Christopher Okigbo insisted on bringing a bargirl back to our hotel, where he installed her Muse of the Makerere Conference. She earned her night's fee – it was all negotiated – but the entire episode was quite chaste. Her task was to look elegant and play hostess (obviously bewildered, but delighted, too) to a bunch of noisy writers who stayed up all night, drinking and eating peppered chicken and *kabobos*, occasionally declaiming poems, all the while throwing something called "Negritude" back and forth.

Did she secretly regard us as an idle bunch of idiots? She floated around in someone's *dansiki* like a wrath while Christopher played chaperon, ensuring that no one got fresh with her. Young, artistic, and romantic: what a great time it was for the aspiring writer!

By day, we had been unpleasantly struck by the social segregation of Kampala. Most of the menial jobs seemed to be held by Ugandans, while the businesses and the lushest residences – neatly landscaped on verdant hillsides – belonged to the Asians. But it was also the first time we had seen Asians driving taxis in an African country. It was one thing to know that Asians had settled quite promiscuously in East Africa, but quite another to see them occupy ever lower-skilled positions. When we returned thirty-five years later, we found the Asians still very much in evidence, but Idi Amin's brutal economic "ethnic cleansing" had clearly left some unfilled gaps. And the Ugandan economic landscapes had changed immeasurably.

II

For that matter, nothing has remained the same in East Africa. Yet we could not escape the feeling of *plusçachange...* It was in 1998, and Kampala was calm, but newspapers and television carried daily news of rebel activity in the provinces... school children abducted, some government official held hostage, casualties here and there. But it was Uganda's neighbours that generated the most excitement as well as the greatest sense of tension among those who followed the news. Some kind of realignment was taking place; the regional powers were moving towards an alliance where political decisions, taken in consultation, would lead to collective action. Dissatisfaction was mounting over the conduct of two troublesome states: Congo and Sudan. Something was in the air.

Our delegation had no business in either place, but our Ugandan conversations inevitably returned to these countries, especially the Democratic Republic of the Congo. Laurent-Desire Kabila, Mobutu's successor was generally felt to be a grave disappointment; the only question was what to do about him. We arrived just after Etienne Tshisekedi had been publicly humiliated. Kabila loaded him onto a small plane with a hoe and seeds and dropped him off in his village with a message: forget politics and stick to farming. It all sounded so much like Idi Amin before the terror. It was also considered poor recompense for Tshisekedi, who had solidly resisted the dictatorship of Mobutu and who had a considerable following of his own. Kabila's policy – not merely to marginalize, but to completely alienate the political opposition – had clearly run rampant. That was all. Taking their cue from Kabila, the army had turned themselves into "a commission on dress." Trousers on women or hemlines considered immodestly short earned public humiliation at the hands of soldiers, physical assault, arbitrary fines, or imprisonment.

Kabilia had fallen foul of his former allies in even more crucial ways. It was almost as if he had set out to offend them. Perhaps he felt a need to demonstrate that he was his own master, despite the heavy helping hand that Rwanda, Uganda, and others had lent in his military coup. Our meeting with the Ugandans coincided with a meeting of regional Heads of State, but Kabila was conspicuously absent; he had gone to Switzerland. Generously, I suggested that he might have received news of sudden movements of Mobutu's billions between vaults in Swiss banks: perhaps he had dashed over to stake Congo's claims. Alas, the reason for Kabila's absence turned out to be the need for a brief vacation, or so he announced via telegraph. Mobutu, of course, spent many of his last depredatory years in Switzerland; he claimed the air was good for his system. *Plusçachange*... Whatever is it that gets into the heads of African leaders that they think they must out posture the last vainglorious villain in power? In Uganda, Che Guevara is now thought to have been most perceptive in his dismissive summation of Kabila, briefly his insurrectionary comrade in Congo-Zaire in the 1960s: "Nothing leads me to believe that Kabila is the man of the hour."

III

I wanted to see *Transition's* first home again, but I had little to go on: we had undertaken our mission in such haste that I had not had a chance to contact anyone for the address. Nonetheless, finding an hour or two between appointments, I took a taxi and plunged into Kampala's residential areas. Some hours later, I was forced to accept the truth: the place had changed so much that I stood no chance of finding Rajat's old house on my own. I decided I would do the sensible thing. I would visit Makerere the following day and seek out a knowledgeable guide.

The next morning, however, I learned that I had just enough time to see Rwanda before our next appointment in Tanzania. I would have to leave immediately, though, since the only flight to Kigali that day was about to take off. Nostalgia lost out to nightmare, and I headed off to keep tryst with the dreaded moment, the proving ground of faith.

The "land of a thousand hills" was still as breathtakingly beautiful as I remembered it, so pastoral and idyllic that it did not take long to recall that Rwanda was the land that gave birth to H. Rider Haggard's *King Solomon's Mines* and the legend of Prester John. I could not forget, however, that the same land – the same phrase – had been put to such diabolical use by the party of genocide, whose broadcasts on the "Radio des Milles Collines" had incited the Hutus to kill. On the way from the airport, my guide pointed out the National Assembly building, holed by shells, where the Hutus militia had put up their last desperate stand. When we had stopped in this same town in 1962, we had heard stories of mutual slaughter between Tutsis and Hutus, but they were muted, seemingly localized. There was nothing then, to approach the horror that numbed the world later, when some Hutu leaders dreamed up their "final solution" and brought it, methodically, to execution. That term – "final solution" – was apparently invoked by some of the intellectuals who organised the unspeakable crime; the pattern of command and obedience was modelled on the Nazi precedent. Only the tools and the methods were cruder.

Could any of us, in the sixties have suspected the possibility of a massacre on this scale? Not even the brutality of the killing in Katanga in 1961 approached this abandonment of humanity. Not even the rabid slaughter in Liberia, home of the poet Lenrie Peters, or the random killing in Sierra Leone of that urbane critic, Eldred Jones, had prepared us for this; not the genocide in Nigeria that led to secession of Biafra and the war in which Christopher Okigbo lost his life; not the agonies of Robert Serumaga's and Okot p' Bitek's Uganda. These writers were the representative voices that dominated the 1962 Kampala conference: their humanism defined for us the new Africa. Where was that Africa now? How does a nation like Rwanda overcome its history?

We visited slaughter spots; spoke to survivors and liberation fighters. The survivors included Hutus who had been accused of being Tutsi sympathizers. Some had lost entire families; in some cases they had been treated with greater vindictiveness than the Tutsis – though the Tutsis, of course, bore the full brunt of the atrocities.

We visited one of the killing grounds: a field of wooden crosses, lacking the luxury of headstones. There, at least, the bodies were interred. We proceeded to a memorial museum at Ntarama, an hour's ride on a potholed laterite road from Kigali. It had been conceived as part of an optimistically named "Peace Park" honouring Nelson Mandela. The rough shelves contained only five thousand skulls; I say "only" because there was a larger museum that we could not visit for lack of time, that housed fifty thousand remains of Rwandan humanity. Bulldozers had been commandeered to heap earth over the corpses. After liberation, the bulldozers came back to disinter them. Human hands cleaned the skeletons, pieced them together, and made a record of them. In Mandela's park, a church where victims had holed up seeking sanctuary was preserved. They had been slaughtered in the church, and that is where the bodies lie. As skin and flesh fall away, it is only blood-caked clothing that remains to shroud the bones. Very few skulls bore bullet holes; most of these people were slashed to death with pangas. Embedded in the hilt in one child's skull was a crude knife.

There was, apparently, a going rate for the privilege of being killed swiftly by a bullet. For thousands who could not afford it, or who were not given the chance, it was a painful, cruel death: death limb-by-limb, disembowelment. Sometimes the tendons were severed first, to ensure that the victim stayed in place as his or her torturers took time off to attend to others, drawing out the tempo in the dance of death.

There are landmarks and physical scars for nearly every story in Rwanda, including stories of heroism and self-sacrifice. I understood the UN Secretary-General who could only convey what he had witnessed in the words, "I know now that there is a God, because I have seen the face of the Devil." In 1962, we believed in goodness, because we, too, had seen the face of evil. But in 1962, evil wore the face of the Belgians (who share the blame for the Rwandan massacre of 1994); it wore the face of the Portuguese; the British settler, and the Boer. We were the good, the repressed, the cubs of a continent's transition, waiting to spring into creative vistas of a limitless future.

The flight schedule obliged us to return to Uganda for the night, and then continue on to Tanzania the following day. I chose to remain in the airport town of Entebbe declining the thirty-minute drive to Kampala. There was only one reason to go back to the city, but I found that I no longer cared, particularly, to look for the building where *Transition* was born.

Wole Soyinka
Abeokuta
Nigeria

Foreword II

I was born in a country, which was a British colony. In grappling with issues of identity and place as I grew up, my understanding was forged through looking at the history of slavery and Britain's relationship to its former colonies, but most crucially, through my interest in the struggle for independence and the discovery of the post-colonial literature of the countries of the Caribbean and Africa. The writing of Chinua Achebe, Wole Soyinka and others helped me to connect some dots but it also helped me to explore – push the boundaries of my understanding.

This anthology marks the 55th anniversary of the 1962 historic Makerere Conference of African Literature in Uganda – an event which brought together post-independence writers, many of whom would play major roles in defining Africa's literary history. And to mark that significant milestone with an anthology of the next generation of African writers from seventeen countries – Anglophone and Francophone and from countries often absent in such celebrations such as: Botswana, Burundi, Rwanda, Senegal, the Democratic Republic of Congo and Zambia, is worthy of history.

Ivor Agyeman-Duah, a SOAS alumnus and currently a Centenary Research Associate, has brought this collection together. Agyeman-Duah's previous work, *All the Good Things Around Us: An Anthology of African Short Stories*, (Ayebia, UK: 2016) was the source of an international conference on African literature at SOAS: *One Continent Many Stories: Creativity and African Literature*.

SOAS has a long history and relationship with the African

continent. Since the admittance of our first students in 1917, Swahili and Bantu languages have been taught at the School. By the mid-1930s the School offered courses in Hausa, Yoruba, Zulu, Twi and Xhosa. And in 1938, SOAS added 'Africa' to its name in recognition of its teaching and research in African languages. It was through the study of languages that it became a place where it was understood and appreciated that connectivity and multi-disciplinarity added weight and depth to scholarship but also that culture, politics and society had to be understood from the perspective of the regions and peoples in which the School specialises.

It was the place where some of the brightest minds from Africa met. It provided a space for students to discuss and debate the future of their countries. As Professor Wole Soyinka recalled: "Each time I come to SOAS or one of the watering holes around Goodge Street where the West African Students' Union met, I think, "This is where we conspired, talked and urged each other to go back and change Africa. We felt we were born to transform the African continent – we had a focus, something to bond us together in a progressive and radical way."

The School is also the custodian of the history of some of the great African writers. Our Heinemann African Writers Series collection in the Library is home to an extraordinary collection of more than 70 manuscripts, typescripts with authorial corrections. These include the pre-publication typescripts of Ngũgũ wa Thiong'o's *Weep Not, Child*, Chinua Achebe's *Beware Soul Brother* as well as some of Nelson Mandela's speeches and articles. These are available for scholars, students, the public – and importantly future generations – to explore.

We have celebrated and hosted many of the great African writers. In 2008, the School had the honour of hosting Chinua Achebe. He spoke at a celebratory event on his work *'Things Fall Apart* at 50' and was joined by Chimamanda Ngozi Adichie. Princeton University Professor Chika Okeke-Agulu described the event as "one of those rare events you feel infinitely grateful to have witnessed, especially if African literature means anything to you."

A very successful literary agent told me recently that the most exciting and interesting writing in the world at the moment is from the African Continent. At SOAS, three students have launched Afrikult, an online platform that discusses, explores and celebrates African literatures. The aim of the platform is to address the gap between the growing interest in African literature and the lack of knowledge of its richness and diversity. It is about opening up minds, sharing different perspectives.

I am delighted that we continue to be the place which brings together some of the best new talent. In 2016 for instance, the Caine Prize shortlisted authors came together here to discuss the future of African writing. They were Abdul Adan (*The Lifebloom Gift* from *The Gonjon Pin and Other Stories*), Lesley Nneka Arimah (*What it Means When a Man Falls From the Sky*), Tope Folarin (*Genesis'* from *Callaloo*), Bongani Kona (*At Your Requiem'* from *Incredible Journey: Stories That Move You*) and Lidudumalingani (*Memories We Lost'* from *Incredible Journey: Stories That Move You*).

This latest and wonderful anthology edited by Agyeman-Duah is a fitting tribute to those who attended the 1962 conference and over the years inspired all of us to read and write. I hope you enjoy it.

Baroness Valerie Amos
Director of the School of Oriental and African Studies
London

Foreword III

The literary arts have always had a powerful influence among people in search of freedom and in campaigns for social and political rights – in fact fundamental rights. Rome had its literary culture of the past as did Greece and Europe and civilizations thereafter.

In particular, the novel and poetry were popular tools for Africa's de-colonization in the 1960s as the writers of the time had strong opinions on colonialism's effects as they craved bigger space for their craft.

Literature's role in the ending of Apartheid was partly fuelled not only by writers from within but those from without with unmuted voices and affordability of freedom.

The Nigerian Nobel Laureate Professor Wole Soyinka dedicated his Nobel Prize speech to Nelson Mandela still in prison in 1986. Other poets and playwrights paid similar respects to the collective imprisonment including in particular to: Oliver Tambo, Walter Sisulu, Govan Mbeki and other freedom fighters. We witnessed before this the role of 'resistance literature' in the Frontline States as Rhodesia transited to Zimbabwe. The inspiration that writers from especially East and West Africa gave southern Africa to complete the continent's de-colonization under brutal oppression is an important part of imperial history.

When Mandela out of prison and on reflections of politics and literature said, reading Chinua Achebe's *Things Fall Apart* in prison was like the opening of its doors, it was an expression of how novels became non-violent weapons for the hopes of liberation.

But that was what that generation of writers, some of the

continent's best in their budding form and youthful interest sought to do in Makerere: be people of influence. They interpreted lack of freedom in South Africa as against their own space.

Ivor Agyeman-Duah's editorship of *The Gods Who Send Us Gifts: An Anthology of African Short Stories* published by Ayebia is in remembrance of their efforts and deeds: Chinua Achebe, Wole Soyinka, Christopher Okigbo, JP Clark, Kofi Awoonor, the only woman who it is said was among that gathering, Frances Ademola, Ngũgũ wa Thiong'o and of course the exiled South African participants: Dennis Brutus, Lewis Nkosi, Ezeikel Mphahlele and Bloke Modisane.

The contributors to this very important anthology are most representative of the continent including two generations of South Africa's writers: Njabulo S Ndebele and Zukiswa Wanner. Now a free nation and people in the third decade of being themselves, South African writers can reflect on both the past and the challenges of the present.

As this anthology's multiple themes reflects, they are a basis for questioning cultural values that impede progress and there is the need as well for preservation of literary history and the efforts of the elders.

South Africa's relatively better economy should put her at the forefront of this.

It is one reason among others that the University of Johannesburg, is working with the editor of this anthology, Agyeman-Duah towards the hosting of the Wole Soyinka Foundation at the University.

For as we write on the current, we preserve as well that which is behind us; the future literary direction is also about the receded as it is about what is at hand.

Pinkie Mekgwe
Executive Director of Internationalisation
University of Johannesburg
South Africa
May 2017

Prologue

THOSE GONE AHEAD
I dreamt again this recurrent dream
of my father
taller ever than he has ever been
in the dream
I travelled on the seventh night
To Awlime, the land of spirits
to visit my people,
those I know and those who know me

On a mat in a corner
under a shady Gbaflo tree
lay my sister Comfort

A bit leaner, her beautiful
smile, frozen by death
as radiant as ever

Oh, how I recall
her capacity to turn
an insipid rabbit
into a festival of delight
the lowly partridge seared
in the oils and onions
of the field
her generosity of spirit
stamped upon her willingness to give
of herself
large and relentless,
kindness was her middle name

When the night fell on her
her startled eyes
of inquiry, set upon me
and I, helpless as the leaf
in the storm
could not save her
nor give answers
to her terrible questions

I believe a love
died here some years ago.
Across a bay I can
hear the distant music
haunting, sweet remembrance
of good happy days
of innocence hung in a bar
at Osu;
of the girl who fainted in my room
out of sheer joy

There is surely a living time
when the recollection of death
slightly shudders
especially when I remember the burial ground
where the house now stands
among mimosa and nim.
the second gnarled
the first tender
as the first day
the second the companion
of death and dying
sinewy, arrogant, persistent

Truth, long my friend
does not deny
and ah, what matters

the despair, the disaffection
of this engagement
when liars, bums
ambitious mountebanks
and certified crooks
short on memory
and basic decency holds sway.

They say misery it is
who acquaints man
with strange bedfellows.
In my case it is not misery.
When I die, I believe
the sun will rise
the morning after,
radiant;
it could be wet
in the afternoon
a cool breeze
meandering through the tree
regular;
what will they be saying
when I am gone:
quite a bit;
that I was a son of a bitch
arrogant, intolerant

But I shall go
perhaps to seek the lost rest
roam the wide vistas
of my afterlife.
savour the welcomed
boredom of eternity
where they say the skies
are pure blue,
and rivers never run dry
and the day lingers on

and on and on
and no one hungers
after food or righteous

Will I see loved ones
gone ahead
relatives and kinsmen?
I expect the boatman
will carry me over
without a fee, my companion and minder
on the road to the place of rest.

Kofi Awoonor

Introduction

African Literature has survived the vicissitudes of the continent's development challenges. Its leadership in poetry, drama and the novel have been an armoury for its cultural frontier. A united purpose of this was from the political fashion of the 1960s Pan Africanism. The writers lived anywhere on the continent that they fancied and practised their craft: Makerere, Kampala, Nairobi, Lagos, Accra and elsewhere. Some even made their families away from their birth homes and gave their children names from their adopted countries.

Sovereignty of nations and lack of limitation of criticism of African political leaders was equally fashionable. In East Africa, many made Makerere and the University (because they were also teachers and intellectuals) their home. President Idi Amin in Uganda, self-decorated Emperor Bokassa in the Central Africa Republic, Siad Barre in Somalia and later, Mengistu Haile Mariam in Ethiopia suffered vitriolic commentaries from their pens. Even the sometimes-visionary ethos of Kwame Nkrumah in Ghana was not spared in the ensuing ideological rift of the time as to whether he was a Leninist.

Yet, they were young writers in their mid twenties and early thirties when in 1962 many of them gathered in Makerere from the corners of the continent in what became known in history as the 1962 Conference of African Writers of English Expression. That conference may have united their purpose and increased the spirit of their creativity and resistance to what they perceived as the coming dictatorship of the post-colonial leaders.

That congregation which included expatriates like the British literary scholar, Gerald Moore and the German Jewish editor, writer and scholar, Ulli Beier (their co-editorship of *The Penguin Book of Modern African Poetry* was published a year later) was a major pioneering work. The other collaborations between European Africanists and that generation of Africans in Literature and the Humanities were landmarks.

From West Africa in 1962 to Makerere were: Christopher Okigbo who would perish in the course of the Biafran War, JP Clark, Chinua Achebe, Wole Soyinka, Cameron Duodu, Segun Olusola and others and from South Africa, its exiled writers: Ezekiel Mphahlele, Lewis Nkosi, Bloke Modisane and Dennis Brutus.

Lewis Nkosi as a literary critic would later write of the conference that the writers were "mostly young, impatient and sardonic, talking endlessly about the problems of creation and looking, while doing so, as though they were amazed that fate had entrusted them with the task of interpreting a continent to the world."

A budding Kenyan writer at the time and a Makerere student participant Ngũgĩ wa Thiong'o, remembers it this way: "the writers sensibilities were shaped by their experience of colonialism, apartheid and anti-colonial nationalism… we were also united by a vision of the possibilities of a different future for Africa."

That defining moment is fifty-five years old this year (2017) and its memorial is the gift of this anthology, which contemporary African writers or ones working have created to remember.

There are many proverbs in Africa that express the deeds of the forebears. One among the Asantes says:

Osaman pa na yeto no badin
[It's a great-departed spirit after whom we name a child.]

We tend to take the writers of English Language Expression in Africa with Britain for granted. Many of those who met in Makerere and from Anglophone Africa assumed so. But we also forget that that generation explored and expanded the frontiers to the Americas especially in the poetry of Kofi Awoonor in *Before the*

Journey (1970) and most famously, JP Clark's *America, Their America* (1964).

America was the idyllic new world in the popular imagination while growing up and then, *America, Their America* had this angry diatribe and a literary nemesis which doused a sense of the nation's power. Some in later generations fell into a dilemma of cultural values and in JP Clark's shadows: *Paradise Regained*? A country of multitude pilgrims?

First published two years after the Makerere Conference and over half a centenary old, it finds America a unipolar power but a vapour of its heavenly belief. Clark's boldness of a critique was in post-McCarthyism; a period of phantom witch-hunt and curses on "destructive" ideologies; and between the tiger's teeth of the Cold War.

Ironically, some of the major African writers of today live there – beyond the enclave of the great metropolis that Britain became for them. They are accountants, university professors, development specialists and diplomats and either as citizens, dual citizens or have the right of abode – a wider spectrum perhaps from those before them. Migration did not just occur. In fact some of the major Makerere participants that included Chinua Achebe, Wole Soyinka, Ngũgũ wa Thiong'o and Nuruddin Farah, had to go into exile from the 1980s because of political dislocations or for economic reasons

Generations of writers since Makerere have had their challenges in the productive processes – from writing to publishing and markets. Fifty-five years have changed much. South African writers in their thirties may be respectful of the contribution that Lewis Nkosi or Ezekiel Mphahlele made towards resistance literature under apartheid. They may not see the African National Congress anymore as Nelson Mandela's sacred cow. Economic constraints of widening inequalities and gender discrimination have created a common front for women – black and white and against a rapacious culture of political corruption. Ezekiel Mphahlele's writings on poverty in Soweto or Alan Paton's *Cry The Beloved Country* would be read with more mitigated emotions now than when they were used as weapons against apartheid.

That is how the world is supposed to be: you live and confront the good and challenges of the present but show gratitude to the deeds of the past.

In response to an email I sent to the Ugandan writer, Monica Arac de Nyeko, currently living and working in Jordan, she wrote, "The gods who send us stories, choose their own time." In other words, good stories are not just written but thought through with perhaps an unseen spirit or guarding mind like the muses of poetic exercise: power of meditation in characters as in situations or plots all coming together brilliantly.

I was at work on an earlier anthology, *All the Good Things Around Us* when de Nyeko's response came with an earlier written story for inclusion and not an anticipated new one. Obviously, the gods had not visited and chosen their time.

Her apt response fascinated me and fitted into my own conception of fictional anthology – of preference to multiple themes and free space to a common theme for rotation. The localities of the gods are as different as their numerous gifts of stories. That is why our muses are not the same.

Without prejudice to what these memorial stories are, whether you enjoy the ones from the East and Central – Uganda, Rwanda, the Congo, or from the West – Ghana, Nigeria, including the one set in Senegal or others from the South – Zambia, Botswana and South Africa echoing the cultures they are created from; they are all meant to be enjoyed. These stories are gifts in memory of those before this generation and to the blessed names of the same ancient gods who visited them with stories as they do to us now.

Osaman pa na yeto no ba din.

Ivor Agyeman-Duah
Kigali
Rwanda
March 2017

ONE

Gravisearch

Ama Ata Aidoo

It started a long time ago one early evening. As usual, I didn't go straight home after school, but stayed out for what my mother always considered "a very long time." I entered the courtyard from the back entrance, hoping to sneak into the bathhouse first before working my way very carefully in. I could then avoid getting seen, and if seen, give my normal excuse. That I'd been peeing. In retrospect, that was the dumbest, because, how did I expect anyone to believe me, especially a grown-up; that between when I should have returned from school and when I emerged from the bathhouse, I could've spent more than one hour just peeing?

Ma was back from the farm and already sitting and sorting out the fresh produce she'd brought, but also waiting for me and very alert. I came from behind her and saw an especially beautiful half-ripe pawpaw; skin speckled with green, gold and a hint of purple. I smacked my lips.

"What's the story today?" Ma asked rather calmly as if she was not really interested in my answer, while I busily screamed.

"Ma...Ma...Ma!"

"Calm down," my mother said. "What is it?"

"It's this pawpaw," I'd already picked it up, "can I have it?"

"Yes," Ma replied easily, "and you need not shout for it?"

She was wrong. I wanted to, not only shout for it, but jump and dance too. I picked the pawpaw up. It not only felt smooth and cool that warm early evening, it was gorgeous. Plus, I knew that peeled, the fruit would taste the way I liked it: farm fresh, ripe but only enough to still have some crunch in it. On the other hand, my mother preferred it properly ripe so that she would make her favourite snack with it.

For the next few minutes, I completely ignored my mother's plea that I help her to organize the produce. Rather, I contemplated the fruit and why my mother had parted with it so easily.

"Ma," I began again after a few more minutes.

"Aha?"

"Why is it called *borofer?*"

I could see and hear whatever she was holding fall out of her hand back into the large *apampa*.

She lifted a startled face to mine. "What kind of a question is that?"

"O I just wanted to know why we call this fruit *boro-fer*."

"Why do you want to know?"

"Because, I have noticed that the names of some other foods and even birds also begin with *boro*, while the names of most other foods and birds are just names..."

"You know what?" my mother asked softly, with something like a combination of alarm and irritation, "I don't know." Then after a slight pause, "why don't you find that out from your teacher when you go to school tomorrow? Or even find time to go and ask your grandmother?"

So I got up immediately and ran across the village main street to Nana, and while still standing and panting, asked her why the name of some foods and birds and other things begin with "boro" but the names of most other foods and birds and things are just names.

"Sit down," she ordered. I sat. Then she began, "When the white men came, our ancestors called them *aborofo*. Soon, they began to add the *boro* to anything they thought was from overseas.

"Nana, is that why we call pawpaw *boro-fer?*"

"O yes, hm... Because *fer* is pumpkin and pawpaw is a sweet version of pumpkin!"

"...and a dove is an *aboronoma*, the bird that came from overseas?"

"Yes." My grandmother was looking at me with a mixture of puzzlement and appreciation.

"But wild doves are *ebubur*? Nana, there is no *boro* in that name?"

"No, and it's because they are wild and they were already here in our woods before the white people came. The others are house doves."

"That's when and how it happened. E..eh?" I asked myself, while Nana stared at me. It was big, although I didn't know how big it was then.

Until, as a post-graduate student in History, I found myself researching the *Origins of Ghanaian Fauna and Flora*. Of course, it took me only the first quarter of the first year to admit that that was just too broad a topic for one research endeavour. So I lopped off fauna completely, thinking I could concentrate on the flora half. Eventually, I had to shrink even that to just the food bit of flora. Guided by Nana's very useful hint, things went quite well. For example, I could conclude easily that vegetables like hot pepper and most of its over two hundred species, as well as the garden egg/egg plant and some of its aubergine cousins are all indigenous. Indeed, I could also not only conclude but even accept a stranger hypothesis; that whereas all kinds of bananas are absolutely indigenous, plantain is a foreigner, a wanderer to these shores!

I was happy. I was very happy; not just with the final conclusions, but even more with the information I gathered along the way. The sea and the role he had played in the distribution of food around the world enthralled me. Ha, I wonder why people think the sea too is male! But the sea had helped humanity to share their food, carrying vegetables and fruits from the land to the shores from where the sea had swept them up and distributed them, long before people built ships and sailors took their foods on board to other lands and their peoples and returned home with foods from other lands and explorers carried foods from their lands on their voyages in search of other foods they suspected existed but whose specific nature they had no idea of…

… and slaves hid the likes of rice and yams on their persons and struggled to keep them hidden through the beatings, the raping, the birthing of rape results, other travail, but through them all clutched at those precious seeds for dear mind and life, so they would not be tempted to throw themselves into the sea as they had seen others do, or otherwise bring harm to themselves, or just so they could keep a little of the taste of home for comfort and plain old nourishment, wherever they eventually got thrown.

I was very happy with my research, although quite a lot of the stuff I came across was rather cruel, scary, or just plain nasty. But as everyone knows, in research as in life, sometimes the journey is the thing; and I was extremely happy.

Until one day. You know what I discovered? You won't believe it. You won't believe me. I was on the internet chasing after *aboboe*, aka bambara beans, aka Congo goobers aka *gurjiya* aka *okpa* and literally, hundreds of other names by which it is known across Africa, when I came upon some research paper produced in a US university in which they claimed that unlike the bambara bean, the peanut was imported to Africa from the United States of America. Eiii, hmm, yes o, the peanut, aka groundnut, was imported from the United States of America to Africa! How about all those people aboard those truly wretched schooners, chained, whipped, starved, who against all odds, had hid the peanut in unmentionable parts of their anatomies throughout the horrors of the Atlantic Crossing, I kept asking myself?

That's how come I lost my happiness. At least for a day. I just crawled into my bedroom for the rest of that day whimpering like a wounded puppy and stuffing my face with roasted peanuts: otherwise known as

adzui
atwee,
nkatse/nkatie…
geerte bi
amendoim,

and literally, hundreds of other names by which it is known across Africa and not a *boro* in sight. By the next morning, I had recovered enough to want to attempt to deal with the internet before those Americans got there first and told me that because they make the meanest gumbo in New Orleans, they had exported okra/okro/derere/bamia/e momi/fetri, etc., etc., etc. to Africa.

RECIPE FOR EDUYAA'S MOTHER'S FAVOURITE SNACK (EMOFS)

A. PLAIN (ORIGINAL)
1 large fully ripe papaya pawpaw
1 cup fresh tom brown (roasted corn flour)

Scoop out the pawpaw fruit and mash in a bowl until smooth. Add the tom brown to the pawpaw, mash and mix thoroughly. The result should taste naturally cool. Chill if preferred colder. However thick, never add water. Just add more pawpaw, or make sure to use less flour the next time you try it out. Serves three.

B. (EMOFS) BASED ON A., INTERNATIONALIZED, & EXPANDED.
However thick the plain version, never add water. Mash in more papaya and/or add milk.
– For spicy, crush 1 half hot pepper, a bit of ginger and add.
– For extra sweetness add sugar to taste. (Frowned upon.) When fully ripe, papaya is very sweet, so it should not be necessary to add extra sugar to any EMOFS preparations. Except on the most "foodpornic" occasions. Like when it is the sign-off for the most elegant and formal dining, or a wedding. Such presentations may call for even more extravagant fortifications: such as heavy cream, grated or powdered nutmeg and honey.
– Saner possibilities for adding to the original or as substitutes for the tom brown (roasted corn flour) may include any dry breakfast cereal, e.g. the following:

Crushed groundnuts/peanuts

Muesli

Crushed Weetabix
Granola mix

Trail mix
Med mix
Pumpkin seeds
Sesame seeds
Shaved almonds
Singly or any combinations of broken Brazil nuts, cashews, pecans and other known nuts, raw or roasted and yoghurt.

TWO

The Conference

Sefi Atta

In April I attended the African Literature Association conference in Illinois. The conference was on African women's literature and the convener, Lateef Adeyeye, was a professor I had known in Nigeria. He was in his sixties, soft-spoken and had an air of detachment from the general commotion in the university union, now occupied by a few hundred African Literature scholars. There was a concourse and food court on the first floor, conference rooms on the second floor and a banquet hall and union motel on the third floor. Even though the conference was on African Literature, Anglophone African writers dominated the panel discussions. A few sessions focused on Francophone African writers whose works had been translated into English, but there were none on writers who wrote in African languages.

A number of Nigerian academics were present. The keynote speaker, Tanimo Imana, was a Nigerian playwright who had enjoyed a lot of popularity in her day. She, too, was in her sixties. She had a PhD in Theatre Arts from the University of Ibadan and had taught at the University of Ilorin before she retired.

Professor Imana was born into a polygamous Yoruba family. Academics often described her plays as provocative. I personally found them painfully protracted. She had her characters reciting long soliloquies in the form of praise songs. I could see why Professor Adeyeye would invite her, being a Moslem from his part of the country, but I couldn't imagine Professor Imana getting involved in that kind of cronyism. She was against Sharia law practices relating to marriage; polygamy in particular. Her stance was personal. She left her husband when she found out he'd married a second wife without her knowledge.

Outside the panels, Osaro may have been absent from the conference, but he was the main topic of discussion. *Last Word* had recently won an American prize for non-fiction, which was accompanied by a monetary award of $25,000. The general consensus among the attendees was that Osaro didn't deserve the prize. I found that out when I met up with Ranti Shonubi, a fellow student from my PhD years at the University of Ibadan. She was the first person I recognised in the concourse, which was like a marketplace when I walked in. I'd just picked up a conference brochure when I saw her.

"Lukmon Karim," she said. "What are you doing here?"

I told her my family had won the green-card lottery and that I'd left academia for banking in Nigeria, but couldn't find a banking job in America.

Ranti was one of the most beautiful women I knew. She wore a tight *ankara* outfit, so low in front her breasts looked liable to pop out. Her hair was shorter than mine. I wasn't usually attracted to bald women, but I'd never seen a more perfectly shaped head.

She was as contrary as I remembered. We had barely greeted each other when she launched into an attack on Osaro.

"He is a liar," she said. "Plain and simple. As for these *oyinbos*, any far-fetched story any African tells them, they believe. Can you imagine? He said he fled Nigeria to escape political persecution and they couldn't even verify that information before giving him a major literary prize. The book wasn't even that good! The runner-up's was much better! But oh, no, she was African American and all she was writing about was depression. Don't mind these *oyinbos*. That is how they are. They're always trying to cause confusion with their random acts of tokenism. That was all this year's prize was about and Osaro's book was published at the right time. I'm sure PEN America will be calling him soon."

When we were doctoral students, Ranti was one of the women I listened to in silence. I thought it was wise to. She could lash out unexpectedly. She was a feminist back then, yet she was always in one revealing outfit or another. She walked as if she were daring someone to call her a slut and made every woman around her look boyish.

She, too, had had literary aspirations. She had written short stories. They were probably still unpublished. She and Osaro had left Nigeria in the same year, so they must have encountered each other in the small circle of African Literature academics in America. I couldn't rule out the possibility of professional envy.

"Everyone is talking about him," she said. "Of course some people are defending him – you know how Nigerians are. Someone wants a favour, so they keep quiet and hope he might do something for them. Then you have those who might support him for tribal reasons. I wouldn't talk to him if I saw him today! He is a disgrace! What is it? He's calling himself an academic and he's behaving unethically, lying all over the place and giving the rest of us a bad name. Honestly, *oyinbos* are ridiculous. It is unbelievable to me that they buy his story."

She stopped for a moment as an *oyinbo* academic walked by. He wore a *dashiki* and a string of wooden beads around his neck.

"You see what I have to deal with?" she said in Yoruba. "That one calls himself a specialist on African women's literature. The only African woman writer he recognises is Nadine Gordimer."

Ranti was in the women's caucus and I imagined that caucusing, for her, meant getting into academic disputes. She was of the impression that Professor Imana was ignoring her because she had criticized her negative stance on polygamy. She felt the professor's stance was rooted in Western thought. I could easily have challenged that. First, an African academic who lived in America had no right to criticise an African writer who lived in Africa about being influenced by Western thought. Second, I knew plenty of Nigerian women who weren't in favour of polygamy and their exposure to Western culture was at best limited. But they accepted polygamy because they were raised to or because they had to. My mother, quiet as she was, would never have put up with competition in our house. If my father had had other wives, she might not have quarreled with them, but she would have found a way to make life difficult for them.

Ranti was no longer a feminist. Or, as she explained, she was now in favour of African-centred womanist ideology that was less hostile to men. I was just relieved.

"You remember how I was in Ibadan?" she asked. "Ra-di-cal. Remember? I used to go to feminist conferences when I first came to America. Now, you won't catch me at a feminist conference in this country. These *oyinbos* don't want to know what African women have to say. They don't even want to hear that you might have a different point of view. All they want you to do is patronise African women with simplistic messages of empowerment and demonise African men…"

The more she talked, the more challenging it was to concentrate on what she was saying. Why did women do that? Expose their breasts and expect men to listen to them? If my chest were exposed, hairs and all, wouldn't she look?

"They think feminism begins and ends in the West," Ranti was saying. "Once I realised that, my eyes opened. Look at the most powerful women in this country. How many female CEOs of major corporations do they have? How many female Managing Directors? Let us not bring up the fact that America hasn't yet produced a female President. Their First Lady, Hillary Clinton, is not even allowed to talk. All she is allowed to do is smile and wave. If she does more than that, they vilify her. In Hollywood, they make more money than other women in the world, but they're retired by the age of forty. So what do they do? They mutilate their faces and bodies. America is a sexist country. In fact, I would go as far as to say it's misogynistic. Yes! But they're always ready to point fingers at Africa…"

Now, she sounded like a proponent of cultural relativism. She stopped talking for a moment as Professor Imana approached us. I had not seen Professor Imana since I left the University of Ibadan and had forgotten how tall and regal she was. She wore a *boubou* and head tie. She walked straight past us without acknowledging Ranti.

"This is serious," I said.

"Don't mind her," Ranti said. "She thinks I hate her. Why would

I hate her? I'm just doing my job. She is a prime example of what I'm talking about. Feminists here love her. I'm going to her panel today, whether she wants me there or not. When I've finished with her, she won't be able to ignore me anymore."

I'd never understood academics who took pleasure in hounding writers, but Ranti was soon off on another tangent, this one about how she was denied tenure. Someone delayed her application. Someone else discredited her work. Things got so bad for her that an *oyinbo* academic accused her of reverse racism.

"The politics in this place is too much," she said. "I can't stand half the faculty in my department. I don't talk to them unless I have to."

She couldn't stand her students either.

"They call me 'Rotting'," she said. "Can you imagine? I tell them, 'Call me Professor Shonubi if you can't pronounce Ranti and if you can't pronounce Shonubi, just call me Professor.' Common courtesy they don't have and you can forget any knowledge about Africa. You have to start from the very basics with them, providing them with geographical maps and social statistics before you begin to discuss African Literature with them..."

I wondered if she was married. She wasn't wearing a ring. Making allowance for age, she was still in good shape.

"So how are you coping in America?" she asked, as if noticing me for the first time.

"So-so," I said.

"Do you like it here?"

"It's not too bad."

She sighed. "I'm telling you, I would go back to Nigeria today if I could. It's just that it's hard to make the move once you get stuck in academia."

The concourse was filling up and it was harder to hear her above the noise. I could barely maintain eye contact, given the number of people walking past. I leaned over and spoke in her ear.

"Forgive me for saying this, but I'm here to look for a job. After I get one, I might be more willing to talk about the disadvantages of having one."

She laughed. "Look at you! You haven't changed! Still sarcastic!

Sorry. It's all the *wahala* I have to deal with here and I don't have anyone else to talk to. Don't worry. We will talk more about that when you're settled. We should have lunch together later. Are you coming to the Imana panel?"

"I'll try and make it," I said.

Her perfume smelled great and for a bitter woman, she had a lovely smile.

She left and I leafed through abstracts in the conference brochure, craving the banality of business words like "profits" and "revenues" as I skimmed over words like "womanhood," "gender" and "sexuality." Then, just as soon, I went in search of my next contact.

Pascal, Osaro's Congolese friend, was presenting a paper on Assia Djebar's *Vasteest la prison.* I headed for the conference room where he was scheduled to be, but it took me a while to get there because I stopped to greet several academics I knew. Some couldn't remember my name and vice-versa. One of them stood on a stair above me and barred my way.

"Don't I know you from somewhere?" he asked.

He was a scruffy-looking man with freckles.

"I'm not sure," I said.

"Your face is familiar," he said. "Yes. I know you."

It turned out we did know each other. We had met as students in London. I took his card and said I would email him.

He was Urhobo. Most of the Nigerian academics were Yoruba or Igbo. I'd never attended an ALA conference before, but politics in American academia was nothing compared to politics in Nigerian academia, which at its worst had been known to degenerate into juju curses and physical altercations. In the department I'd worked in, relations between faculty members had very quickly become strained whenever a trip overseas was at stake, but I left before I was senior enough to be considered for one.

I found Pascal in the first-floor lobby with his colleagues from the Francophone caucus. He wore a black turtleneck and beret. He remembered me from Osaro's dinner. I told him I was looking for a job and it turned out we were staying at the same hotel, so we arranged to meet later.

"Have you heard about Osaro's prize?" he asked.

"Yes," I said.

"He's the talk of the town," he said.

"So I hear. I should email him tonight to congratulate him."

I was curious to find out what he thought about Osaro's prize but not enough to ask. He introduced me to Helen Darko, Steve Gilbert and Chinedu Obiora, who were presenting papers on Anglophone African writers. Steve was the *oyinbo* academic in the *dashiki*. He had just returned from South Africa. Helen was Ghanaian. Her personality was as colourful as her appearance. She laughed so hard at something Pascal said to her in French, her *kente* stole fell off her shoulder. Chinedu looked out of place in a suit. He seemed friendly enough until Pascal mentioned I was job-hunting, to which he responded, "Things are tough."

There were noticeable circles at the conference. Igbo, Yoruba and Ghanaian academics stuck to their groups. African academics were the majority and *oyinbos* were the minority. My perception may have been wrong, but the *oyinbos* seemed to gravitate towards non-Africans. Everyone was united on how disorganised the conference was, though. The panels ran late and into each other. Some of them were cancelled at the last minute, so conference rooms were empty when attendees arrived. Meanwhile, our convener, Professor Adeyeye, walked around seemingly calm in his blue *agbada* and matching cap.

I was late for the Imana panel. She was at the centre of the table, flanked by a presenter and a moderator.

"Okay," the moderator said. "This session is beginning to get out of hand, and there is no need for that. We can exchange ideas without getting heated up. So, can we move on to the next question please and not waste any more time on this topic?"

I wondered if the topic had involved Ranti, who was in the front row with a notepad and pen poised. I sat in the back row as a man raised his hand.

He cleared his throat and looked downward. I could already tell he was a time waster.

"Um, your plays," he said.

"Yes?" Professor Imana said.

"They are … rather dramatic."

"I should hope my plays are dramatic."

"Sorry, I meant to say…"

"What is the question?" the moderator asked, after a moment.

"Her plays are way over the top," the man said.

"And?" Professor Imana said.

"Why?" the man asked.

"Why what?" Professor Imana asked.

"Why are your plays so … intense?"

Professor Imana couldn't disguise her irritation.

"Have you read any of my plays?"

"I've seen one or two," the man said.

"Yes, but have you read any of them?"

"They're not available in the United States."

"Read my plays, please," Professor Imana said. "Then we can discuss them."

The man folded his arms. I doubted he was an academic. He may not have even seen any of her plays.

"Next question, please," the moderator said, checking her watch. "Actually, this has to be our final question because we're running out of time."

Ranti raised her hand and the audience laughed, which told me that I might have been right in thinking that she had caused trouble earlier.

"I'm just wondering what you have to say about my, uh, assertion that you and other playwrights of your generation have failed to, uh, capture the attention of a new generation of Nigerian theatre enthusiasts. You never quite addressed that."

"I've certainly captured your attention," Professor Imana said. "You've done nothing but bombard me with questions from the beginning of this panel."

Ranti nodded. "Yes, you could also say I've done a lot to draw attention to your works. But since you refuse to, uh, speak to the issue, my question to you is this: 'What would you like your legacy to be'?"

"What is your name again?"

"Ranti Shonubi, Associate Professor of African Literature.

You might be familiar with my most recent essays on your works, 'Feminising Our Fathers' and 'Politicising Polygamy'."

"No," Professor Imana said.

"You're not familiar with either essay?" Ranti asked.

"I'm not familiar with anything you've done," Professor Imana said.

"I could summarise —"

"That will not be necessary," Professor Imana said. Then she addressed the audience. "You know, in my forty years of writing, most of which I've spent examining the inequalities that Nigerian women face, it never ceases to amaze me that my toughest critics are educated Nigerian women. I understand their concerns. They don't want to be regarded as victims. But in being protective of ourselves, we cannot ignore women whose voices are not heard.

"Heard by whom?" Ranti asked.

"They don't have the platforms we have," Professor Imana said. "You cannot deny that."

"They have their own platforms," Ranti said, "which may not be visible in the West, where every African platform becomes a spectacle."

Professor Imana turned her face to the moderator like a child refusing to take more medicine. I was sure Ranti had more to say, but she took her cue and kept quiet.

Women were their own worst enemies. That was no cliché. I agreed with Professor Imana. Whenever I talked about Nigerian women, I was referring to women I knew. Ranti, too, was right. Disadvantaged Nigerian women did have voices and it was presumptuous to speak for them. So why were they confronting each other? They ought to be confronting men. I sometimes didn't consider women when I talked about Nigerians.

"Well," the moderator said, rubbing her hands together. "That was a highly spirited and enlightening session. If Professor Imana would be kind enough to end it with a few closing remarks …?"

"Listen," Professor Imana said, facing the audience. "I've never been of much use in forums like this and maybe I should have stayed away. To be honest, I don't think about what we've discussed today, or my legacy. If anything, I think about whether my work is worthy enough to belong to the tradition of African Literature. The professor here said the future of African Literature is in the hands of academics and I disagreed with her. I didn't mean to offend anyone, but the dependency is the other way around. It's just a fact. None of you would be here but for African Literature. It is true that African Literature has been restricted to classrooms and lecture rooms, but it will find its way out. It's a matter of time and you'd better be ready when that happens, or else it will be out of your hands. So if indeed you are the guardians of African Literature, remember the standard that was set at the conference at Makerere University in 1962. I wasn't privileged to be there, but it was attended by the best African writers and Literature scholars of my generation. Now, here we are today in 2000, holding an African Literature conference in Illinois. Ask yourself why. Give that your time and consideration."

The moderator thanked her and the audience for coming. The audience clapped. A few people approached the table as Ranti sat where she was, scribbling notes.

Ranti and I had lunch at the food court. She wasn't impressed by the array of fast foods on offer and shared the general view of Professor Adeyeye's mismanagement of the conference.

"Ade *yeye*," she said, diminishing the meaning of his last name from "the crown befits its titles" to "a joke of a crown", with a change of tone. "The man doesn't know what he is doing. The whole place could be exploding and he would be walking around like this."

She imitated Professor Adeyeye's calm expression.

I worried about Ranti's sanity. She had always been trouble, but not to this extent.

"It's not exactly Makerere University in 1962," I said.

She hissed. "Don't mind that woman. She was just trying to insult me. The point I was making was that African writers need African scholars. What is wrong with saying that? Who else but us can analyse African Literature with any depth of understanding? Who else but us can be the guardians of African Literature? Even if African Literature does find its way out of classrooms and lecture rooms, it will only be because of writers like Osaro who write under the Western gaze and they will be nothing more than exotic appendages to the literary landscape. What is she talking about? What did half her generation of African writers and scholars end up doing when they came abroad? Sleeping with *oyinbos*. Before they knew it, they had forgotten all their revolutionary ideas. I'm telling you, facing West has never benefited Africans."

Ranti wasn't interested in hearing about my job search; she just wanted to vent. I could have told her the dependency between African scholars and writers was mutual, but perhaps because of the racket in the food hall, the fluorescent lights and the sight of Africans queuing up to buy dubious pizzas and tacos and greasy burgers and fries, I wasn't inclined to respond.

I nodded now and then, hoping I wouldn't become preoccupied with the dangers of Western thought while teaching in America. If I had come all the way from Nigeria to do that, I was better off packing up and going back. Western thought wasn't responsible for the disorganised conference. The conference itself reminded me of the Nigeria I'd left. We had contentious panels, attendees gossiping about Osaro's literary fraud and a convener walking around as if he was unaware of the chaos around him.

One aspect of academia I didn't miss was listening to colleagues who took a certain position, knowing it wasn't absolute and defended it to the end. So what if African writers wrote under the Western gaze? They couldn't help that. Osaro had written purely for Western consumption, which was unusual, but he would only end up alienating African readers. If they bought his book, they wouldn't finish it. If they finished it, they would be as pissed off as Ranti. Her staunch Afrocentric stance was perhaps due to her displacement overseas. Academics in Nigeria were not that consciously Afrocentric. It was no longer fashionable or useful to be. A cosmopolitan approach to literary criticism was more practical. They were teaching students who were born at least two decades after independence, students who looked up to hip-hop celebrities and didn't know or care about Diop and other African scholars whose works we had studied. Yes, their schooling was Eurocentric, but they might argue that Afrocentric culture was dominant nonetheless because the African diaspora influenced culture worldwide.

Again I wondered if Ranti was married. We'd had a longstanding flirtation in the university. She would walk up to me and hug me. I called her "talker thief woman" back then. "Talker thief" was what my aunt, a perpetual settler of family quarrels, would say when she meant to say "talkative."

My mind was all over the place. I put down my burger. Ranti had already given up on hers. She picked up a French fry and ate it.

"Do you like Oprah?" I asked.

She tucked her chin in. "Winfrey?"

"Are there others?"

She rubbed her forefinger and thumb together. "Why are you asking me about her?"

The realisation that I'd been lonely at home.

"My wife likes her."

Ranti pulled a face. "Really?"

"Are you married?" I asked.

"No," she said, looking askance.

"How come?"

She lifted her chin. "My choices aren't that great."

"Any children?"

She nodded. "One. Only one."

Her daughter, Morayo, was a freshman in college. She'd never married Morayo's father. She didn't want to. Nigerian men were all mad, she said.

"Not all of us."

Afrocentric culture was dominant nonetheless because the African diaspora influenced culture worldwide.

"I thought you were one of the nice ones. Why are you asking me about Oprah? Are you having problems at home?"

I shook my head. Ranti was too much trouble.

"Can't a man complain about being misunderstood?"

"Not to a woman like me."

"Why do women here worship Oprah?" I asked.

She pointed. "Hey! Respect your wife and stop stressing me out! Asking me questions about my private life stresses me out! Look at you. I was hoping for some intellectual stimulation and all you can come up with is, 'Do you like Oprah?' Since you ask, I'm not an Oprah Winfrey fan. Would you like to know why?"

There was a time when I would have taken her answer to mean she was interested in me.

"I hear too much about Oprah at home," I said. "Tell me about jobs."

She was helpful. She suggested I apply for fellowships and promised to tell me about any opportunities she heard of. She was planning to sleep in, the following morning, but would stay until the end of the conference. She had films to watch and the final dinner to attend. I told her I had to head back home first thing in the morning.

She gave me her card and we went our separate ways. Our next panels were concurrent. I attended a session on Nawal El Saadawi, followed by one on Tsitsi Dangarembga and Yvonne Vera, after which I went to a conference room that had been set up for book publishers and sellers. There were books by Francophone African women writers like Mariama Bâ, Calixthe Beyala, Véronique Tadjo and Anglophone African women writers like Ama Ata Aidoo and Buchi Emecheta. Bessie Head was duly remembered and Nadine Gordimer wasn't left out.

Gordimer, like Coetzee, was sometimes absent from the category of African Literature because her works escaped into World Literature. I'd read her books in England, so I bought books by other African women writers and then I treated myself to books by Zakes Mda and Nuruddin Farah. As I paid for their books, it occurred to me that I would never describe them as African men writers. There would be no need.

In the evening, I returned to my hotel. The hotel restaurant was only marginally better than the food court, but I had dinner with Pascal there. We ordered steaks and baked potatoes. He thought I should apply for a visiting position while looking for a permanent one.

Pascal was a political exile. The real deal. Laurent Kabila had wanted him killed. He told me only because I brought up Osaro's prize, about which I was ambivalent. On the one hand, I thought Osaro's colleagues could do more than talk about the matter. On the other hand, if Osaro had written about his authentic Nigerian experience, no one would publish his book, let alone give him a prize.

"You must have heard the rumours," I said.

Pascal nodded. "Oh, yes."

"What do you think?" I asked.

"It is unfortunate," he said. "Osaro is merely a victim of his own imagination."

He did not say more about the book, but instead revealed more about himself. He had fled to France. He had been in the United States for two years. He was married to a Frenchwoman who stayed in France with their son because she didn't want to live in America.

"You prefer to live here?" I asked.

He wiped his mouth with his napkin. "For now? Yes."

One on one, Pascal was the kind of academic I found easy to be around. He was intellectual without being pompous. The truth was that I was insecure about returning to academia because I'd peaked too early in my career and my banking detour had left me rusty.

We had almost finished eating when Helen Darko joined us.

"Ah, Madame," he said, "*Ça va?*"

I stood up with him and they kissed each other twice. She asked for a menu, and Pascal ordered a bottle of wine. I decided it was time to excuse myself.

THREE

What Could the Matter be?

Ogochukwu Promise

A cold pale sky and a soft breeze, blast of trumpet as Nick blew mindlessly into it were all I could think of after I heard the shocking news. There was also the tremor of my fingers on the piano keyboard. Lizza was faltering as she played the harmonica. The sucking sound she made irritated me. Nick kept casting curious glances at me each time I missed a note or struck the wrong chord. When he got the chance to speak to me as soon as choir practice was over, he leaned across and whispered, "The rumour is rife, but it's still rumour. We don't know with absolute certainty that he did it."

"What difference does it make? It's true anyway."

"Have you confirmed it yet?"

"Can't you see that he didn't come to supervise choir practice? Very unusual. The news is making the rounds in the church already."

"Did you notice that Whitney didn't show up either? She's been granting interviews. She's becoming a star. You'd be in the limelight now if you'd been brave enough to tell someone."

I shoved him off and began to walk away from the music room, from the saxophone and especially the cello, which I preferred to the piano. I was made to play the piano only when Whitney was absent. I remembered the ugly expression on Lizza's face the day she told me I loved to play cello because I was black anyway. I had restrained myself from striking her because Father Bloomsbury never tired of teaching us how wrong it was to hit one another. Instead, under the pain of repeating himself every so often, he patiently taught us to accommodate one another in love and charity – a lesson that was hard to assimilate. Even though I had always been quite hot-blooded, I did my best to tolerate all the young people who upset me, especially in church.

My sanctimonious mother, Nana Ama, always insisted I be of good behaviour, especially in church. She would remind me she was from a family of nuns. Two of her sisters were nuns. The only reason she was not one herself was because my father swept her off her feet before she could think of going into the convent. After my father's demise, my stepfather came along. And she said my stepfather's love was so good she took the even bigger leap of marrying him, a non-Catholic. But she was quick to point out that he became what she always knew he would be: a pastor of one of the fast-growing churches in the diaspora. He never let anyone forget how international and spirit-filled his church was. He would subtly allude to the fact that he was a minister in this "transnational" church only to show how important and godly he was regarded. One of the things my mother loved about him was that he was liberal enough to wed her in the Catholic faith and even let her attend Mass as often as she wished. She also counted as a plus for him that he married her despite the fact that she had me for her childhood sweetheart – who had drowned in the river the weekend he was to seek her father's permission to marry her.

It did not matter if I liked him or not. My mother didn't think my opinion counted. She didn't really regard me much. Not then. Not now. She simply made up her mind that I had no reason to dislike her choice of a husband especially since he was living abroad and was going to take us both with him. While I liked the fact that I was going abroad, I cried at the departure lounge because I was already missing my friends. Nyoka's mischievous wink when someone we had gossiped about passed by, the telltale sign all over Selasie when he stole my tom-tom and looked away as I searched his pocket, the sideway glances of Kwesi when all of us burst out laughing as Kwesi's mother declared a whole carton of Indomie missing. But I was consoled when I got into the aircraft and settled into its luxury. As it went up the sky and I wondered at the height it had attained, I hoped I would experience many beautiful things in England, make great friends and grow to be an accomplished lady, like my grandmother, Tidaiya. I hoped also that I would one day fly a big aircraft like the one I flew in.

It took me a while to get used to the intensely cold weather in London. People kept saying it never snowed so badly in London as it did the December we arrived and had to wade through eighteen inches of snow. But my stepfather, Kessie, took us out to a restaurant that night and filled my plate with some garden vegetable quiche while my mother ate boiled Irish potatoes and Brussels sprouts which my stepfather said was very good as he wolfed down Singapore noodles with whipped potatoes. It was that night when I knew I would miss home food, especially *akple* and peanut soup, *kokonte* and *nkontomire* stew as well as *banku* and okro stew. Those were my favourites and I missed them greatly.

My mother ate ravenously as though she had eaten that sort of food all her life. She was that kind of person. She would speak endlessly about how she preferred hotdog to *kaakro* and *tatale*, how she could bet that vanilla-coloured custard was certainly better than *koko*. She would say it with her nose turned up as though *koko* smelt, as though she did not enjoy it when Grandma Tidaiya made it along with *akara* and told us she thought it was unfair to call *akara* bean-cake because *akara* would always be a better name for it.

As soon as we left the shores of Ghana, my mother began to speak English with an inflected accent and reminded me very often that I had left Ghana and would do well to discard my thick Kumasi accent. When I looked at people longer than she considered necessary, she would remind me that I was staring and that I must behave like the well-brought-up child I was meant to be. The next time we ate out, she tasted the Riesling first, sniffed the wine gently from a crystal glass and smiled broadly at the butler as she said, "Mmmmmn, brisk, light and dry." She tilted her neck to the left as she waited for us to endorse her appraisal of the wine. My stepfather smiled indulgently and winked at me. I smiled too without knowing why. With relish she ate hot meatball sandwich and sprinkled grilled cheese on it. I marvelled at the speed with which she adapted to our new environment and seemed to reign over it. I tried to copy her but I did not like marinated cucumber salad and preferred grilled *kielbasa* to honey-baked ham on sourdough. But as the years went by, I began to love Scandinavian vegetables and salmon croquettes. When my stepfather asked what he would get for me on his way home, I began to happily ask for Lemon meringue pie and butterscotch pudding which he always brought home with the sort of glee that seemed to match my enthusiasm. Then my mother's stomach began to swell. She seemed elated and would often repeat that ours was a pretty joyous family.

I thought so too until that night my door handle suddenly depressed and a flurry of snow blew in as a head appeared by the door. I opened my mouth to scream, but a broad palm covered my mouth and his voice flooded my ears. "Don't shout and disgrace your mother. Remember you are no longer in Kumasi. Be good and let me in. It will be nice and easy. And I'll get you all you want. Just make a list." He was breathing heavily. He sounded desperate, his eyes roving all over my body.

"Let go of me! What do you want?" I asked, conscious that people do not shout in London as Mother had told me.

"Just to see what you've got down there. It'll be fun, I promise," he planted his knees between my thighs, pushing them apart.

"What are you doing?"

"Shush. Be a good girl and shut your mouth nicely, my dear."

"Leave me alone! My mother won't like it."

"She might not, but you will, I assure you."

"What is it you want with me?"

"I'll show you nicely. And I will take you out and show you the city. I will make sure you go to school this fall. Don't you want to go to school anymore? Don't you want to make friends instead of being locked up in the house? You've been in the UK for a year now and you've hardly seen the outside of this house. Now, don't you shout, don't you shout! Remember the cops, they'll come and get you!" He was now speaking under his breath and quickly too as though he was running out of time.

Fear flooded my eyes as he said he would call the cops if I screamed and woke the neighbours. I let him have his way, closed my eyes all the while surprised at him as he promised again to make it worth my while, even as he forced shut my mouth and kept pushing something of his inside me. He was sweating profusely and acting like a mad fellow.

The moment he was done, he headed for the door and forgot to shut it behind him. The whole exercise was cheerless. I was partly in shock and overwhelmed with fear. It had snowed all night and I was cold and wary of the night, not knowing what else it held. I was left feeling like someone who had just experienced a theft, the magnitude of which I was neither aware of nor could fathom. But the weather improved the following week, with sunlight and the beginning of a thaw. It was also that bright week he enrolled me in a school and filled my palm with coins totalling twenty pounds, which he told me to keep from my mother's prying eyes. "Be mindful of letting anyone see it, OK? Say nothing about this to anyone either in school or at home. I will always protect you at all costs."

I nodded, thinking that it was a little price to pay for going to school. In Kumasi my teacher had said I showed promise and could be bright if I was assisted. She said I had a great faculty for absorbing information and she encouraged me to read voraciously. When I told my teacher I was leaving for the United Kingdom, she urged me to make sure I continued my studies. I promised I would and since I arrived, I had been pleading with my mother to enrol me in school but she kept putting it off till she had had her baby. She said she needed someone to assist her and that I would resume school after she had weaned her child and was able to get a child minder.

I overheard her quarrelling with my stepfather when she learnt I was to resume school.

"And what signal are you sending out there, Kessie? That you love Afua more than I do? Is that it? She is my child, remember?"

"Nana, calm down," came my stepfather's voice. "I've told you time and again that I am no longer comfortable seeing this child wasting at home when she should be in school."

"And did I tell you I didn't have plans for her to go to school?"

"We've been talking about it for a whole year now, Nana. She came here when she was eleven. Let her join other kids in school, please, so she won't fall behind educationally. My conscience can't take it any longer. This is your child, for crying out loud, not some babysitter."

"Then get me a babysitter, Kessie."

"I will hire one as soon as you have had the baby.

That was how the matter was resolved. Or so it seemed.

Pastor Kessie received thousands of invitations to talk to various groups in different branches of his church. He was a persuasive and emotive preacher. He often cried, danced in the pulpit and drew crowds who referred to him as a "powerful man of God." He was energetic too and jumped about a lot as he encouraged people to come to his healing ministry. Many who went claimed they were healed of ailments. His church members said he was an enigma and that he went about like his master, the Christ, doing good. On one of the few occasions my mother and I attended his healing ministry, I was taken in by the crowd that surged after him, reaching for the hem of his garment. A woman sitting by me was feverish and throwing up. But when he laid his hands on her, the fever dropped and she was able to sing and dance all night. At some point, she turned, smiling fully at me and said, "Pastor Kessie is awesome!" She was overwhelmed with joy.

I might have agreed with her, had he not kept coming to me oddly any night he wanted to be with me. As for my mother, whose cold stare and aloofness never ceased to amaze me, she only came alive when I did something wrong. She not only frowned at me but I would get a telling off. She spoke to me meanly as if I was the cause of all her woes.

On one of the nights my stepfather came to my bed, I asked him if he was sure his wife was my mother. I complained that she wasn't demonstrative and never hugged me. He nodded and muttered something about the need for me not to hold it against her. He assured me that she loved me very much, that she was just being a little self-centred and erratic because she was about to have a baby. Her hormones were all over the place and she was afraid and anxious. He said she needed to be understood and forgiven.

Then I noticed he was coming to my room more frequently and that he had a way of being in a hurry to leave each time he had got enough of what he came for. When he was with me, I liked it when he talked. I wished he would only talk and not lie on top of me. I liked all the gifts he gave me. There were so many: a near complete set of Harry Potter, a video game, shoes, clothes and a book on love and romance, which he said I should keep out of my mother's reach. But I didn't like what he did with me, perhaps because the pain that came with it never quite subsided. Yet I wished he would not be so much in a hurry to leave. It made me feel so lonely, so forlorn.

At home, I withdrew into myself. In school I was a loner. In the Catholic Church my mother and I still attended, I joined the choir and realised that I liked to play musical instruments, deriving much joy from them. I went to church often in order to play those instruments.

Reverend Van Stephen, who used to be the youth chaplain in our church, was a strange fellow! He had a stern appearance and spoke brusquely. He always insisted that things be done in certain ways: you sang only traditional songs, the traditional way and no theatrics. And at the confessional, you made a penitential confession stating when you last went to confession and how many times you committed a particular sin. You got admonished sternly. You got a tough penance. Father Van Stephen would listen carefully as you recited the act of contrition. If you mumbled a word, he would make you repeat it and tell you how costly your salvation was purchased. In a little while, the older women talked about his high-handedness, the fact that he hardly smiled at anyone, that he summoned the Mass servers to the duties he assigned them as though they owed him allegiance and that he would sooner do all the work in the parish house than share a joke with anyone.

So the older men got together and put pen to paper, stating as his offence his inconsiderate silence as though he were a hermit of some sort. They said his human relations were too poor and that no one could actually hear him at Mass, as his method was too drab, making the Mass too mournful. It wasn't long before he was transferred to some place where nobody cared to find out. But it was certainly not his hometown, somewhere in South Carolina. I came to Mass one day and was told that Father Van Stephen was gone. I did not care really even though I was not sure I liked it when Whitney haughtily said, "Good riddance to bad rubbish." I thought those words unnecessary. At the same time I thought I might have felt that way because Whitney was always acting as though she was smarter than everyone else and I hoped that by disregarding her words, she might be slighted.

The following week, a new priest arrived at our parish. I could tell we all liked him. From the first day he set foot there and word got round that we had been given a brilliant and handsome priest, I noted that we all wanted to be his friend. He would celebrate Mass joyously, making elaborate gestures as he drove home his points. Within a few days, he knew everybody's name. After Mass, he would stand by the door of the church sharing handshakes, hugs and pecks and blessing everyone.

He reorganised the choir and got the youth to participate actively in it. He made us play various musical instruments and kept telling us we could be good with just about anything we were convinced of.

We giggled a lot when he was around and would compete for his commendation, which he gave effusively with his deep, resonant voice: "Kelvin that was a beautiful sound you produced there. Enrica, I strongly believe you'll make a great soprano soloist. That rendition was incredibly beautiful! Whitney, you are splendid with the tambourine. Lizza, your handling of the xylophone was exceptional. You should also try the guitar. I am sure you'll make something good out of it. You all need to be versatile."

I was hurt that he hardly mentioned me. I asked my stepfather to buy me the cello and he did. I did extra practice at home to improve on my skill at playing. After school, I played all evening. My mother grew curious about my new obsession with the cello. Of late, she had been going on about the fact that Kessie was spoiling me, buying me too many things that took up my time so that I was starting to act as though my house chores were some unbearable burden. To this, my stepfather would remind her that I was only a child. "Let her be, Nana. As long as she does the work you give her."

"Yes, but the way she does it matters too. See, this dishwasher needs a good clean! And look how untidy her room is, littered with all manner of things. I don't want Maami Tidaiya to quarrel with me when she comes here. You knew how hard it was for me to take Afua away from her. She has always been afraid I would not give Afua much love and training because she believes my eyes are not fully open to my duties."

"That's precisely why I keep buying her things that will help her develop her mind and talents for which you fight me, dear."

"I just think that you sometimes give her a little too much."

"Trust me, I give just enough."

"I hope so."

"You worry too much. Go to bed and get a rest, my dear."

My mother would go to bed, her podgy stomach resting languidly on her side of the bed as she lay her back. I pitied her then because she could hardly work smartly. She got tired too often and her face and feet were swollen. She looked twice her age with too many pimples bursting at the same time on her cheeks. When I first noticed the way she walked, like someone with a wound around her lower abdomen, I was alarmed. I remembered that I walked like that when my stepfather first pushed his "sugar cane," as he called it, into me. But he took time to teach me how to walk straight. He said. "Yes, walk like a lady. Don't you know you are a beautiful lady? Don't bring disgrace to anyone around here by walking like someone with a wound between her legs!" He had examined me thoroughly and told me I was okay. When I showed concern over my mother's condition and expressed my fear of becoming like her with that gruesome stomach that wouldn't let her lie down properly, he was alarmed and gave me some pills. Then he avoided me for some days, during which I enjoyed some respite. But he soon returned with some funny-looking transparent rubber, which he wore over his turgid "sugar cane" as he complained about the "pull" he had towards me. He said I was privileged to be loved by him and that he would make sure, someday, I would have all the music instruments I wanted. And if I still wanted to be a pilot, he would help to make it happen. I didn't know how he would accomplish all that since I was only just starting school and he gave me a lot of "don't do, don't say, don't think" instructions that filled me with fear and kept me from making inquiries.

But I loved my cello and thanked him again and again for buying it for me, for prevailing on my mother to get me a lot of things. Ever since my mother got pregnant, she hardly noticed anything else other than her massive stomach, which didn't let her see beyond herself. Even though my stepfather was worried she might notice the way I walked when he initially started visiting me at night, my mother took no account of the things that were of interest to me. I suppose she doted on me in her own way by occasionally asking if I had eaten, ensuring I ate up my baked beans, green peas and broccoli, which she said would nourish my body and keep me healthy. She forced me to take siestas and read good books that she bought for me. She taught me good manners and worried endlessly about how I behaved in school and especially in church. When I became one of the Mass servers, she said the robe looked good on me and that at some point, she actually thought I appeared like one of those cherubs everyone imagined waited on the Lord Jesus.

At home when she told my stepfather about it, he chuckled and said something about how untraditional it was for the Catholic Church to let girls parade the Lord's sacred altar in the name of serving Mass. His face was ugly as he said it and I realised then that he had two molars missing. I wondered why my mother never noticed anything, why she tolerated him. It grieved me that she took no offence at his utterance, probably did not even notice he expressed a negative opinion about her faith, about one of the ways of her church. She merely sat there, gazing in abstraction at the flickering fire.

That night when he came to me, I began to cry and insist I was aching all over. He pleaded with me and said he was getting more attracted to me each passing day. I opened my mouth to scream, as I didn't care if he called the cops on me. He mumbled something about me being unkind, ungrateful and that I was not being fair. I pushed and pummelled him savagely. His eyes widened in surprise. "What has got into you?" he asked, withdrawn.

"I don't like you anymore," I retorted.

"Please be a good girl. I have been good to you. You don't need to be aggressive with me. Tell me what else I should get for you and you'll have it at the break of dawn."

I thought about it and shook my head.

"What have I done to you?" he sounded sombre as he tried unsuccessfully to disguise the fact that he was cross.

I wondered at him. Then I said, "You said ugly things about a girl serving Mass, even when you knew I now serve Mass."

"Oh, that. I am so sorry. By all means please go on and serve all the Mass you want. If there are things you need to do it well, I'll get them for you."

I liked the power I wielded over him at that moment. I waited until he made so many promises before I allowed him to snuggle up to me. I must have tasked him so badly that he indeed went into spasms as he danced crazily on top of me before he collapsed on me, breathing heavily. This time, he didn't leave in a hurry. He said he had fallen in love with me and didn't know what to do about it. I thought his falling in love with me meant he was going to be buying me more things and I felt it was okay.

He got me a music teacher and I practised everyday at home and really improved. It wasn't long before Father Bloomsbury singled me out for commendation, which made my head swell with pride. I even closed my eyes as I pulled the bow rhythmically, flaunting my skills especially after I had caught a glimpse of Father Bloomsbury earlier staring at me momentarily lost in admiration. In my belief, it was there and then that he set his heart on me. I thought I was the only one that saw that stare. But I was wrong. Nick saw it too and drew my attention to it as soon as the Reverend Father left.

"Afua, that was a brilliant performance," he imitated Father Bloomsbury as he made his comments and gave me a knowing smile. "You really impressed him."

I couldn't help a broad smile. "Tell me, did I earn his commendation?" I asked.

"You sure did."

"I'm glad. I've been practising at home."

At the sacristy as we prepared for Mass, Father Bloomsbury held my gaze and smiled, his eyes appeared moist and very kind.

I wondered if he knew we all thought him a handsome Englishman, though we later heard his mother was mixed-race from South Africa; we marvelled at the loveliness of his features, especially his straight nose, large, warm eyes and narrow, almost grim lips. I even wished he were my brother, someone I could look up to. I wished I could tell him about my mother's indifference and have him tell me if he thought as I did that I might have belonged to another mother who would pay me a little more attention. I knew I could never tell her about my stepfather, though I felt the need to tell someone. I wanted to tell Father Bloomsbury about the fear that tugged at my heart each night I prayed that I would not hear my stepfather's surreptitious footsteps as he crept into my room. I badly wanted to discuss the fact that I felt lonely often and wished I were home with Grandma Tidaiya, with Nyoka, Kwesi and Selasie. I wanted to tell someone I didn't like what my stepfather did with me, that sometimes I wished I need not go home and that my heart skidded each time I felt that familiar depression of my door handle at night. I wanted to tell someone that I felt like screaming all the time in that house, at my stepfather, at my mother, at the washing machine, even at the easy smile on my mother's face as she bought me things and told me casually that she loved me.

"Day dreaming!" Nick whispered into my ears, startling me.

I picked up my robe and hurriedly wore it to catch up with the others who were dressed for Mass and ready for the entrance procession. I fell in line at once, my hands clasped together in penitential attitude.

I did not know that I looked dazed all through the Mass until Father Bloomsbury told me. But he also said something to which I did not know the response to give. "You are beautiful, child. You sure are. Can you see me at The Chaplaincy at four?"

I must have looked dumb at first before I began to nod. He moved away then, as though I made him shy. I felt elated that Father Bloomsbury said I was beautiful. That meant I really was, even though no one had told me so before. My stepfather never said anything about my looks. My mother merely concerned herself with discovering when I was untidy, when she didn't think my teeth were as clean as they should be, when she worried about how well I washed my panties. On a number of occasions she took the trouble to inspect my armpits to make sure they were clean enough. She smelt my clothes and sniffed at me to ensure I had no body odour. She always warned me not to disgrace her in any way, as though she saw in me the tendency, however obscure, to dent her well-groomed image – the well-dressed, well-mannered, elegant and sophisticated Mrs Nana Kessie-Appiah, wife of a revered gentleman. She never bought me perfumed roll-ons because she said I was too young to use them. I was glad she didn't notice I had been stealing her perfumes, spraying them into used bottles and dabbing my skin with them on my way to school or church.

I was glad I was smelling really good the day Father Bloomsbury asked me to see him. I was impatient with the dull passage of time as we did our rehearsal in the left wing of the church. When Father Bloomsbury came to supervise us, he stayed too long pointing out areas that each person needed to improve on and he spent so much time praising Lizza over the deft manner in which she handled the banjo. He also praised Whitney for doing a fantastic job with the violin. He said nothing about how smart I was with the harp, though I played well to impress him. Nor did I like it that he hadn't let others know I was to see him at four, which would have been a big boost for me and would have raised my standing in the choir class if only slightly. I thought about how he said I was beautiful in a shy manner and I wished I could tell everyone. I could imagine the envy that would be on Lizza's cute little face. I wondered if he meant that my face was also cute, though no one ever told me. Well, I assured myself that even if Lizza's face was cuter – especially as I had heard one or two people, even Nick tell her she'd got such a lovely face and an abundance of wavy red hair – I was the one invited to see Father Bloomsbury at The Chaplaincy. That was precisely why I was not happy that Father Bloomsbury didn't announce it. It dampened my spirits a little especially as he stayed on until it was almost four. I feared he might have cancelled the invitation without informing me. I was starting to look miserable when he said, "Afua, kindly keep the envelopes in my pigeonhole." He left without glancing back.

I was puzzled. I had no clue what envelopes he was talking about. His little utterance was not what I expected. It was bereft of the dignity it ought to bear. It had no sense of importance attached either to the message or the messenger. I sat back after everybody had left and tried to figure out where the envelopes he talked about were. I was still there when Nick ran back to tell me that Father Bloomsbury was asking of me.

"Who did he ask?" I inquired.

"Lizza and me."

"And what did Lizza say?"

"Nothing," he shrugged.

"I bet she didn't like that she wasn't the one being sought after."

"She offered to let you know the Reverend wanted to see you."

"She did?" my face lit up in excitement.

"You are getting quite some attention lately. Good for you."

"Would Lizza think so?"

He nodded.

That lifted my spirits – the fact that I got something I knew Lizza would have wanted to have. It also made me feel warmer towards her, to learn that she actually meant to come looking for me. I told myself that I was going to smile a lot more at her and do my best not to feel awry when she beat everybody to the guitar.

I hurried off to The Chaplaincy and was almost there when it dawned on me I had not yet given a thought to why I was needed there, what I would say and how I would behave. I had been to The Chaplaincy only three times since I started attending Mass at St Paul's Catholic Church. On the three occasions, I went in the company of other members of the choir and we sang to the delight of the Bishop and the delegates he came with. Today, I was going alone and feeling somewhat awkward.

It was that day I realised the building had a penthouse where Father Bloomsbury lived. It was at the penthouse I saw him. He was seated in the pantry when I arrived. A broad smile spread over his face as he asked me in. I settled on one of the settees in the living room. "Come and sit with me," he invited with a winning smile.

I went and sat with him and he held my hand.

"What have you been up to lately?" he asked.

"I've been developing my skills," I responded.

"You've got such full lips. Has anyone ever told you they are inviting?"

I was taken aback by his blatant admiration.

"They are terrific. Perfect!" he said as he got up and moved towards the dining section of the living room. From there he asked, "What shall I get you, a Coca-Cola or Malt drink? There is also Pepsi and pineapple drink."

I kept wondering to what I owed this attention. I was glad to be its sole recipient. My back began to gradually relax on the soft backrest of the settee as I said, "Pepsi, please."

"On the rocks?" he teased, with a soft chuckle.

"No, Father," I found myself smiling broadly as he winked at me from the dining area. I shook my head.

He served the Pepsi, filling my glass gently after which he held it to my lips and asked me to take a sip. I did and was startled by his next words, "Can I kiss your luscious lips?"

"Father!" the word escaped my lips before I knew it. The drink in the glass I held spilled on me.

"Yea, Father," he repeated. "Why don't you call me Tom? That's my name, you know. And I am just like you – human," he whispered the last word and smiled broadly. "So, give me a kiss, if you don't mind."

I told myself that would have to be an advanced form of a holy kiss especially as he waited and got my nod before he leaned over, kissed me long and deep, his tongue warm, intimate, probing. It totally relaxed me and I found that I was no longer shy. I was curious but not afraid.

"Have you been to confession lately?" he asked, licking my neck.

"No, been a long time I went."

"I find we'll be better off if we avoid putting it off often."

"But I can't go to confession now."

"No, no, not now. I can't hear it either. Say no more, come and sit on my lap. You are such a dashing young woman."

I liked the things he said and the gentle and kind manner he said them. They made me feel special. Even the way he did what he did with me later was so tender as he whispered into my ears until I experienced a frisson of joy, which pleased him greatly. I was responsive to his affection and I felt that in him was everything a girl could possibly desire. I held him the way I had seen my mother hold my stepfather in one of their private moments. I had seen them because I sneaked up to the pantry and peeped through a tiny hole on their door. She was all wrapped around him, her head resting on his shoulder, her lips forever kissing his chest. The first day I saw them I was upset that my stepfather could be so gentle with her yet rough with me. I kept sneaking up there to see them when they were alone in their room. I stopped only after I narrowly missed being caught by my stepfather who suddenly leapt out of bed and said he was going to get some wine from the refrigerator.

"What are you thinking about?" Father Bloomsbury asked.

"Father, I really want to go to confession now," the words tumbled out of my lips.

"Please, please, dear," he clasped his hands pleadingly; "I know I can trust in the love of God and his mercy, but this is a bit too much for me. He is a just and holy God as well. In fact, woe betides anyone who dares to trifle with his justice and holiness. Pardon me. I am afraid I can't hear your confession right now. I myself am in dire need of one," he said, his eyes growing dim as though he was holding a conversation with someone else.

"But I need to tell you something, Father," I said drawing up my skirt to cover my nakedness.

"Afua dear, please don't insist. Just lie down beside me and be calm."

"No, I don't mean that sort of formal confession. I just want to tell you what I've been up to lately."

He gave me an indulgent look and shrugged as though beginning to understand that I did not have the sort of mature mind to appreciate his sudden need for silence.

I told him about what I was doing with my stepfather. I told him about my insensitive mother, the drab house I lived in and how I missed my friends. I told him also that I found solace in singing in the church. Then I told him that I liked him very much.

He drew me to him as though meaning to console me, as though he thought I had been through a lot. I was not sure what he was thinking as he held me, saying nothing, caressing my right shoulder, squeezing it after a while with a faraway look.

Then I began to wonder what would happen if someone came there and saw me in his arms. While I was proud he invited me to the penthouse, I was not sure I could hold my head high should I be discovered in his arms. I told him what I was thinking and he said something about my being right but added that he had taken care of such an eventuality. Then he lapsed into silence again. Time passed and he managed to rouse himself as I stroked his hairy chest, my head resting on his shoulder.

"You are a sweet child," he muttered.

"Aren't you going to say something about what I told you?" I propped myself up on one arm in order to get a glimpse of his face, which remained calm.

"I'm afraid I am not fit even to give you advice."

"But give me all the same," I nestled to him.

He began stroking my hand again, "I would like to tell you what I would tell myself, 'Don't do it again.' I know it's hard but we need to keep trying not to give offence to people, to God." Then he seemed to be speaking to himself, "I know the importance of chastising the body. And believe me, I've been dealing with this obstinate and insatiable body all my life, starving it, punishing it by engaging in all manner of acts of self-denial, but it is pretty stubborn. It always devises new ways to indulge itself. Yet I must take responsibility because I am the one who should be in control. I should steel my will and fight all my battles, particularly those of the flesh. I know. I know. I have stifled my spirit-man and have been overfeeding the mortal man. What a shame indeed!"

"You started saying something to me," I interrupted him.

He gave me a peck on the right cheek and smiled, "What do you know, child!"

"Enough to know I don't want my stepfather anymore," I tried to look serious. I wanted him to see that I could act maturely.

"Why?"

"You just said it was wrong. I shouldn't do it again. I read somewhere that such a thing attracts retributive justice."

"But you know that retribution does not always come in this lifetime. Let's avoid wrongdoing for the offence it gives rather than the punishment it attracts."

"My problem is that I do so many wrong things. You just pointed out one of them."

He held me to himself, "Yes, it's easy to point out things that are wrong, isn't it?"

I nodded.

"But you've got to see why it is wrong and be convinced about it. And I don't want to saddle your little head with St Paul's teaching about the body being the temple which should not be desecrated and all that. No, I don't want to go into anything of that sort. But did it *really* feel right, what you did with your stepfather, what we just did? The truth is it *really* doesn't. I don't know what you think, but when you give it profound thought, you'll agree with me that it isn't something we should be proud of. Sure, on the spur of the moment, I enjoyed it absolutely. You probably did too, I hope?"

"He gave me a look that seemed desperate to assure itself that it had not been completely taken over by the devil. He wanted to be certain I had as good a time as he did, to which I nodded vigorously. I liked listening to him. I thought he scintillated with wit. In any case, sitting quietly and listening keenly is one of my many accomplishments. So I gave him my full attention.

"Would I do it again, I hope no. Would I like to do it again? Certainly yes," he answered coldly, calmly, looking into my eyes. "Such is the level of the idiocy of the flesh. Shall I continuously strive to resist this surging idiocy? Oh, yes. And will I succeed? Who knows? I pray so because I *honestly* want to succeed."

"You mean you don't want me anymore?"

"Far from it, my child. I want you even now." He chuckled. "Aaah, the body is terribly vulnerable, so unreliable. It constantly seeks pleasure and comfort. That's why it needs a wise mind to take charge, a powerful mind to tame it. St Augustine fought fiercely against his body and disciplined it. I have to sit up and face my struggles considerably. Give me a kiss and let's get something to eat."

He made a turkey croissant sandwich for two and we ate in silence. Before I left, I asked him when he would like to "see" me again. He hesitated, before telling me we would see the following week. Then he asked me to keep him in my prayers.

The following week as we made love rather wildly, my supple, smooth brown skin a sharp contrast to his very light, tight skin, he seemed to have overcome his little sense of guilt, for he said nothing about St Paul, nor did he ask about my stepfather. Instead he gave me loads of books on self-development and made me promise to study them and act on them. Though I was not his equal in intelligence I was willing and determined to improve.

Our next appointment was in a fortnight and I asked him why. He said they had a diaconate meeting that week and he asked me to pray fervently for him as he was going to be preaching at a retreat as well. I studied those books diligently, rising at night to try and assimilate them. I was going to keep the promise I made to Father Bloomsbury by also applying the knowledge. I did not want to fall short of his high standards. Before long my mother began to tell me that she could feel the effect of my learning in school. My classmates asked me who my home teacher was so they could recommend her to their parents. My class teacher awarded me impressive marks and Nick stopped me several times to repeat the same words, "You haven't told me which of the angels has been coaching you. Girl, you're well improved in every way. What have you been feeding your mind with?"

Even Lizza stopped short one afternoon, after I played the guitar with renewed dexterity and said, "Afua, the way you're going, you certainly will represent the entire province, not just with the cello but every damn musical instrument. How do you do it?"

I shrugged and said, "I've been reading a lot lately and practising."

"What sort of books?" she asked.

"I read Ziglar, Robin, Clancy, Twain."

"You do? But I read them too."

"I don't just read for the knowledge. I live the knowledge."

"What do you mean? Don't be haughty," she sounded piqued.

"If I am, real success will elude me. And I mustn't let that happen," I said.

"I'm impressed, Afua. Thank you."

"You sure are welcome."

II

Three months had passed since I stopped seeing my stepfather. I could see he still had not accepted it especially as he kept going on about the love he felt for me even after my mother had given birth to two lovely boys and named them Oko and Atsu respectively. Perhaps what hurt and at the same time strengthened me was the way he kept lamenting all he did for me. Sixteen times, he called me an ingrate and said he made a mistake by bringing me to the United Kingdom. He said that were he not a man of God, he would have thrown me out of his house, since I spurned his kindness and generosity. But he did keep quiet when he sensed my mother's movement around the house. He certainly didn't want her to learn of his anger at my ingratitude. Not that my mother was keen on finding out anything, she seemed content just sitting there, rocking the baby in her hand gently with a faraway look. Yes, always with a faraway, sometimes puzzled look.

He began to stay out late, choosing to spend more time at the church than the house. He did get the nanny – a middle-aged woman – he promised my mother. He seemed to have taken his preaching ministry very seriously too as he was always away on a preaching tour. Then my mother began to give him problems. She began to complain that he was hardly home. She began to insist on accompanying him on some of his trips. At first he gave countless reasons why he couldn't go with her – the children being very tender, the risks involved in his job, the many hazards of travelling, how bored she would be waiting endlessly in a hotel room for him to get back, the cost of taking a nanny along with the kids. But my mother insisted there was nothing better than being with him even if it meant going through the ball of fire to stay with him.

Then one day he said: "And this daughter of yours, aren't you bothered about leaving her here while you hop from place to place with your husband?"

"You should think of that, Kessie, you know," she said in a matter of fact manner.

"I have been thinking of that!" he blurted out.

"It beats me that you speak of it in that way," she sounded serious in a casual way.

"Well, you should care what happens to her when you are away," he said pointedly.

"Not only when I'm away, Kessie," she walked up to him and stood in front of him with a deliberateness that suggested she was not as complacent as he thought. Then she flung emphatic words at him, looking him in the eye: "I do bother about what happens to her even when I'm here. I care about what happens to her right under my nose. How could you, Kessie? How could you! And if you're waiting for my reaction, I can tell you right away you'd not like the taste of it. So you better stop, do you hear? Stop right now!"

My mouth hung open. I saw my stepfather's did the same temporarily too, even as he managed to say something that sounded incoherent.

My mother turned and went upstairs to her room. My stepfather did not go out that evening. I was gripped with fear. I kept telling myself that it was possible my mother knew all along. Good God! She wasn't fooled! Or was she? I hoped I was wrong. I couldn't fathom how it was that she took things coolly.

I stayed in my room waiting to be summoned but no one summoned me. I told myself that nobody could understand my mother, let alone predict her. I began to feel awed by her and could not tell whether it was respect or love I was starting to develop for her. I watched the way she looked at me, listened to her tone of voice when she spoke to me, noted the way she sent me on errands; and I observed that nothing much had changed. It made me wonder a great deal at her, for I was beginning to feel she was not altogether laid-back, insensitive and careless.

I think my stepfather probably realised this earlier than I did and was so deeply affected by this realisation that he became much more cautious. He avoided me as much as he could and began to spend more time with my mother so that often I wondered if his preaching ministry was not suffering. But he didn't seem to mind that it was, as he did say to my hearing that he had been training a lot of assistants lately and wanted to give more time to ensuring stability in his family.

I was glad that whatever was going on in my house did not affect my programme at church. My stepfather still bought me things he felt I needed, though now he would give them to my mother to give to me, rather than the way he used to do it which was to give me things that I would then show to my mother who would thank him and say something about how he was bent on spoiling me.

Sometimes I pitied my stepfather, especially when he was not angry with me and was not cursing under his breath; he would occasionally pull me aside, by the toilet door and snatch a kiss and tell me that I was denying him pleasure because I couldn't imagine how much he was in love with me. He kept insisting he had made his feelings towards me abundantly clear and did not understand why I refused to be "his little girl." He even told me that if it were possible to marry me, he would have loved to. He said he sometimes wished he were a Moslem with such liberties to marry up to four wives provided he would love and care for them dedicatedly. It never ceased to amaze me that he could think of such a thing as marrying me when he was married to my mother with whom he appeared very much in love when they were together. He would lick her all over, tirelessly whispering his unending love. It used to make me both sad and happy. But now it made me really happy for my mother, that she had a man who could love her like that. I was glad too that I had a man who loved me like that. I couldn't bring myself to tell my stepfather that. But I let him know again and again that it was all over between us. I did not bother to tell Father Bloomsbury. I simply loved him with renewed intensity. He had a way of making me feel special each time I was with him; even when it was only once a month, he still made me feel loved, cared for and he seemed determined to make up for his absences. There were also periods we saw each other almost every other day. I cherished each moment with him. We would cling to each other as though in each other we had made the best discovery that we couldn't afford to let go of.

Unknown to Father Bloomsbury, I was preparing fervently for the first anniversary of our love. I could never forget the first day I was alone with him in his living room, the first day he held me as though I was all that mattered in his life. It was my first time of feeling loved and truly important. Out of the money my stepfather gave me I bought fruitcake and vanilla ice cream and some candles, which I would take to Father Bloomsbury. I planned to drop the cake and my gifts in the cabinet by his door and stick a note to his door so he would see it and take the gifts in. I wrote in the note that even though I would love to see him, I did not want to ruin the surprise by asking for an appointment. I was prepared to leave it to chance. If he was home and it was okay to see him, I would be delighted if he could put a call by 5pm to The Chancery where I would be seated by the phone waiting. I said that if I didn't get his call by 6pm, I would go home pretty sad. I ended the note by indicating that I would not like to be sad on the first anniversary of our love.

I dressed in his favourite shades, the outfit he liked to see me in, the very one he bought for me on my birthday: a burgundy lacy top with a flared skirt. I remembered that the first day I wore it to see him he had spread his arms in excitement to receive me as I flew into his embrace, jumping high so that he caught me in mid-air. He held me as he looked up at me, his eyes beaming with joy. It was that day I bemoaned the fact that he was a Reverend Father. It was that day I asked him innocently if he could marry me. He was surprised at first. Then he laughed over it and said that the only way that could happen was if he left the Priesthood. And the manner in which he said it indicated that was unthinkable.

"Or the church," I had said.

He shook his head and muttered something about how improbable that was. In my eagerness, or perhaps childishness, I had suggested he wrote to the Pope for permission to marry me, to which he smiled and shook his head vehemently at my obvious naivety. "Marriage is not for the likes of me," he said.

I was sure I looked hurt but he soothed me as he said, "You are a delightful girl. Any man would be grateful for the opportunity to be your husband. It's just that I am not cut out for marriage. Personally, I can't deal with the intricacies of married life."

"What if the church approves of her priests marrying, won't you marry me and learn that vocation?"

"Do you want to know the truth," he had asked, his eyes glittering under the glare of the chandelier in his living room.

"Yes."

"No, because I will not encourage any woman to go through the torture of marrying a restless soul, flighty spirit and blighted body like me. Besides, I sincerely believe that priesthood has enough pains and pleasures and should not be saddled with those of other vocations especially a complex vocation like marriage. You know, as tough as celibacy is, it is good for priesthood even with all its trials and torments. The character, discipline and nobility it bestows should not be dispensed with. I do not think a priest should be fettered by family responsibility," he had finished as though talking to himself, as though I was not there with him. I had left it at that, though I never stopped dreaming of someday being his wife, perhaps when I grew up, when I was at least sixteen. He seemed a person who would always be there, watching and helping me grow.

I had all my dreams in mind as I approached The Chaplaincy on our important day. When I reached Father's house, I gently placed the cake in the cabinet. As I stuck my little note to the keyhole of his door I heard a faint noise at the background and was tempted to investigate it. However, I assured myself it meant he was at home. So I went to wait patiently at The Chancery, glad he did not see when I dropped both the cake and the note, which would have ruined the delightful surprise I had planned for him. The phone did not ring until seven o'clock when I finally dragged myself home. Tears blinded my eyes. Twice I missed the 177 bus going to Woolwich. When I did get on a bus, I missed my stop and had to walk back. I consoled myself all night that Father Bloomsbury was probably out of town and would make it up to me; but I was unhappy that he forgot the anniversary of the day we first made love. I did my best to hide my tears. It was possible that my mother had noticed and chosen to ignore my mood. I liked it that way. I stayed in my room for the rest of the day, especially since the nanny didn't ask for my help in any way.

At the choir practice the next day, Nick startled me out of my chair with the worst news I had heard since I was born, "Have you heard that our handsome Rev Bloomsbury is making out with our dear soft-spoken Lizza? They were together all yesterday. People are starting to think she's pregnant!"

I managed to sit back down, feeling numb. I could have died then, yet I found myself still breathing, even as a cold wind flooded my entire body and made me feel sick.

"What's the matter with you, Afua? You suddenly look pale."

"I'll be fine, Nick."

"Have I upset you with the ugly news?"

"Are you sure about what you just said, Nick?"

"Pretty sure. My respect for him fell when I heard it."

"Then say no more. Let no one else hear it. I'm heading home. I feel sick."

"You're acting strange, Afua! This is some juicy tale and you're walking away from it! It's impossible to understand you girls!"

"You're a voyeur!" I shouted at him.

He regarded me wryly as I stomped off.

My mind was in turmoil. I wanted to head straight home but, as luck would have it, Lizza was at the bus stop when I got there. It must be the very devil that led me up to her and before I knew it, I hit her across the face, to the chagrin of the man who was standing by her side. The man started to make a call, but Lizza pleaded with him to let me be. "She's in the choir with me. She just made a terrible discovery and needs to take it out on me. I'd do the same if I were her." Then she turned to me, "Afua, shall we talk about it, please?"

Her calm humbled me and made nonsense of my fury. She began to walk away from the bus stop. I followed her. We got into Finsbury Park and found a suitable place to sit down. "I read your note," she began without looking at me. Her voice was tearful.

"So you know everything then. You ripped the envelope open to read the note in it? You saw the cake?" Tears welled up in my eyes.

"Yes," she nodded. "The envelope wasn't properly sealed. I saw the cake too, but I didn't let him know I had seen them."

"You've been dating him too, right? "I choked back tears.

She nodded, tears streaming down her crestfallen face.

"For how long?" I asked miserably.

"Almost two years now. How long have you been with him?"

"Yesterday was exactly a year. The cake was to celebrate our anniversary," I burst into tears. The frigid air made it difficult for me to breathe well.

She hesitated and then held me until gradually our heads touched and we found that our tears fell relentlessly. I did not know how long we were in that position, watching our thighs collect our tears of pain and hurt.

"I thought he was a man of God," she said.

"I don't know what to think now. I had all my hopes on him."

She looked faintly surprised and then fiercely said, "How could you? Our hope ought to be in God!"

"You can afford to be self-righteous. Little wonder you dated him. That man means the world to me."

"I've been hurt before, you know."

"So this is your second time of having heartbreak?"

"Third time, in fact. I thought because he is a Reverend Father, he would be more responsible and know that the heart is not to be toyed with."

"Are you going to leave him?"

"Certainly! What would I be doing with a lecher, some wretch of the earth!"?

"Careful, he's still God's anointed!"

"To you perhaps! He lost my respect yesterday."

"Did you really love him?"

"If I didn't, I wouldn't have stuck with him for two years. Who knows how many other people he's been screwing while I was loving him."

"You don't have to talk dirty. I'm leaving now. I have a headache.

I don't seem able to deal with this matter here and now. I feel like smashing his head. At the same time my heart yearns for him."

"That's because we are fools. But I don't want to be a fool anymore."

"So what did you do with my note after reading it?"

"You know I sensed someone was at the door. I waited for the person to rap and come in but that didn't happen. After listening to surreptitious movements, I felt that the person left. Out of curiosity, I opened the door. The note fell down. I read it then put it back neatly in the envelope and I returned it where I found it. He was all the while in his workstation preparing a document. I didn't get to leave until 8.30pm."

"How did Nick see you?"

"I don't know and I am past caring."

"Well, the news is fast spreading," the words merely fell from my lips.

"Who cares!"

"Tell me, please don't lie to me, after you read my note, did you make love to him?"

She was taken aback by the question. "Afua, why are you tormenting yourself?"

"Answer me, please."

"If you really want to know, I didn't. If you know him well, you'll know he wouldn't go working if he hadn't done all that. I'd been there three hours before you left your note."

I couldn't bear the thought that she indeed knew him that well so I started to leave.

"Listen, Afua," she ran up to me, "if it will make you feel better, I'll never have anything to do with him again. He's all yours if you still want him."

I turned then and took the hand she offered. "I still love him," I sobbed. "Please let's protect him. Don't tell anyone what you went there to do. You could say you were helping him with some work."

She looked at me pitifully and said, "Afua, be wise."

"Do it for the love you once had for him and for your reputation too." I began to walk away quickly to keep from breaking down again before her.

I was ill the whole week and didn't leave the house. Just when I was starting to pull myself together I got flu and had to stay back at home for two more days.

Things had taken a different turn by the time I got to the church. The news of Lizza and the man after my heart was already obsolete. Instead, everyone was whispering that Whitney had taken him to the cleaners. He did not come to supervise the choir that evening because an investigative committee had summoned him from The Deanery set up by the Bishop.

I had just left the music room when Nick ran up to tell me. I was asked to appear before the committee at once. He said Whitney was in there and it would be my turn after that some people had actually gone to my house to bring me to the church. Just then, we saw Whitney leave. She wore a look full of courage. When she saw us, she gave a faint smile of acknowledgement and then turned away and walked jauntily down the lawn, swinging the cord from her earphone as her frilly skirt flirted with the wind. She was a tall girl with straight brown hair and a fringe. I wondered at that brief moment what it was Father Bloomsbury saw in her to make him fall so cheaply for her. Maybe it was her confident gait, her queenly carriage and lovely blue eyes. I had to admit she yielded nothing in splendour. Nick started to say something to distract me as I had my eyes glued on her. He pointed out a gentleman in brown suit who was standing far off beckoning. He must be the one who had sent for Nick earlier on. Nick was speaking rapidly. I could hardly pick out all his words, "How can a man of God abuse his body for years in sex? If I were you, I'd tell them the whole truth, as Lizza and Whitney did. You have nothing to lose."

I shrugged and turned in the direction of the man in brown suit, who led me silently into the meeting-room. There another gentleman and two ladies were seated, their demeanour devoid of warmth. Before them was Father Bloomsbury looking pinched with infamy and grief. The glow in his eyes was gone, in its place a gloom that seemed to overshadow his entire being. I could not take my eyes off him until the lady in green called my attention to the gathering of "humble delegates" from the Bishop's office who she said, were on a "fact-finding mission" and needed me to assist them.

"We are all brethren in the Lord's vineyard," the man who appeared to be the leader of the team said, introducing the others and then himself. "I suppose you are Afua Appiah."

I nodded, feeling awkward.

"We have a few questions for you and we would appreciate it if you answer candidly without fear or favour. Please bear in mind that the good Lord is here with us and expects you as his beloved daughter to help us make headway on the matter that brought us here. This is not a courtroom and we are not a panel of judges. We are ordinary church members, the body of Christ desirous of helping one another to continue to be Christ-like. So please relax and let us have a chat with you."

I looked from one to the other and assured myself that they looked ordinary enough, though I wondered how ordinary people could be on such a crucial mission.

"Father Bloomsbury here," he pointed at him, "has told us a couple of things about you and him. Tell us what you know of him."

Tears filled my eyes as I looked at him seated there, his head bowed remorsefully, his eyes glistening with unshed tears. "I love him," I sobbed, startling them.

"You know he is a Reverend Father, don't you?" asked the man who had walked me in, his face expressionless.

I nodded, "Yes."

"Are you aware that he is attracted to several other young girls?" he said cheerlessly.

I nodded, sobbing so badly that I dropped from my seat to the floor. Father Bloomsbury hurried from his seat to try and help me to my feet.

"You can trust us to take care of her, Father," the lady in blue said, frowning.

There was a moment's silence. Father Bloomsbury went back to his seat, still wearing a dismal look. He quickly wiped away a strand of tears that had escaped his eyes. I wanted to rise from where I lay to tell them that whatever I did with him was of my own accord, but I felt too miserable.

"It's possible the poor girl is pregnant too," the lady in green sighed, her face set like someone doing all she could to contain her anger.

"Father Bloomsbury," the mean-looking fellow called, "you have told us that you dated six girls in the two years you have been in this parish and your dates are all aged between nine and twelve. As far as we know, your last attempt was Whitney, who just turned eleven. But she's been such a resolute child. The reason we are here is because she resisted you violently and made bold to report you to the church's Council of Elders."

Father Bloomsbury shifted uncomfortably in his seat. The team members before him were not falling over themselves to help him and the look on his face showed he did not expect any form of leniency. His gaze fell before their stares and his cheeks remained blushed with abashment, making him look pathetic even as he seemed willing to bear the brunt of his misdeeds.

The mean-looking man appeared determined to press his point: "I am certain you are aware that the church relies on you to be discreet." He paused as though allowing the pain of this betrayal to be soaked in the sweat that dotted the embattled priest's forehead, waiting for some gratifying small reaction. Getting only the priest's stare into space, he said: "Did it ever occur to you that you could harm these little girls, could jeopardize their future? They might have been your children! They need protection, not molestation! Did you show them any consideration as our faith demands?" Then he stopped, regarded him pitifully and asked in a voice both soft and sorrowful, "Father Bloomsbury, what on earth is the matter?"

That question seemed to ring aloud in the room leaving very disturbing echoes as the man sat down, drained of the spirit to remain detached.

"You must respond, Father Bloomsbury. It is important you do," the team leader continued dispassionately from where the mean-looking man left off. It was as though he wanted me to hear it even though I was still on the floor sobbing, with the lady in blue attending to me.

As tears streamed down my face while I was being led out of

the room, I heard his response, "I have been constantly aware of the possible consequences of my action. I have tried to get out of this malady. I have been grieved by my many failures. It is a thorn I have neither been able to shake off completely, nor contain. I regret the disrepute it brings to the church. I wish I alone could be dragged in the dirtiest mud or be cut out like cancer. I will submit to whatever measure of reparation the church recommends. I am truly sorry."

I was led out of that place by one of the catechists, a middle-aged woman who was charged with the responsibility of taking me home. She led me to the front of her office where I waited as she hurried to the garage to bring out her car. She had barely turned her back when I realised that some two women standing away from me were discussing the matter. Try as I would I couldn't help overhearing their conversation.

"How did it go?"

"Very badly. I hope for his sake the press doesn't get a wind of it."

"The news is already in the foreground. His conduct has made him fair game for even the tabloid press. He's a bloody frigging sensualist. A total disappointment!"

I cringed at the statement. A huge strand of tear ran down my face.

"No. I think he hardly has the heart. I learnt he wept. You should have seen how he looked today, like someone blown about by the wind! Poor soul."

"He should have known that paedophilia is not for the faint-hearted."

"Isn't that one of the girls he abused?" They looked in my direction.

"Poor thing! I heard she loves him despite his failings."

"She's just a kid. They have to get this lecher out of here at once. I hope the church knows she can't afford to pussyfoot over a matter capable of destroying our young ones."

I was relieved when the catechist's Nissan Sunny pulled up in front of me. I thanked her as I got into her car. But I couldn't stop crying. The harder I tried to stop, the more I cried. Perhaps if I had been able to keep a straight face like Lizza and Whitney, they would not have had to take me home and tell my parents what I had got involved in. Perhaps that reporter from a top-rated cable news network would not have put my mother on the spot as he said, "It must be hard for you."

"The whole world has gone crazy!" she responded, throwing her hands up in exasperation.

It was my stepfather who stretched his anger to the rooftop, shouting at the top of his voice, "Pretenders! That's what they are! Just think of it; celibacy and paedophilia are becoming synonymous! How could we let this go on? That fellow ought to be castrated!"

I was not only pained by the fact that his words rang true but his superciliousness nauseated me.

"You really think so?" the journalist pursued. "Expunge celibacy to retrieve the church from ruin?"

My stepfather was elated, almost as if mildly drunk. "That's some way we can start looking forward to a regenerate society. You can't begin to imagine…"

I raised my head then and held his gaze until his face dropped.

An awkward silence reigned. The reporter whose sensory organs were hyperactive inched forward towards me as my stepfather stepped back.

I told him it had to be some other time, turned and walked miserably to my room.

FOUR

The Good Ones

Ivor Agyeman-Duah

Angelina was lying in bed at the Top Tower Hotel room weary from travel; not so much jet-lagged as from the hustle of airport pre-departure formalities which come with sleepy hiccups and waiting. She did not remember the process of freshening up in the shower and collapsing into the bed. It was two hours after that a waiter with a seductive smile knocked at the door, momentarily startling her to the indifference of her new surroundings.

"Welcome to Kigali," he said: holding in hand a tray with glasses of orange and pineapple juices. The thought of: "Don't trouble the long distance traveller,"came to mind, more so as she had hung the "Don't Disturb" tag on the door's knob.

"Thank you so much," she found herself saying instead, as she took the pineapple juice. "I will call when I need some assistance."

She could not sleep again and sat by the window to discover a panoramic view of the city and it's much talked about cleanness. She glanced through *Inzozi,* the Rwanda Air in-flight complimentary magazine, which she had picked up as the flight transited in Lagos for more passengers who would later be travelling from Kigali to the Democratic Republic of Congo, South Africa and Zambia. That the airline operated effectively in eastern and southern Africa was an impressive record for a country whose airport was, in 2009 a big container with a poor runway. But you are reminded in the airport advertisement that it's now the seventh best in Africa!

Angelina put the magazine aside and flipped through the television channels with the remote control, to a local station. She wondered at the same time whether she should send a text to her mother about her safe arrival. To call her was not appropriate under the circumstance. She had engaged in a tense argument, in fact, disagreement over the choice of her boyfriend, which is what had brought her to Kigali.

Afua Sarpong Bonsu, as they call her mother, thought it a prank when one weekend a little over a year ago, Angelina called her from St. Louis, Missouri, where she was completing her studies at the University of Missouri's School of Journalism. She had found a boyfriend. They met at an African Development Summit organised by the Washington DC-based think tank, Trans-Afrika Forum in Missouri. She did not discuss him in subsequent calls, so Mrs Bonsu thought it was one of those lonely moments of friendship that dies after studies.

She was therefore surprised when Angelina returned to Accra and started playing Rwandan music and talking about Alex, the boyfriend who was likely to emerge top in his graduate class in Economics; she could even talk of the causes of the genocide with some authority even though she was only eight years when it happened. Mrs Bonsu became alarmed later when on a Thanksgiving weekend, she called her two sons, Angelina's brothers to send them good wishes for the occasion; having missed her call, they later called back to say they had been on another phone line with Alex.

"Mum, I am sure Angelina has told you about Alex," Osei, the elder son said.

"Who?"

"Alex!"

"She did some time ago but I thought it was one of those things."

"From Rwanda and she is supposed to live in Accra; how can it work seriously ... and who will entertain that?"

"Well, it's serious Mum... and so it means Angelina has not told you she is travelling to Kigali next month for a holiday with Alex?" The shock was clearly expressed in Mrs Bonsu's face. There was growing anger in her voice.

"She has said nothing to me."

For days, Mum hardly spoke to Angelina. Mr Bonsu, her husband, found it all amusing. He was not too bothered about Angelina's choice but had to be careful between that and his wife's feelings about Angelina being her only daughter. She cannot be allowed the liberty of a foreign marriage, let alone in far away Rwanda, known as a ravaged country. Its seemingly confusing cultures had already led to genocide, a situation she could not handle if love is gone and responsibilities remained.

"We do not marry for fun and love only."

Mr Bonsu's intervention, without it being seen as on Angelina's side, was that the genocide ended twenty years ago, but the bad thing was the scars it left after the acute media coverage. An image of savagery – a media psychology which is what people remember takes time to go away. He could not even bring himself to cite their own similar example.

When he completed his graduate studies, he was employed as a United Nations A3 Officer posted to Addis Ababa at the Economic Commission for Africa. Mrs Bonsu, then his girlfriend, visited him against her parents' advice and stayed for a month. Her parents' argument had been that Ethiopia under Mengistu Haile Mariam was in the news for all the bad reasons. After the socialist revolution of 1974 came famine, malnutrition and dying orphans became the face of Ethiopia on international TV screens. It was at that time in the 1980s that Bob Geldof made his name. The charity concert, "We Are the World" became a sensation. Mrs Bonsu liked Ethiopia so much that when they returned to Ghana for the marriage rites and then finally settled in Addis Ababa so leaving to another post became a big emotional problem. Of the five other UN postings they shared together in Africa, Europe and the United States on retirement, Ethiopia still holds the best memories. But her argument was different, "We are Ghanaians and no dilemma whatsoever of children born of such marriage. Rwanda? Who's heard of it but for the war?"

II

Angelina settled on sending her Mum a text message copying her dad as well of her arrival in Kigali. She could herself not believe the visit and so was not surprised by her mother's protest against it. The airport pick-up by taxi and the hotel reservation had been paid for with Alex's credit card through Expedia Travel in Missouri. It was something she thought could not be done electronically and so her mother's other complaints was something she would have thought about as well if she were a mother too. But just when she was about to send another text to Alex, her father's response came, "Thank God. Keep safe." At least Mum would know. She smiled to herself. She would have to wait for at least a day before Alex arrives from Missouri transiting in London and then in Nairobi from where he would fly to Kigali.

Her mind again shifted in a monologue to their first meeting, then to Alex's impending employment as research economist at Rwanda's Ministry of Finance. It is one reason for the visit: an interview for him and for her, to see the country for the first time. He would be working if all goes well with the Chief Economist at the Ministry who they had met at the conference in Missouri and have since become friends with. The Chief Economist has promised her an arranged interview with the Minister of Finance. She had done an internship with *The Wall Street Journal* in New York. They had praised her highly, especially the Bureau Chief, for insights on commodity reporting in West Africa and on cocoa in particular. If she was able to do a good economic profile on Rwanda, when she told them of the visit, they could use it. Seeing herself as an economics journalist and writer already, Angelina had edited *Africa*, the monthly students' publication, whilst an undergraduate in economics at the Imperial College London.

III

When she heard the knock on the door in her deep sleep almost midday the morning after, she did not need to ask who that was – Alex! She opened it still in her velvet nightdress and then a speedy embrace and kisses oblivious of the presence of the porter. He still looked handsome though exhausted.

All he wanted to do was have a prolonged shower which he set himself to whilst Angelina ordered pork chops, rice and vegetables with some *pilipi* – the oily pepper sauce Alex had spoken about endlessly.

"Do we eat or make love first?" Angelina found herself asking after his shower. They burst into laughter and cuddled up in bed. Suddenly there were thunderstorms as is often the case in Rwanda; rain falls just like that.

"I just like the scent of dust mixed with rain water. It's so romantic. Alex drew her closer and she felt his warm embrase.

"The first time you made love to me was in my apartment in Missouri, it was raining like this and I remember and you were a bit shy." She slapped him lovingly and gently as he indeed did so again, silence taking over, in this long-awaited moment.

When the waiter announced her presence with their room service order (too long on arrival but good timing all the same) they were exhausted but still smiling at each other. Angelina signed and received it. Over lunch, Alex talked about their trip to the southern province the following day and Angelina's interview, the day after, with the Minister of Finance, Ambassador Gatete, who before that portfolio had been Governor of the Central Bank after serving as High Commissioner to the Court of St James's in London. The profile intimidated Angelina but she was most eager. She had only five more days to spend with Alex before his trip back to the United States and return to Kigali to start work. He had told her about how beautiful the outskirts of Kigali were if you were driving towards the western part to Goma in the Democratic Republic of Congo or the south.

"The driver comes at 7am and so we leave at 7.30am," Alex said after the lunch, his head in the skies... He fell asleep there until deep in sleep, she positioned him well, admiring the face of the man who boasted of being older than her by two weeks in their twenty-eight years of life.

IV

They sat at the back of the rented Prado with the driver, Charles in front and in charge as they set off to the south province. Negotiating traffic in commercial parts of Kigali unto the outskirts and Kigali like every city has its brisk movement of people. These days, the billboards advertisement of transnational telecommunication companies adds to them: MTN, Airtel and multi-racial crowds – Indian, Chinese, Rwandan and Ethiopian all mingling freely. As the commercial hurdles are cleared, the journey of hill climbing begins: Rwanda they say is a country of 'a thousand hills.' Angelina was afraid of heights but those were the things that spelt the beauty of the country. Hundreds of horticulturists were seen at work all along their route constructing terraces and planting trees against soil erosion and landslides, pruning outgrown weeds in their orange overalls. Although one witnessed a lot of poverty along the way the environment was very clean. These community workers earned their keep from this through the Local Government. Some had diversified from this employment into supplementary livestock rearing cows, goats, chicken with coffee cultivation and thatched houses giving way to concrete or brick type houses.

"In much of Africa you see the poverty of the people in their environment but here it is not so bad," Angelina said.

An hour and half onwards in a town called Kabgayi, she thought she had seen the most beautiful part of the country. The weather was cloudy and many people were walking about in jackets. On both sides of the road, you could see irrigated vast waves of rice farming and manicured beds; hills convolute and the driving was zigzagging parallel to the hills and the road pavement with trees lined along avenues. They drove about an hour more through Nuanza District and to the next one – Huye District whose *Buture* town was their destination and the tree-lined avenues still continued.

"Charles, what is the name of this tree with a long trunkand leaves that sprout from the middle to the apex that line this long avenue?" Angelina asked.

"It is the *Inturusi* and it goes as far as to the border town with Burundi. Its lifespan exceeds a century. And they cannot be cut without authorisation from the district council."

In Buture, Charles drove on the instruction of a yahoo map to The Vineyard Lodge built inside a forested grove like Martha's Vineyard in Massachusetts. It had, in place of small lakes more hedges neatly cut and had only ten rooms. Built with bricks and owned by a Rwandan and his African American wife, the Simpsons, it had been recommended to Alex by a friend in the United States.

The Simpsons were hospitable and after they had been shown their room and Charles to one at the outer house, they shared orange juice as they placed an order for lunch.

"What can we do this evening or see before we go back to Kigali tomorrow?" Alex asked.

"Well, we plan going out for a musical concert. You can join us in your car and get the ticket at the gate," Mrs Simpson proposed.

"It's a wonderful musical trio and it is at the recently built Arts Museum at Rwesero in the Nyanza district which is about 20 minutes drive from here. They are called, 'The Good Ones'…"

Angelina screamed with delight but she immediately apologised for the uncontrolled emotion.

"The Good Ones, my God!"

Alex smiled, surprised himself at the coincidence.

"My girlfriend has always wanted to see a live concert and it never occurred to us that it would happen here."

Angelina had missed their live performance when she last visited with a cousin in Britain during the end of the university term; that performance was at the Charlton Park in Wiltshire was featured in *The Guardian* Review pages as "Rwanda is My Home" and was described as "mesmerising close to harmony."

Alex's difficulty was, if he would be able to control Angelina's emotions at the concert. Since the *New York Times* first wrote about these genocide survivors, the musicians were so poor they roamed the streets of Kigali and still played their guitars with missing strings. Their so-called "worker songs from the streets" had no audience to entertain let alone an income. They barely spoke any other language apart from Kinyarwanda, the medium of their ancient traditional songs of love and peace. To patrons and the American Emmy nominee producer, Ian Brennan, these songs were overshadowed by unparalled rhythm. Brennan had discovered them as he travelled around the world in search of unique music.

Angelina later bought the CD of twelve songs, "Kigali Y' Izahab." It made her sad every time she played it and sometimes made her quite emotional. Alex found her once in tears at her apartment in the university and at first was alarmed until he realised it was the music.

"I think the empathy you have for the survivors of the genocide (the last one in the twentieth century) is vested in this music. Others have fainted on coming to terms with it as on a visit to The Kigali Genocide Memorial Centre."

"You do not know the feeling that overcomes me when I hear those voices," she said as Alex looked at the CD poster of the trio: one with a bewildered face, another of relief and the third of hope; all holding the wretched instruments before they became famous and toured the world.

Angelina was surprised to find a small audience when they drove to the Arts Museum with the Simpsons in their small car. When the concert began, Angelina realised how good they looked compared to when the CD photo was taken. They started with "Sara" and by the time they got to Track Ten, she was sobbing and so emotionally charged that the Simpsons were concerned and didn't know what to do to help. Alex cuddled and held her. Other patrons saw the emotions. When it was over with Track Twelve, Alex was so relieved. All he wanted to do was take her to the Lodge but she wanted a photo with the trio first. After that, he went to apologise to the Simpsons who were drinking at the Museum's bar. They thought it needed no apology.

"It's inhuman not to cry out or show strong emotions about something that touches your heart this way," Mrs Simpson responded and explained her own first encounter with the genocide to Angelina.

"I fell ill for three days after I visited the genocide museum. My human instincts totally appalled the inhumanity I lived through in the hour tour; the slaughter of mothers and their innocent children. When I got to know that the 23-year-old confident tour curator who took us – an Albanian group and I, was a genocide survivor, I wept bitterly. Some like me fell on the floor with our lit candles, as witnesses of the historical past but also as its pilgrims. It was this survivor, called Phillip, who in front of other distraught souls comforted me.

I was told Phillip was only five, ill and being nursed by his mother when the hatchers entered their family compound near Gisozi, the central gory point. His mother knew the end was near. She hid the sleeping baby in a bedroom hut and partially covered Phillip's body against suffocation before facing her fate with ten others in the compound.

When Phillip woke up hours later, he cried out from the room into the compound and onto the scattered corpses. He sat by that of her blood soaked mother innocently trying to wake her up. The vultures hovered below the sky onto the rooftops as they saw the carcases of a family. Their hovering and the noises they made frightened Phillip who intensified his cries. It was also that which led the UN soldiers patrolling the neighbourhood to trace the cries to the house and go to his rescue. As they were taking Phillip away, he continued crying pointing his hand at the murdered mother."

Mrs Simpson was eyes was welling up at this point now and she became rhetorical, "Do you know what Phillip told me when I asked why he would curate such tours to remind himself of what should certainly be, horror of horrors? He said, 'Vengeance is the Lord's!' I will never forget his touch on my shoulders as he gently smiled at me lifting my broken down body from the floor at the end of the tour.

So I understand how you feel Angelina.

They finished their drinks and departed in their different cars. Angelina laid her head on Alex's shoulder at the back of the car on the drive back to the Lodge as he continued to comfort her.

"I hope everything is fine?" Charles the Driver asked as he drove.

"Everything is fine Charles and thanks for your concern. Only a little emotional issue to deal with."

When they got to bed, Alex told her how beautiful she was, bringing smiles back to her face, but she was surprised how small the audience there was compared to the number of tickets sold abroad at their gigs.

"The Good Ones are more popular in Europe and America. Like many things that happened after the genocide, outsiders are discovering Rwanda for the first time and realising its gifts too."

She smiled at him and they smiled together, in each other's arms. They made love twice before cock crew at dawn.

V

The drive back to Kigali the next day was less exciting and they slept almost throughout. They were also tired and got back to Top Tower in the evening after having dinner in town. For dinner they had been torn between the American-owned, Heaven Restaurant which also houses the contemporary Inema Arts Gallery, the Silk Chinese Restaurant and the Indian and Greek, Sphere Sardar and Hellenique; the elite joint which is normally full of expatriates in the evenings. They ended up at the Mama Africa Restaurant in Kimihurura that specialises in West and East African cuisine.

The following morning, they walked within Kacyiru South – further down towards The Village Urugwiro, the State House where President Kagame's office is. As they did, they had to deal with a sudden fleeting drama: some pedestrians stood still in anxious anticipation as drivers aware, parked their cars on the side road to give way. Alex and Angelina turned their backs and saw three police and security-filled patrol four-wheel drive cars. The first one was top-opened and flashing red and blue light. Another followed with some armed police and soldiers, their heads pulled out with intimidating countenance. The third was a black Mercedes Benz obviously an armoured one, with the flag of Rwanda waving briskly. Then there was the surprise of seeing President Kagame through the visible window, dressed in a suit and driving himself. A last security detail followed.

"Rwanda is interesting!" Angelina observed.

"Everybody in Kigali knows the President drives himself."

They turned to another road some few minutes later to go to the Librairie Ikirezi Bookshop which also has a coffee bar. The Dutch businessman who established it said it was the best bookshop in Central Africa though it's difficult to know even if it is impressive. You find foreign customers mostly European at the coffee and the book sections, some working with their laptops. Angelina and Alex shared a pot of Rwandan tea. He bought a perfume present for Mrs Bonsu and a book, *As We Forgive*, an anthology of genocide survival stories for Mr Bonsu and newspapers, Rwanda's leading English daily, *The New Times* and *The Wall Street Journal*.

They walked back to Top Tower two hours later as Angelina needed to prepare and freshen-up for the 4 pm interview with the Minister. They read the newspapers before then, with Angelina reading the foreign affairs sections of *The Wall Street Journal* in particular.

She later changed her dress and went under the bathroom shower. The room suddenly turned dark and Alex peeped outside and reported that the skyline had completely changed with heavy rains hitting the rooftop, even as he was still talking to her. He changed as well and joined her under the shower as they laughed at themselves, kissed each other under the running water, changed position and went back to make love on the bed, in each other's arms. Still laughing, they did not know when sleep dawned.

It was a waiter on a routine supply of bottled water to the floor's occupants who knocked on their door to save them time. Angelina screamed with trepidation at that and checked her phone: it was twenty minutes past her interview appointment.

"My goodness," she shouted and checked a message on it from the Chief Economist at the Ministry which said interview is postponed to 5 pm as the Minister was held up in another meeting. She still had 40 minutes to make it and thankfully she needed only seven minutes drive time. She quickly dressed up and in no time was on her way downstairs to the car park.

"Good luck," Alex wished as she left, still smiling.

"Naughty boy!" uttered Angelina

VI

Gatete combines the experiences of diplomacy with economics, she thought, as alone and waiting at the Ministry's boardroom, she looked at the portrait of President Kagame hanging on the wall.

"Good evening Angelina," Gatete announced himself as he walked in ten minutes later, tired from a parliamentary defence responsibility in Parliament House.

"Thanks so much for receiving me," she got up to acknowledge his presence. "I listened to a bit of the defence in Parliament in the morning and thought it interesting of retired Rwandan civil servants to come back from Burundi to receive their pension allowances from the government of Rwanda."

"It's not normally the case, this is under a special circumstance. Under a Memorandum of Understanding in 1978 between Member States of the Economic Community of the Great Lakes Countries, portability of pension benefits between countries is possible. Member States of the bloc are Burundi, DRC and Rwanda.

"These monies have come to us without interest on the pension contribution and the Rwandan government cannot pay the pensions of the 1,800 people because they were not working here and the deduction did not go into businesses here to build on future benefits… without interest benefits from a pension fund, the individual contributions from workers are negligible."

Angelina asked if her tape recorder could be on. She was told to feel free to record and to sit, as they were standing by then. Ambassador Gatete asked if she could be served with any drink before they start the main interview but she had been served earlier and so thanked him for asking.

"Thanks… again for receiving me but I am very interested in Rwanda's growth strategy. This economy is largely donor dependent but utilisation of donor funds have won praises from the donor countries. It also means growth could be artificial in a way. If donor interventions stop for some reason how do you carry on with your small export receipts of $600 million… and what are, if there are any indigenous strategies that you use for poverty reduction if we overlook the classical strategies of the multi-lateral institutions?"

An hour into this, Angelina was very satisfied with the unique insights of the Minister; and experienced a feeling of triumph. He walked her finally to the door as she waved good-bye to Josephine, the Minister's helpful advisor.

"Well, we look forward to working with Alex and hope we will see you again soon." Angelina, shy of possible gossip around her said, "Thanks so much for this."

With forty-eight hours for them to depart Kigali, they spent the last two nights talking about the meeting with the Minister and the assurance from *The Wall Street Journal* that should the interview meet the editorial standards, they would use photos from Getty Images for it. They also discussed Alex's visit to Accra in a month's time from the United States to meet with her parents before work started for him in Kigali.

They however decided to have their last dinner at the Heaven Restaurant in the beautiful and most secured Kiyovu neighbourhood, not very far from the official residence of President Kagame. Angelina had read about this small restaurant and hotel in a review article in *The New York Times*. They were not surprised to find American tourists at its small garden eating hefty burgers and chatting. As they walked into the main restaurant from the gate, Angelina turned to the reception and with a presence of mind walked to someone she thought looked like Josh Ruxin whose photograph, she remembered from *The New York Times* review article on the restaurant.

"I guess you are Ruxin?"

"Indeed I am!'

"God bless my soul… and congratulations for many things."

Ruxin was bemused for he was not sure what it was for.

"For which of my many sins Madam, if I may ask?" They stretched hands to greet each other with smiles.

Ruxin and his wife were American Jews. He was a faculty member at Columbia University and contributed opinion pieces to *The New York Times* and *Forbes* magazine. They also owned the restaurant and hotel and had over the years been living in Kigali. As he offered Angelina and Alex bamboo traditional chairs to sit on, his wife and three kids joined them. They ended up united by their varying American lives and one conversation after the other, led to a shared dinner over love stories.

"The question we asked ourselves when we wanted to settle here was," Ruxin said over dessert, 'Can a country with scars as deep as Rwanda's be healed?' These were just some of the questions which dangled tantalizingly in front of us, newly weds at a Manhattan rooftop in New York. Could we really make a difference in a country with such a troubled recent history? We had no idea but got on a plane anyway, determined to try."

Fascinated with their well-known story, it was something else to hear it from them. As they got ready to thank them and go to their hotel, someone approached Ruxin to autograph a copy of his well-received e-book now turned into a paperback. *A Thousand Hills to Heaven*, is a story of their love and hopes of a humanitarian assistance turning into the making of a lucrative restaurant. Angelina could only do likewise: she bought a copy from the hotel's small gift shop to be autographed. They left for their hotel promising to lodge there on their next visit.

The following morning, they left for the airport, Alex via Nairobi to London and the US as he had come and Angelina via a direct flight to Accra.

VII

It was with the same anticipation and increasing joy as in her travel to Kigali that Angelina looked forward to Alex's visit. They had twittered, emailed and spoken on phone in between. She had looked around hard in West Airport Residential Area to find a small but lovely hotel not far from their house. The Bonsus' house, on the Akosombo Road, three houses away from the Embassy of Zimbabwe was in one of Accra's exotic neighbourhoods. Lavender Lodge, which she chose for Alex was about ten minutes' walk from home; it is on the same road, with a right turn to Adomi Road. Down Adomi was Angelina's favourite coffee shop and bistro, Cuppa Cappuccino, a recreation joint for the expatriates living and working around the area.

Mrs Bonsu was not much enthused about all this. When

Angelina went to her parents' bedroom, she realised Mum had not opened Alex's gift. When she informed or reminded her of his coming the following day, she was less concerned and responded in the same mood. Between asking and giving information Angelina said, "Can I invite him for dinner the day after?" Mum remembered she had a St Mary's Guild meeting at church but said she could.

In the evening, Angelina borrowed her Dad's car to pick Alex who had travelled on a British Airways flight from London to the Kotoka International Airport. As expected, he looked exhausted and looking around as the passengers got to the arrival hall. She saw him first and rushed to embrace him with a kiss. "Welcome to Accra, my dear!" Angelina took the main luggage and they walked to the car parking lot. Accra's traffic normally heavy from the Osu Ministries area towards the Airport and East Legon, the middle class enclave was dying down as she drove at 8pm. The hawkers were winding down their business and the beggars in wheelchairs assisted by their paid pushers knew the sun had set on pedestrian kindness. Alex absorbed these many scenes as much as a first time visitor would.

They dined together at the Lodge and discussed plans for the visit especially the family dinner the next day. They kissed goodnight as it was getting late and Alex was looked tired.

Angelina drove home to find her parents drinking tea and watching the BBC TV news – their usual routine before bedtime.

"Everything okay?"

"Yes Dad! Alex is at the Lavender Lodge close-by and he sends his greetings."

Mum continued to sip her tea while concentrating on the TV images.

"Okay, good night Dad, Mum!"

"Good night," they responded almost simultaneously.

She could not sleep when she tossed herself onto the bed and wished the night would turn into sunrise so that she could to do whatever she needed to do for her Mum.

The morning did come as it always does. She made her parents' breakfast after serving them with orange juice in bed. It was something she excused Joyce, the house help from, anytime she was back home from abroad.

By 9am she was done and went to the Lavender Lodge to have breakfast with Alex. The time difference had affected his sleep and so he still looked weary when they got back to his room after breakfast downstairs to watch TV. He fell asleep heavily and so she left a note on the side promising to come back to take him for dinner at 6pm and drove home.

They arrived at the Bonsus' house at 6.30pm and Alex was overwhelmed with the aristocratic ambience of the garden house: it's perfectly manicured state, the different scents of the blossoming flowers in aerial float of this obviously refurbished British colonial building. He looked at Angelina, surprised at her modesty. They had drinks in the garden, near the poolside under a palm-laden hut close to a hibiscus flower avenue. They went into the living room when Angelina indicated that her father had come downstairs. Mum had gone to the St. Mary's Guild meeting.

Mr Bonsu was very warm towards Alex who stood up to greet him. He drank white wine whilst they made do with pineapple juice. Conversation shifted from conflicts in Africa and issues to do with democracy and development to Accra. For an hour or so they spoke, as Angelina shuttled between the hall and the kitchen to supervise as Joyce laid the table. Alex made a huge positive impression on Mr Bonsu, his good looks aside.

As Angelina suffered the internal pain of Mum's snobbish boycott, she was surprised to hear the door knob turn and see Mum enter, back home before the time the meeting would normally close. She later learned her friends had persuaded her to come home when they got to know of her decision. Alex stood up for her and Mrs Bonsu looked him twice over with a kind face that Angelina did not expect. Obviously, Alex made a first good impression.

"Mum, you finally meet Alex; you are just on time and can we have dinner?"

"Welcome Alex," Mrs Bonsu said.

Dinner was in silence and Alex only spoke when spoken to or asked questions. The television footage was covering with the

Ivorian elections declaring Alassane Quattare as winner for a second term as President of Cote d'Ivore. It was at that moment that Mr Bonsu asked Alex to tell them how come he grew up in Abidjan the capital of this cocoa-rich growing economy.

"It is a long story," he said, which started with his father. When the 1964 onslaught against Tutsis began, many left Rwanda for nearby Uganda but his father and a brother had worked with an Anglican priest from Ivory Coast who advised that they leave with him to Abidjan. They lived there for about five years until Alex's mother joined her then boyfriend in Abidjan from Kampala where she had escaped to with her extended family. Alex was born in the Ivory Coast and grew up there but his father's brother, his uncle – worked with his father as cocoa researchers. "Uncle Tommy came to live in Kumasi and worked with the Cocoboard. He married a Fanti. My father visited him from Abidjan from time to time."

"That is interesting," Mrs Bonsu responded with her chin partially resting on her open palm.

"Which part of Kumasi does Uncle Tommy live … I am sure you know we come from there right?"

"Yes I do." They all laughed.

"I think in a place called Adum and the house is opposite another which has a small Indian restaurant… Babubaza?"

"Goodness! … The other house adjacent to the restaurant is our family house. What a small world!"

Mr and Mrs Bonsu were overwhelmed with the disclosure of these surprises.

"Did you know this?" Father asked his daughter.

"A bit of it."

"So where is your uncle?" Mrs Bonsu stepped in again.

"He passed away a year after my Dad died. It's just recently I made contact with his family – two of his daughters still live in Kumasi and the son is in the United States."

"…And your Mum?" Mrs Bonsu asked.

"She still lives in the Ivory Coast but has decided after my Dad's death that she will go back and live in Kigali possibly within a year."

The table's absorption of this dramatic conversation was

unending and even though Angelina knew a bit about some of the revelations, she did not know them in as much detail as Alex had revealed. His confidence and poise were brilliant. The short-sleeved jumper, an indigenous wear made to fit from the Woodin fabric she had bought at Osu's Oxford Street in Accra made him look elegant. It was unknown to both Alex and Mrs Bonsu that it was psychological to make Alex look Ghanaian in the eyes of the latter that this choice of clothing had been made. How he handled his cpmversation and elegantly wore his Longines watch, the prize for winning the Longines Graduate Essay on Development Economics at Missouri, made Angelina feel so proud of him. She was unconsciously looking into his eyes through his polished multifocal lenses as the conversation progressed.

"So what do your cousins do in Kumasi?" That was Mrs Bonsu again.

"One is a medical doctor with the Komfo Anokye Teaching Hospital and the other teaches Art History at the Kwame Nkrumah University of Science and Technology. I spoke to them extensively yesterday. It has been agreed that they would come over and take me to Kumasi on my next visit to Accra, since this is only a short visit. If it is alright with you, they would also, when next in Accra, come over to say hello to you." "They are welcome to visit," Mrs Bonsu responded as her phone rang. She ignored it but it rang again. She realised it could be Osei, her elder son. It was. He spoke in an agitated voice to his mother and wanted to talk to Angelina immediately.

"We are all having dinner here but hold on and talk to her…" She gave the phone to her, alerting her Osei was on the line.

As her brother spoke, Angelina let out one of those screams of joy, thanking him. They could hear from the phone's speaker from Osei's end: "Again congratulations!" With broad smiles Angelina unplugged her phone from charging and put the phone's power on, proudly revealing that her article on Rwanda that had been prominently published in *The Wall Street Journal* with beautiful photos had been well received, especially the online version. She put her laptop on to see it.

"For *The Wall Street Journal* to devote three pages for this means a lot," she proudly said aloud as she thanked Alex for arranging it, scrolling down the many messages on her phone which had been off for almost a whole day, as the laptop turned on its power at the same time. Many of the congratulatory messages were from friends in the United States. And the one that made her scream even louder, creating an irritation and joy at the same time from her parents was a message from the newspaper's Africa and Middle East editor. He was asking if she would be interested in being employed as their East and West Africa commodities correspondent based in Accra or Nairobi.

"Of course I would be delighted," she said to herself before finally reading the message to the hearing of all.

Too many stories in one evening. It was late, almost midnight when Alex had to say goodnight to the Bonsus.

"Lest I forget, thanks so much for the lovely present," Mrs Bonsu said, but Angelina knew it had not been opened.

"It's a pleasure and once I settle in Kigali and start work, I will come often."

"Always welcome."

Angelina was surprised about her mother's turn-around attitude and was glad she never told Alex about her earlier resistance.

Mr Bonsu suggested that the security at post help Angelina walk Alex through to the hotel. Hand in hand they walked, with the security before them through the coolness of the midnight scent of the flowers of the gardens in the neighbourhood wafting through the air. The evening had been a success and there was nothing more to say other than perhaps sleep over its goodness. They kissed each other goodnight at the hotel entrance before Alex disappeared into his room.

When Angelina got back home, Mrs Bonsu had locked the living room door but opened it for her.

"Thought you were sleeping over!"

"Alex said it would not be courteous," replied Angelina as she sat in a chair smiling at her mother and looking a bit tired.

"That is thoughtful, courteous and gentlemanly of him."

"But Mum... there is an issue... I think I am pregnant!!"

Mum and daughter looked at each other and burst into simultaneous laughter.

"That's discourteous and ungentlemanly. I suspected that some few weeks back ... but the good ones come home and are polite to the core."

They climbed upstairs to their rooms, Angelina to a night of joy to the world.

FIVE

Good Night, Prince Koroma!

Boubacar Boris Diop

I had been waiting by the roadside for quite a bit and I was starting to fume over it. From time to time, a cloud of red dust whirled over the acacias and the sound of an engine heralded an oncoming car. I would then stand up, expecting to finally catch sight of the visitors approaching in the distance. As they would be coming from the capital, they could only enter the town from its north end, via Kilembe. Shortly before sunset, a blue Volvo, turning its headlights off, slowed down to a full stop near the wooden bench I had been sitting on for nearly two hours. Someone slammed a door open, then I saw the driver advance towards me. He was all by himself. In spite of his resolute air I first thought he was some traveller lost or seeking shelter for the night.

He was neither.

"Sorry for being late, Mr. Ngango," he said tersely.

We shook hands. I was still sizing him up, whereupon he asked me to confirm that I was indeed Jean-Pierre Ngango, Chief Medical Officer of the Djinkore Commune. I nodded, while carefully examining his features. He was lean and wiry. His wide glowing eyes, as if they were on constant alert, suggested that he was a man of strong character, accustomed to bossing people around. That initial encounter set the tone: a vague feeling of unease that kept me puzzling over it.

He introduced himself, "My name is Christian Bithege. We have seen each other once, at a meeting in the office of the Minister of Rural Development, in Mezzara…"

No sooner had I told him that I didn't remember the occasion than his face turned cold as stone. For a moment we just stood there in chilly silence, both embarrassingly confused. Then he said in a soft voice, "I'm here to represent the government at the Imoko Ceremony…"

He must have thought the phrase was some kind of password meant to facilitate our secret partnership as government employees. In Djinkore, a small town lost in the middle of nowhere, he and I were indeed the eyes, mouth and ears of the State. So what? Was I supposed to understand that by joining me, he was also, more or less, entering enemy territory? I knew the particular cast of mind of these big city folks and sometimes I would tell them, tongue in cheek, that I was a double agent covertly working for the local authorities in Djinkore. They would threaten to have me hanged, but in the end we would heartily laugh about my anti-republican pranks. This stranger was different, for I quickly sensed that he wasn't the type to take such joke slightly. He must be a fanatic, I felt, one of those die hards determined to act out their bigoted madness to the bitter end.

Firmly convinced that he was coming ahead of the other officials, I said:

"I guess the others will be here tomorrow…"

"What others?"

"Your colleagues, I mean."

"As you can see, it's just me," he snapped, his thin lips curled in a tight pinch around the corners.

I pressed the matter: "I'm talking about the official delegation sent every year to represent the government at the Imoko Ceremony."

As I try to recall what happened back in those days, in order to relate them truthfully, I now realize it was at that moment, there and then, that things slipped through my fingers. Here was a good opportunity to corner the newcomer, to instill in him the feeling that his cover was blown and maybe even his life was at stake. Unfortunately, I always lose my momentum when it really counts and this proved to be no exception. Seeing that I was thrown off balance, he eyed me with a mixture of irony and compassion. I was to find out, later on, that this guy, this Christian Bithege, had a deep understanding of the human soul.

It was time to get on our way to Djinkore. His Volvo wasn't in great shape: the top was crisscrossed with slash marks, wires were hanging low under the wheel and the interior smelled strongly of gasoline. The floor mats and the little corners in between seats were littered with mandarin peels and small bottles of our "world famous Montana mineral water."

We stayed silent during the whole trip. He looked grumpy and in any case I didn't feel like chitchatting either. All kinds of questions were running wild in my head. Why did the government decide, this time around, to send only one delegate to the Imoko Ceremony? This was odd and rather unprecedented. Before my assignment to this small town, I knew that every seven years ministers, MPs, high-level business executives and even the President himself would flock in droves to Djinkore for photo-ops with its sovereign. My readers know as well as I do why it has always been so vital for our politicians to curry favours with this old mercurial, greedy monarch, so I won't dwell on the matter. However, I would very much like to know why, all of a sudden, the Imoko Ceremony had lost all significance in the eyes of our rulers. Maybe they had issued a decree stating that there would be no more elections in this country and they forgot to send me the memo? The only thing I knew for certain: the inhabitants of Djinkore wouldn't be pleased with such a decision, because they had elevated the Imoko Ceremony to the status of a planetary event. I began to fear the worst for Christian Bithege and for myself. I simply couldn't picture him standing up to address the whole royal court on behalf of the President. Such an offense could cost him his dear life, on the spot. Like him, I was just a public service employee and since he was lodging at my house, my life was also on the line.

As we entered Djinkore, I gave him the directions to my house, almost grudgingly. When I saw him put his personal belongings in a corner of the living room, I couldn't help going back over the topic that was bothering me so much: "You know, I had my servants clean and prepare many rooms for you and your colleagues…"

"One is enough," he cut me drily.

For all government workers posted in the hinterland, my house was quite huge and roomy. I wanted to put up my guest in the master bedroom reserved for senior government officers, but after a quick glance he declined the offer: it was too close to the kitchen. Gilbert, the houseboy, made arrangements for another room.

Dinner was a boring affair, as would be expected. My guest barely touched the meat platters – mutton and pheasant skewers – and feasted instead on *biraanjóob*, those local mangoes with a sweet juice and a peculiar aftertaste, like fresh sourdough. He would cut them up in little slices, before letting them melt on his tongue, one by one. I proposed to pour him some wine. "No alcohol," he said, gesturing toward the Montana bottle in front of him. Ah, the little caprices of this fruit-loving, only-bottled-water-drinking health nut were really starting to get on my nerves…

How I missed, there and then, the noisy soirées with other government officers from the capital on some assignment in Djinkore! Best good timers I know of, if you are asking me. They would raise so much brouhaha that, by the end of the first evening, my house was a complete mess, but I liked that. At least they were injecting blood and lively colours back into a place that had sunk in a morose, gloomy atmosphere, ever since my dear wife Clementine ran away with Sambou, one of the nurses from my section. Conversations were always light, funny and full of sleazy trivia. They would get drunk on *tiko-tiki*, our local palm-wine, so strong, as everybody knows, that a little sip could bring the dead back to life pronto. I can still hear them pledge, in their slurred voices thick with drunken stupor, to clean up the pigsty that was our country's political life. First and foremost, they would put an end to the dizzying carousel of crassly opportunistic, treacherous political alliances and reinstate the death penalty. Then the show would begin.

Do the people complain of economic crimes? Take this crook to the gas chamber! Come again? What's your claim? This building contractor is corrupt, why? You think he did a sloppy job with the hospital, because the dilapidated walls are now crumbling? Ok, we'll handle that right now: bring on the firing squad in here, double quick! Right on, brother, you know, these hard truths have to come out, once for all and if white people don't like it, they can kiss my black ass. Human rights? Fuck that, we do things differently here. As for that shameful aid money coming with all strings attached, they can wipe their white asses with it and lace those strings around their dicks, we just don't give a shit.

After trotting out those grandiose designs of moral and political reform, we would play loud, banging music, frantically shaking, twisting, and bouncing on a makeshift dance floor with a couple of Djinkore party girls, until the break of dawn. As the sun rose, we would collapse from exhaustion; our sweat-drenched bodies slumped under the girls' arms.

I also remember that my colleagues from the capital used to ask all sorts of questions, at times quite naïve, on local customs in Djinkore. Above all, they were dying to check all the crazy stuff that was rumoured about the Imoko Ceremony. Was it true that nobody ever saw the king eat or drink? And the story about him, you know, *actually* sleeping among the stars? That's just insane, man. Really, you think he can do *that*? Was it also true that he flew back up to the heavens with the queen mother, who kept complaining about her arthritis during the return flight, saying that she was more than sick of the whole damn business, that this wasn't for old folks like them? My guests were always wagging a skeptical finger: "You know what, this is too wild to be true. Come on, man, you can't be serious!"

As I didn't want to get mixed up in such complex matters, I just told them what they already knew. In Djinkore, every seven years, the Two Ancestors rise from the dead and for a whole night, called The Sacred Night of the Imoko, they tell their descendants how they should rule for the next seven years. It was as simple as that. On that night, the Two Ancestors, in a voice seething with scolding anger and indignation, expose all criminals and evildoers, bring to heel all the unfaithful wives, worthless husbands and tyrannical chiefs. The town is then stricken with a paralyzing angst for everybody is scared stiff that the Two Ancestors, in their mad fury, might simply destroy Djinkore under the flames and lava of a volcanic eruption. So from sunset to sunrise, the kingdom is holding its breath. Before space-travelling back to their cloud-covered celestial mansions, the Two Ancestors would reveal the name of the monarch who was destined to be installed on the millennial throne of Djinkore.

As I said, my guests knew all of this. After all, they weren't randomly selected to represent the government at the Imoko Ceremony. However, they were always fishing for little details, odd bits and pieces, the kind of stuff one likes to tell friends after a long trip or at night, around a campfire. For instance, some of them enthused over the fact that the Two Ancestors were a man and a woman. They saw in this an innate sense of fairness among the inhabitants of Djinkore, a prescient "gender-based approach" and all in all, not to put too fine a point on it, a masterful lesson of good governance, for the benefit of humankind at large. My colleagues' nonchalant, cavalier attitude always came as a shock to me, but I found them more amicable, easier to get along with.

How different was my evening with Christian Bithege! Under the dim light of the living room, comfortably seated on a couch, he was going through some documents, every now and then staring into the blank space around him. The mood was so austere that even the usually cheerful houseboy looked sad and depressed. Later on, Gilbert told me that from the moment he saw Bithege step out of his blue Volvo, he knew, deep in his guts, that he didn't like this man.

The next morning, we went to buy bananas and guavas at the market. Gilbert could have handled that errand for us, but Bithege wanted to visit the town centre. The Imoko was only four days away, so on both sides of the main thoroughfare – actually, just a tiny stretch of laterite – people were busy with activities and preparations ahead of the ceremony. We met several groups of dancers mounted on stilts, making strident, chirpy noises as they blew on whistles. While humming ancient work songs, young women tossed millet on a basket, to remove the chaff, or pounded it in a mortar. The Imoko was the sole topic of conversation. Some railed against the sudden price increase for sugar and oil, while others predicted that at least two million people would come to Djinkore for the ceremony. As we passed, many raised their heads from whatever they were doing to greet us cheerfully, although not without casting furtive glances at my companion. Bithege always acknowledged them with a faint nod, but his mind was visibly elsewhere. Today, in retrospect, I wonder if, at that very moment, some didn't foresee the tragic course of events bearing down on us. The truth is, as the Imoko Ceremony draws closer, the inhabitants of Djinkore grow restless. Waiting for the coming of the Two Ancestors takes a toll on them, it makes them nervous, to say the least. It's like, you know, they can't get these two ancestral monkeys off their backs. Once they have landed on earth, the Two Ancestors must then say something, but what will it be? Nobody has a clue whatsoever. In their angst-fueled expectancy, the people read into every unanticipated event, such as the presence of Christian Bithege, a good or bad omen.

"People here seem a little edgy," said Bithege.

"What makes you think so?"

"It's just obvious, hard to miss it."

This fellow was definitely special.

"You're right," I concurred, "there is always some tension in the air before the appearance of the Two Ancestors. This will be my third ceremony and I'm sure it will evoke the same feelings as the first one, fourteen years ago. It's an experience like no other, you just can't forget it."

"There is no need to worry, everything will go as planned."

He said it in a rather contemptuous tone, as if implying that all this effervescence surrounding the festivities was mere smoke and mirrors to keep the rabble in line. I was more or less in agreement with him, but all the same felt a bit slighted in my self-esteem.

We stopped in front of a fruit stall and I introduced him to the vendor, Old Casimir Olé-Olé. "Mr. Bithege is here to attend the ceremony. This year, he is the government emissary."

Bithege nodded, then slightly bowed in deference to Old Casimir. For a few seconds, as they shook hands, the two men sized each other up. Old Casimir was what you would call an oddball. He had built a little cabin near the entrance to his house, right in front of the market. There he would sit all day long, waving a flycatcher over his merchandise – mangoes and *ditax*,[1] coconut slices and dried fish. He was at pains to appear like a simpleton, a completely insignificant fool even. I believe Old Casimir's biggest dream was to turn, overnight, into a shadow, so that he could be privy to everything without being seen. His whole demeanour seemed to be saying: "Call me Casimir Olé-Olé. As you can see, I'm right in front of you, but please forget that I'm here, act as if I don't exist." The clever fellow was even pretending to be deaf. No matter what he was told, he always asked his interlocutors to repeat themselves, while he cupped the palm of his hand around an ear pavilion – his trademark gesture. But while acting up this little comedy, his eyes, beaming with mischief, hinted that he had perfectly heard you. Besides, every time I secretly watched Casimir Olé-Olé, I had the feeling he was keeping an eye on the comings and goings of all the inhabitants of Djinkore, as if he was keen to know what each one of them was thinking, at every single moment of their lives. A solitary man, always suspecting some foul play against him, Casimir Olé-Olé was definitely intriguing for me. Although he lived in abject misery, I anticipated that after his death, people would find a huge sum of money stashed under his bug-infested mattress, hundreds and hundreds of bills, maybe worth millions. At other times, I was convinced he was an undercover police agent, or even one of the big wigs from the secret police stationed in Djinkore.

If I'm telling you all this, dear readers, it is to convey my excitement at staging this encounter between Christian Bithege and Casimir Olé-Olé. Would the latter finally lower his guard? It was all I cared about and I wasn't disappointed – in a way.

Uncharacteristically, Casimir Olé-Olé was rather considerate vis-à-vis our guest. In a casual tone, he had the conversation shifted towards the Imoko Ceremony. According to him, letting the dead decide on all matters of life for the living was a sign of great wisdom.

"I also think it's a good idea," declared Bithege, as he carefully

---

1 Local name for the tallowtree and its fruit (T.N.).

weighed and checked, with his bare hands, each banana he picked from the stall.

The tone of his voice was so bland that I couldn't determine whether he was saying this in earnest or just to make fun of the locals. But I could tell he was a little annoyed when Casimir Olé-Olé asked him to repeat what he just said. Yet he did so, without demur. Then the merchant exclaimed:

"Yes, that's how we can live in peace! The dead always know better!"

The stranger then remarked that nowhere else in the world were people behaving as they did here, in Djinkore. After a few seconds of thoughtful silence, he added conclusively, "But who am I to say who's right or wrong, right?"

For once Casimir Olé-Olé forgot his play-deaf-and-dumb routine, looked at Bithege long in the eyes, and said:

"I, Casimir Olé-Olé, don't know who's right... But let me tell you this: why should we be in the wrong, we the people of Djinkore? Who can tell me why everybody else would be in the right, one way or another, and not us?"

It was time to pay and leave. Bithege gave the merchant a five thousand bill. The latter tried to trick him by pretending to be short on small change. This drove Bithege into a cold, terrifying, but nearly indiscernible fit of anger. He was trying hard to hide it, but it was then that I sensed in Christian Bithege an unpredictable and unlimited capacity to inflict great violence. I could see he was ready to make a scene, even hit Casimir Olé-Olé. Extending his right hand, Bithege obstinately demanded the change he was entitled to. I looked up towards the old vendor and as he locked eyes with me, I realized we had just sealed a bond of silent hatred for the newcomer. I felt that Bithege, too, was aware of this, but he couldn't care less.

After we left, he observed off-handedly, "Quite a character, this Casimir Olé-Olé." The fruit seller was intriguing Bithege too, yet he was counting on me to better figure him out. I felt some satisfaction at the prospect of not obliging him, but back then I had no idea the stranger had already set up his little network of informants. He must have been doling out thick wads of banknotes, for he even enlisted sources from inside the Royal Palace, where I had never set foot myself.

The word "palace" may draw an amused smile from you, dear readers, but I don't know of another one to designate the king's house, although this sovereign, an alcoholic given to pomp and excess, had only one thing preying on his mind: make sure his subjects cast their votes for the most lavish candidate, come election day.

II

I will never forget the day I first heard Christian Bithege call Prince Koroma by his name. It was no offense to do so, but it wasn't wise either. In Djinkore, we don't interfere in the affairs of the royals and their underlings, we do as we are told, without even pretending to know who they are, where they live and what they are called. So I advised Bithege to watch his mouth. Instead of shutting up, he went on to ask my take on the chances Prince Koroma stood to become the next king of Djinkore.

"The Two Ancestors haven't spoken yet," I said feebly. I didn't expect Bithege to fall for that – he was no fool.

"These things are always known beforehand," he said calmly, but with finality.

"Well, for my part I don't know anything, Mr. Bithege."

I was more and more infuriated by his condescending manners, and I made sure he got the point. Yet undaunted, he kept at it:

"You've been stationed here for almost fifteen years, right? So you must know Prince Koroma fairly well."

"I have told you already, your attitude is putting us both at risk."

"But I must know everything, don't you see that?"

He had slightly raised his voice, but without seeming particularly upset.

"I don't know Prince Koroma. Please, let's talk about something else."

He found my half-hearted lie amusing.

"Well, I'll introduce you to him," he said blithely.

"Introduce me to whom...?"

"To Prince Koroma."

"Yeah, right."

A shame I couldn't be more sarcastic, back then. But in the heat of the moment, my heart was pounding so fast I felt like I was on the verge of a panic attack. "This man, "I told myself, "must be completely mad, to act so brazenly."

"I've had many discussions with the Prince," he said. "He's promised to come and pay me a visit, here in this house…"

I cut it short, almost threatening him with a mean look: "Don't make fun of me, Sir. I don't like it."

We had been together for a couple of days and it was the second time I was calling him "Sir." That's when he addressed me in a rather candid tone, almost as if he were confiding in a close friend:

"I'm not making fun of you. Not at all. I have met the prince twice. Speaking with the powerful is part of my job. You need to understand that I'm not like the ones who came to Djinkore before me."

I got the message, loud and clear: Christian Bithege was asking me to choose sides. After all, I was also in the service of the State.

Perhaps sensing that I was a bit confused, he added, in the same affable tone:

"I'm going to have a third meeting with Prince Koroma. This time nobody must see us together. He will come discreetly to your house, but this must stay between us…"

From that moment on, I felt I was completely at his mercy.

For two or three hours, we conversed about this and that. Without really meaning to and without enough strength to restrain myself either, I told him all he wanted to know about Prince Koroma. He asked me very pointed questions and it was clear to me, time and again, that we were crossing the thin line between a normal conversation and a full-blown interrogation. As time went by, it appeared to me, quite distinctly, that the political future of Prince Koroma was at stake. Christian Bithege wanted to have him replace his father, this eccentric monarch who was soon to be a hundred years old. But Koroma himself seemed to be mentally unstable and that's why my guest was a little hesitant…

"This Prince Koroma, is he really, you know… is he *competent*?"

The question would come up many times during our informal talk, overtly or not. It meant: he will know that he owes us, but will he be strong enough to confront his conniving enemies? Since I liked the Prince, I felt I had to defend him. I decided to disclose to Bithege a little personal anecdote. I told him that the Prince had already been to the house once, to see me.

His eyes lit up: "Really? How did that happen?"

That was the first time I saw him a little bit carried away.

So I told him how. "One night, someone knocked on the door, around three in the morning. I opened. It was Prince Koroma. He was bringing me the son of one of the palace guards. The boy was five or six years old and he was having a violent fit of malaria…"

"The boy was five or six years old…" he jeered, intently looking at me. "Then what?"

"I gave the boy an injection."

Bithege contorted his face dismissively. "He must be thinking that we are both two laughable amateurs, Prince Koroma and I," I told myself. He wasn't interested in my story; maybe he found it stupid, even. A six-year-old boy!

"Quite a charming man, our Prince," he said. "But aren't you telling me about one of those dreamy young idealists who figure they can change the world and the way humans are by nature?"

I felt he was cleverly dragging me into a tight corner. Who was he really, anyway, this senior government officer from Mezzara? He hadn't yet told me what exactly his job entailed, in the capital, but I had a good guess he wasn't glued to an office desk all day. I was probably dealing with one of the higher-ups from the political police. In any case, I had to admit he had seen through Prince Koroma's character. The latter didn't fit in a Djinkore royal house that rivalries and palace intrigues were constantly tearing apart. His brooding, melancholy moods and his innate goodness were out of place there: the prince was an angel lost in a ruthless universe.

Bithege knew all of this. He was only looking for confirmation. Deep inside, I laughed at the thought that the only way to help Prince Koroma was to say, "Look here, between you and me, this Prince is a cold-hearted son of a bitch and the worst of his kind. The bastard will do anything to get what he wants, OK? So you can take my word for it: at the hour of vengeance, his hand won't tremble as it falls upon his enemies!"

I couldn't bring myself to stoop so low.

"You know, in Djinkore people are rather fond of Prince Koroma," I said instead, grasping at a last straw.

"Really?"

"I tend to think so. I don't know."

My answer was elaborate bullshit and he pounced on it, sneering:

"There must be a good reason… what do they say about him, then? Tell me."

"They say he respects the religion of his ancestors…"

Bithege acted as if he were making a mental note of this new piece of information. I went on:

"He is a very self-confident young man, never doubts himself. Many members of the royal family toy with… with…"

I was struggling to find the right words. Bithege egged me on:

"Go on, I'm still listening."

"I admire his strength."

"His strength? What do you mean?"

"You know, when people keep telling you that every seven years, your long-deceased great-great ancestors, rising from the depths of time, come back on foot from the sky, just for a little nightly chitchat, there are moments when you must wonder whether this is all really true."

"Yeah, I see what you mean," he quipped.

"Well, I believe one must be strong to always keep the faith and never allow doubt to creep in. You know, we have all these smarties who think the whole stuff about the Two Ancestors is just childish amusement, yet all the while they're grabbing every opportunity to dominate their fellows and enrich themselves; then we have thousands of good people who stand under the sharp light of hope. Prince Koroma is among the believers, those who never give in to doubt or despair. He is really convinced that the Two Ancestors come out of their graves for an all-night prowl around the streets of Djinkore.

"You can also call it being just simple-minded."

His face remained impassive. I couldn't tell whether or not he was approving of what he seemed to regard as the Prince's naiveté. I gave the matter some quick thought and said:

"It's possible. Maybe it also proves his moral strength."

Bithege nodded slowly, then said, as if he were thinking out loud:

"Well, what's the use of moral strength without sheer force?"

It was hard to argue against that. He continued:

"I agree with you on everything else. You know, thousands of people on this earth are getting the most out of these crackpot fairytales. I think that's what Casimir Olé-Olé meant; yesterday... we can't afford to be the only people in history who are always on the wrong side of the tracks. It just makes no sense, as if we were resigning ourselves to a spiritual death by a thousand cuts. Chimeras for chimeras, why not hold on to those of our ancestors, right?"

He had a good point, but he was also making a strong case for Prince Koroma. I drove the nail home:

"I'm positive Prince Koroma will do good things for the inhabitants of Djinkore. Maybe the time has come for this kingdom to have a ruler who also has such a great purity of soul."

The stranger had a cagey smile, but he was still not letting whatever feelings he harboured show.

"Purity of soul... So you're a philosopher then."

III

On the eve of the ceremony, I found Bithege sitting in the middle of the verandah. He looked fresh, well rested and for the first time since his arrival in Djinkore, was in a somewhat pleasant mood.

"I've been watching these lizards for some time now," he said. "They crawl up and down the wall, then vanish into the tall grass..."

I nodded vaguely, not knowing what the hell he was talking about. He rambled on:

"I'd really like to know where they're headed, these lizards. What is their ultimate destination?"

I smiled:

"Let me know when you have solved the case, Christian. I have to run, we're working off our feet at the community health centre right now."

"Right, right, the Imoko of course…"

"Just diarrhoeas and lots of fainting, nothing really serious, but we need to be cautious."

He volunteered to come with me:

"The prince won't show up before an hour. It gives me enough time to take you to the health centre and come back here."

"Sounds good. Let's go then."

"Give me a minute, I'll change my clothes."

While I was waiting for Bithege on the verandah, I heard a scream, near the main entrance. Then there was complete silence. Bithege immediately rushed out of his room, a towel slung over his shoulders.

"What's the matter?"

"I heard a scream."

"Any idea what that was?"

Maybe I was imagining things, but I felt he suddenly suspected me of hiding something from him. He was staring hard at me, with that same creepily evil glow in his eyes. It was scary how his face could assume different expressions from one moment to the next.

Then there was a second scream, much louder. Bithege threw his towel down and rushed out onto the street. I followed him. After a few yards, I saw him stop to talk with Prince Koroma who was coming toward the house. The prince looked haggard. He kept turning his head in every direction while mumbling what sounded like errant nonsense. Between two broken sentences, he was repeating: "I saw them… I saw them…"

"Who are you talking about Prince?"

"They were playing like children! I swear I saw them!"

"Who did you see?"

"They are making fun of us… Do you know they're really making fun of us? How dare they?"

"Tell us what you've seen, Prince Koroma. What is it?"

Today, nearly a year after the events of that day, there is at least one thing I can say for sure: Christian Bithege immediately sensed the extreme gravity of the situation. As for me, I was completely baffled. I also felt too sorry for Prince Koroma to think of anything else. His face, usually radiant with sweetness, was all doom and gloom. If he moved at all, it was because he had to; his body seemed to move cautiously within some invisible and dangerous labyrinth. His crazed eyes were those of lunatics still under the spell of their haunting visions.

With calm and patience, Bithege managed to get the prince to tell his story.

It was indeed a very disturbing one.

Prince Koroma was walking alone in the Diandio Forest when he heard an unusual sound. He hid behind a bush. Then he saw the Djinkore dignitaries getting ready for the Imoko Ceremony. To put it as crudely as possible, without mincing words, the old bastards were casting the lead characters and staging a performance for the Imoko.

You, you'll play Ancestor One. No, not like this, you fool! You can't walk so fast, remember you're three thousand years old and you just got out of the grave? So here is how you should move. Got it? Same for you, Ancestor Two, and don't forget you're a charming old lady, you got this bloody arthritis, etc., etc.

I readily admit that I'm casting it in rash, broad brushes, but only to remain faithful to Prince Koroma's jumbled narrative. The latter said he had never witnessed such a horrible scene: the dignitaries rehearsed their little shit show while mocking the people for being so easy to mislead into believing any crap. Between two long draughts of *tiko-tiki*, they sang and pranced around, grotesquely twisting their tired old bodies. Ancestor One, as they called him, had to try many times before he could manage to give the impression that his booming voice came straight from the deep abyss of time. His feat elicited loud, thunderous applause from his peers. All had their faces smeared with kaolin, ashes and coal. With the birch from trees they had made traditional dresses. From his hiding place, the prince could hear them say his name many times. Amidst loud inebriated laughter, they were joking that Prince Koroma would be a good king for them because he was such a crazy fool.

Bithege feigned outrage at what the prince had just revealed:

"Prince Koroma, do you know these disgraceful individuals?"

"This is all Old Casimir Olé-Olé's doing, he is their leader."

"The leader of who?" asked Bithege.

We both wanted names. But little did we know that Prince Koroma was no longer with us in spirit. He said, very slowly this time:

"So this is all just a fable."

I wanted to say something, but words were failing me. I found the prince's metamorphosis quite fascinating: he was completely losing his mind and there was just no way he would ever recover any measure of sanity.

"Calm down, Prince. We won't let them do it," said Bithege.

"Dirty stinking lies, all of it!" the prince yelled. "They make the Two Ancestors say whatever they damn please! Casimir Olé-Olé is their leader!"

"Casimir Olé-Olé…" muttered Bithege.

He didn't seem surprised that the old fruit vendor was the centrepiece of this whole business. Still, he remained a bit tense.

"Casimir Olé-Olé must be killed!" the prince commanded, before settling into an eerie calm.

"But why?" I asked confusedly.

Of course, I didn't like what the old dignitaries had just done, not at all, but also I didn't see why one would want to kill them. Today, I can better understand what made me freak out so much, back then: it was the feeling that soon, one way or another, I would be embroiled in a political murder.

"The Sacred Night of the Imoko!" Prince Koroma barked. "The Sacred Night of the Imoko! I'm going to tell the people of Djinkore that it's just a bloody piece of shit! Nothing but goddamn lies!"

Bithege was obviously the more levelheaded of us three and he was particularly anxious to know whether the Prince had had time to tell anyone else in Djinkore about his chance discovery. When he determined that we were the only ones to be in the know, Bithege addressed the Prince with the deepest respect:

"Prince, let's go together in the Diandio Forest. Casimir Olé-Olé and his clique will be deservedly chastised."

I almost screamed at Prince Koroma: "No, don't go, don't do it!" I didn't have the guts to tell him. In any case, he wouldn't have heard me. Nothing mattered to him anymore. Bithege went back inside the house, hurriedly returned with all his personal belongings and gestured for me to get in the back of the Volvo. The Prince, like a robot, sat next to him in the front.

As we were about to enter the Diandio Forest, Bithege requested that I leave him alone with the Prince, for a few minutes. There was no need for such formality: I knew what was going to happen. He took out a brown satchel from the trunk. The man was executing every gesture to a plan. An air of unflinching, savage finality seemed to exude from his whole persona. I watched him as he led Prince Koroma by the hand, and disappeared with him behind the dense shrubbery.

He came back forty five minutes later. "Let's go," he said, as he turned the car engine back on.

"I'm terribly late for work," I thought. "At the community health centre they will start asking about my whereabouts." I was trying to convince myself that life would go on, just like before. But it wasn't that simple. My shadowy double was pestering me, drilling the same question into my conscience: "Now, my dear Jean-Pierre Ngango, what will you become after *this*?"

Bithege announced point blank that he was driving back to Mezzara this very evening. I acted as if I wasn't listening. Then he added: "the official delegation will be here tomorrow. The big boss in person will be leading it. I'm going to debrief him tonight."

The big boss... He really took me for a ride, in the end, this Christian Bithege.

The silence in the car was less heavy than on the day of his arrival. This time, I wasn't talkative out of some vague hostility towards him, but more out of a clear need to stay away from the darkness that threatened to descend upon me, following the assassination of Prince Koroma.

Bithege said, his eyes tensely fixed on the road:

"There was no other solution."

"I know."

I sincerely felt he had no other choice, one way or another, although it was hard for me to admit it. Somehow, my indifference spurred him on:

"Everything went smoothly. He didn't suffer a bit."

"Oh, you're very kind, Sir."

Even today, I don't know how I have come to despise this overly self-assured jerk. He took no offense at my spiteful innuendo. As I was stepping out of the car he simply said, in his characteristically bland tone:

"Thanks for everything. Goodbye now."

He didn't wait for me to say anything in return, but I knew what he meant, as he looked straight at me, one last time: "I did what I had to do. Too bad for you, if you can't get it."

It was almost pathetic.

The rest of this story is still fresh in my memory, as if it happened just the other day. The Two Ancestors flew down to Djinkore, as huge and magnificent fireworks lit up the sky. In the early morning hours, the delirious crowd exulted: "All hail the new king! Long live Casimir Olé-Olé!" Then the President appeared next to Casimir Olé-Olé. The king-elect struck a stiff, stone-faced pose, with that mask of weariness and benevolent gravity that, ever since, has stuck on him like a new skin.

SIX

Upon this Handful of Soil

Zukiswa Wanner

The first time the soldiers came to Salome Kruger's farm, she had been listening to Catharina reading the Bible out loud to her as they prayed for the burghers' success against the English. Dusk was falling. Catharina's daughter Paulina and her daughter Elsie had run in with so much terror on their faces that the tongue-lashing she had on her lips for the interruption died.

"Ma, they are here. The English," Paulina, always more talkative than her Elsie, blurted out.

Elsie nodded her head vigorously in agreement.

"Sit," Salome said with more firmness than she intended, to the girls. Then a little more gently as though to calm them and herself down, "Stay here. We shall deal with this." And turning to Catharina she said, "Let's go."

They walked out just as the men and their horses galloped into the yard.

The man in charge gave a command and they got off their horses. Some of them made their way to her hen house and took all the chickens there. Others shot the pigs and threw the carcasses on one of her carts, which they commandeered and attached to two horses.

Others walked into her farmhouse as though she were not there. She and Catharina followed them and Salome regretted asking the girls to stay in the house. One of the men, exhibiting sheer cruelty, kicked at Paulina yelling, "Silly *kaffir.*"

And then it happened.

Like a lioness whose cub had been grabbed, Catharina ran to him and scratched his face, yelling; all the time yelling, "leave my baby, you English bastard. *Fokof.*"

Salome had never heard Paulina yell, let alone use bad words. She seemed to realize too what she had said, how unladylike she had been, how lacking in decorum as she put her bloodied hand to her mouth.

The soldier, seeing the blood seemed to get incensed. He slapped her and she fell down.

"Bloody, stupid *kaffir.* You think you can touch me? Did your whites here not teach you any better?"

Salome wanted to yell out, she is not a *kaffir.* She is an *oorlamse.* The wife of a Griqua prince. But words died in her throat.

She watched in fascinated horror as this man turned beast unbuckled his belt while Catharina screamed. The noise of the other men taking things from her home seemed but a side issue to this abomination being visited on her mother's *oolarmse* who had been her mother's daughter before she was born. And she was frozen with shock. It was only when he was zipping up his trousers again that power returned to her limbs and she ran and pushed him in futility. He pushed her back and she stumbled on the Bible. Dear God. Not her too? He was not going to…

He saw the fear in her eyes for a moment and leered at her. Then he took out his gun, turned to Catharina and shot her. It was the casualness of it all, the way he appeared to have so little regard for human life and his dead eyes that made her blood turn to ice.

And then Salome screamed. And as she did, she saw her daughter Elsie holding on to little Paulina as the two of them sobbed across the room.

God why? That anyone should witness such violence being visited on anyone but worse, that that violence is being visited on the mother.

And then the British, not content with the horror one of them had visited on Catharina, went crazy dragging clothes and blankets. Breaking plates. Struggling with cabinets and wardrobes antiques gifted to her by her parents when they left for the Cape

Colony. Everything they did not break, they dragged outside. They had put it all in a giant heap outside the house and set the heap on fire. All of them seeming to possess a maddening gleam of cruelty in their eyes.

Poor little Paulina. Poor poor child.

And Catharina?

What would she tell Catharina's husband, Adam? What would she tell the young prince who had generously offered to take her cattle to his grazing lands when he had heard of the approach of the English? How would she tell him that their daughter was orphaned and he was now a widow, that poor, good *oorlams* – though not as much as Christian as his wife? How would she tell his five sons that they no longer had a mother? Where was God now?

When he came with her sons to bring the cattle to the kraal, she saw on his face, the sadness at the devastation caused by the vile British. The fire was still smouldering and she had attempted to save what precious little she could from it but with little luck. But he had no idea what had happened to Catharina so when she looked pitifully at him and told him after he got off his horse, he looked at her in confusion and said, '*Ekverstaannie...*'

She did not understand either.

She did not understand how any human could wantonly violate another human being and then afterwards shoot them. Did those men qualify to be called humans?

Animals. That's what they were.

She hurt for him, for herself, for his children at their shared loss.

She repeated what had happened again slowly, leaving out the shameful violation of Catharina at the hands of that man. What did it matter? The end had been death. That is all he needed to know.

Before he came, she had cleaned up Catharina and attempted to make her respectable in death as she had looked in life. As she wiped the blood between Catharina's legs, she could not help remembering that it was Catharina who had talked to her, washed her and allayed her fears when she saw blood coming from down there and thought she was dying. It was Catharina too who showed her how to cut strips of cloth that she would use for that time of the month. Until she got married in a church to Adam, Catharina would go with her so that she could wash the rags. An *oorlamse* but the older sister she never had. They had maintained their closeness after Catharina's marriage, with Catharina visiting her regularly and reading the Bible together as they had been doing today. And although it was she who had received this farm when her parents moved to farm in the Cape Colony, it was as much Catharina's home as it was hers.

So she told Adam, "We shall bury her here in the orchard under the orange tree." She paused and with a faraway look in her eyes and a distant voice added, "She planted that orange tree." And Adam did not seem to have much strength for fighting.

And later, much later after Catharina had been buried, when Salome insisted that Paulina remain with them, Adam did not argue. Now left with a household of five strapping boys all older than Paulina, Adam probably would not have known what to do with an eight-year-old girl.

It was Adam who gave her and the children more blankets and all of Catharina's clothes and sewing machine. She used some of the clothes to sew new clothes for her children and kept some for herself.

That was months ago.

She had refused to let Catharina's violation and death break her despite the devastation and hopelessness she had felt then. As her neighbours on farms nearby ran into the alleged safety of the camps, Salome Kruger had stayed on. It flew in the face of everything she stood for to surrender and leave. Her Marthinus and her brother Hermanus were out somewhere fighting and she felt that they needed to know that this was home and hearth. A place to keep and worth fighting for. If she surrendered and left, she feared, he would surrender too and then where would they be? Men, she knew, were weak and needed the strength of womankind and belief of the volk to keep them fighting. Many a burgher had already surrendered but she would not be one of them. Her ouma and oupa had trekked so very long ago to this very land she was on and had received this piece of land as a gift from Adam's forbear, Adam Kok, the father. Before there was the Republic of the Orange Free State, this land belonged to her family. They had owned the land from the birth of the Republic to its seeming demise. But she had lived in the hope that the Boer Republic of the Orange Free State would be theirs again. She had been determined not to give those damn British the satisfaction of owning or ruling over what belonged to her family.

But then last night, six months after the death of Catharina and in the dead of the night, Marthinus had come and knocked on her window. Since they had left home to join the other burghers, Salome always left a plate for him and Hermanus whether they came home or not. The night before, he had come home.

Since that time, six months ago, when the British soldiers had senselessly broken her bed and other furniture, she had never bothered to get another bed. In these warring times, it seemed like a luxury they could do without. She woke up and went to open the front door, taking care not to wake up the girls who were sleeping on the floor in her room with her.

She had opened the door for him, blown a fire in the hearth and then warmed some water for him to bath. As he bathed, she warmed the food that would have formed part of the children's lunch tomorrow, had he not come. She watched him as he ate, now clean. He had lost weight and with it, his looks had become more rugged. She would have liked to see him as he used to look before he went into the bush. Before, he had a fully-grown beard. She did not know why he had not shaved while taking a bath. She had put his shaving knife there. But she must not complain. He was here with her, which was more than many other women of the volk had with sons and husbands who had died fighting for the nation.

Then they started talking and what he said came to her as a shock.

He started, "Hermanus has been ill lately. He needs to come home."

"What happened?" she asked trying to sound calm but with her heart beating fast.

"A month ago during a raid on a *kaffir* village when we were hungry, he took the last cockerel from some *kaffir* village woman."

She interrupted, "So?"

"Let me finish," he said, waving his right hand at her. "He took her last cock and she cursed him. One of the *kaffirs* with us said he would not eat that chicken. He sounded scared. So of course we all became afraid." It seemed all of them had been driven away from that chicken and ate other food except Hermanus who called them women. He had braised the chicken on an open fire when they got back to their camp, eaten every morsel of it, relishing every bite. An hour later, his troubles began.

"What happened?"

This time he did not chastise her for interrupting.

He told her.

"Every hour on the hour, that cock crows from his stomach. He cannot stop it. We tried to go back to the village to ask the woman to stop it, but the day we arrived she had died. So the General says he has to leave as that is a surefire way for the British to catch us. He comes tomorrow," Marthinus finished.

Salome nodded.

Then he added, "And when he arrives, you shall go with him and all the children and surrender yourself to the British."

"But why? Why must I go when this is our home?" she had said, tears catching in her voice.

"Because Salome, we are wasting more resources trying to keep you and the other women and children who refuse to leave safe. We cannot go on the attack because we have to be near the farms in case they come again. And look what they already did at this place. When they come again, they may not spare you," he answered gently.

"So maybe the children and I can come with you with the cattle? I can do the cooking. We cannot and will not stay in the camps set up by the British."

"Woman, you are trying my patience now. I am telling you…"

Marthinus had never hit her but he looked as though he was about to strike her now so she lowered her eyes.

Something in her died then.

Something of her love for Marthinus died.

She had heard it in his voice and she knew. His suggestion that she join the camps with the children meant he too was close to giving up.

This was not the brave man who had promised that he would die stopping the bullets of the British when *she* didn't want him to go.

But what could she do? It was no longer safe. The English might come again and who knows what they would do to her this time.

He tried to placate her, "Look at it this way, my skattebol," he had not called her skattebol before the children were born, "look at it this way. When you go in with Hermanus, they will assume he is your husband and Hermanus can get us intelligence from the inside."

She was not entirely convinced, but she resigned herself.

In the morning when she woke up, she gathered the children together and asked them to pack the essentials.

"But Ma," her second oldest, Theunis had tried to object. He always questioned more than his brother.

"Do as you are told, Theunis, you too Piet," she said in a voice that brooked no objection.

As they packed, Hermanus arrived and for a brief time, the packing was interrupted as the children went to hug their uncle Hermanus. She noticed that he cringed whenever Paulina got close to him. Perhaps he was thinking of the old woman who had cursed him?

Paulina dutifully packed everything, folding her clothes quietly. Ever since her mother's demise, she seemed to have exchanged roles with Elsie. She was now the quiet one while Elsie chatted away until she slept as though silence scared her. Little Paulina would only talk in monosyllables but she wrote a lot on whatever scraps of paper she could find. Once, Salome had tried to see what she was writing when she left one of her scrap papers. They were words, not sentences.

Words that would seem random if one had not known what she had seen.

Tarer.

Blood.

Dod.

Tears. Blood. Death.

Elegant penmanship for one so young.

Heartbreaking words.

Among the few things she now packed, little Paulina neatly folded some of these scraps of paper. Salome was heart-sore. Poor child.

Hermanus, Piet and Theunis took the packed luggage unto the ox wagon. The blankets. The biltong. The little flour that remained.

Salome left the children with their uncle for a short time as she returned to her bedroom. She took three bags that the British soldiers had overlooked. She then went to the orchard and knelt on Catharina's grave, seeming to be speaking to her but in fact, burying them in a hole she had dug earlier. She hoped the bags would be safe.

As the ox wagon made its way towards the gate with her driving it while Hermanus, Theunis and Piet drove the cattle, Salome took a look back at the orchard.

Catharina had looked after her when she was a child. She would look after the small bags too.

And one day when the Republic is free again, she would come back and get it.

For now, she would go with Hermanus and the children to the camp as instructed by Marthinus. And she understood now how Hermanus' stomach could have been a distraction for the burghers fighting. Twice already, it had crowed and the sound was loud enough to awaken a village.

This was her home but it was also a place of tears, blood and death.

Maybe away from here, her little Paulina would talk some more. And her little Elsie would get a little quieter.

And away from home too, may be Hermanus would spy and get the burghers the information they needed to defeat the British.

SEVEN

African Connection

Mary Ashun

This is one of the days I initially planned to be a "sanity day." When anyone asks, I tell them it's a day when I try to rejuvenate those brain cells that have died in the course of the school term. They laugh and think it's funny. They have no idea.

I look out towards the ocean and marvel at how endless the sea seems. Palm trees sway in the wind and the sand beneath my feet feels warm and grainy, as it should. This secluded beach on the way to Cape Coast is a gem and like many gems in Ghana, is a pain to get to. The directions given by hotel staff are almost always wrong to begin with. And when you think you've found the right turn off the main road, you ask a couple who are standing at the junction if you're at Apam junction and one nods and the other shakes the head. To which you think, I'm screwed. But here I am and the Aqua Baresort has lived up to my expectations except when it comes to how quickly food arrives. It seems one has to order lunch at breakfast to ensure the food is on time!

I'd left school at six in the evening yesterday after a particularly grueling week of dealing with parent after parent regarding our new report cards. I am the Vice-Principal of a tiny international school in Accra and came here five years ago from Buffalo, NY. The founders of the school intended for it to be so small that the School Head would know every single child; we have one hundred and twelve students from ages three to eleven. As the Vice, the same is expected of me in this primary school of children from fairly wealthy homes. Four years ago, we decided to introduce electronic report cards to cut down on the amount of paper used and also to usher us into the electronic age. Most liked it but it shouldn't have surprised me that one parent decided it was akin to asking Britain to support North Korea's war against South Korea.

"Ms Bannerman? There's a lady on line two to speak with you," said my secretary Jessica. Jessica was one of those girls who acted dumb but really wasn't. She was smart, sassy and much loved by many of the primary children who could have been her younger siblings.

"Did you ask the parent what the call is about?"

"Yes, I did. And she said it was none of my business."

Okay, I thought. It was going to be one of those phone calls where I have to grit my teeth, be on my most polite behaviour and yet deliver a strong message.

"Hello?" I said as demurely as I could muster.

"Yes, is this Ms Bannerman?"

"Speaking. How may I help you?"

"I'm very upset about this new electronic report card. What nonsense is this?"

I moved to the couch in my room, sat on the comfortable leather and let my back easily slide into a position that felt good and I breathed in and counted to five.

"May I know with whom I'm speaking?"

"Mrs Osei"

I got up quickly, rushed to my computer and did a quick search on my school database. Tough since the name Osei in Ghana is like Smith in the West… almost everyone it seems is called Osei! I kept that window open and as she talked, I narrowed the Osei's down to Mr and Mrs Osei, parents of Stephie Osei in Grade 3. Been in the school for just a year. Father works at Resource Gold Mines and mother is the Country Manager for Strong Pharmaceuticals, headquartered in Boston, Massachusetts. Resource Gold Mines pays the child's fees. They have the one child between them. I must remember to do a LinkedIn check on her.

"Mrs Osei, may I suggest we meet in person?"

"I'm very busy and have no time for this."

"I can imagine, Mrs Osei. But I think it would be a good idea for us to chat about your concerns. Do you drop Stephie off in the mornings?"

There was a long pause.

"No I don't – but I could do so sometime next week and then we can talk about many things that are wrong with this school."

I flinched.

"I look forward to it. I will connect the call back to the secretary to book you in."

I reprimanded myself silently for expecting a thank you. The LinkedIn search turned up a few interesting titbits: she'd schooled in the UK, won a management award with a Spanish company and then been scooped up by Strong in the United States. She and the children were in the State of Maryland while Mr Osei was working with Resource Gold Mines in Ghana. I'd heard that Strong was opening a factory in Accra as its way of distributing all over Africa. Mrs Cressida Osei, born in Ghana and schooled in the UK, was made Country Manager and came to Ghana last year.

II

"Mrs Osei, a pleasure to meet you."

The woman who walked through my door couldn't have been more than forty-five years old. She had a badly made up face with inappropriately applied fuchsia lipstick and surprisingly boring shoes; the kind the queen wears. I stretched out my hand expecting a firm handshake and instead got a limpid one. I hate those. Her weave extensions were not very well done; I could see the closure where her scalp had not been fully hidden by the extra piece. She sat gingerly on the edge of the sofa in my office and looked hard at me, trying to size me up and failing miserably at keeping her face from being expressionless.

"It's a lot of nonsense," she started off.

Seems she likes this word, nonsense.

She had a British accent. I tried to place it and thought it might be a contrived East London accent with a layer derived from some years at one of the Russell Group Universities.

I raised my eyebrows ever so slightly but didn't say a word.

"You make the assumption that everyone can log onto a computer and download this and that. What about the children who come from homes where they can't do this?"

A poverty activist, I see.

I still listened, hoping for a decent place to walk in and give her some home truths.

"I mean, I get so many emails a day and it's hard enough getting through them. Why would you give me more to do? Why can't I have a paper one like we used to? That way, I can scribble all over the sheets as I have a conversation with him about his grades."

So this was about her and not the poor children she'd just championed a few sentences ago?

"So it's too much *wahala* for you?" I countered?

She looked surprised I used the colloquial word *wahala*. She relaxed a bit and all of a sudden, East London became East Accra. And all her "h's" dropped as she warmed up to me. I told her I could take her off the email list. Whatever made her comfortable and didn't violate any school regulations would be fine by me. Basically, she could opt out of anything. Then I highlighted all that she'd miss out on and reminded her that it was expected that parents would have that information. *How else would we be in partnership with them?*

And then I moved in for the kill.

"In America, did Stephie get this much positive attention when it came to school? Did children who looked like her and likely came from homes like hers surround her? Were her School Head and teachers this accessible? Did the management of the school communicate effectively with parents and involve them in the many activities of the school? Was the school constantly looking for ways to enhance student learning and seeking to exceed international standards in their policies and practice?"

I paused for effect.

"Did Stephie's former school tolerate abuse from parents like you on a daily basis? So why on earth, do some people think that once they move back to Ghana after several years of being treated like second class citizens in another country, that they suddenly have the God-given right to abuse those amazingly good things that are happening in Africa? We are so tolerant of mistakes made in English and American schools, but immediately flip a gasket when it happens in a reputable international school in Africa. And you know what, it's gotten tiring for those of us who know what a good thing we have in this school. So, Mrs Osei, it's your prerogative what you choose to do, but I find it oddly amusing that you say we are in such a horrible place but continue to keep your daughter here."

She straightened her skirt, as I looked straight at her. For a moment, it was just the strange whirring of the air-conditioning unit that broke the heavy silence in the room. I wondered if I'd gone too far. She picked her Prada purse and gave me a terse smile. I could have sworn her weave had shifted.

"Thank you Ms Bannerman. You've given me much to think about."

I curtsied with my head and made sure I smiled.

She left my office still looking like she wanted to fight but she'd left me feeling quite curious. I searched her daughter Stephie's file and found one suspension last year, for yelling obscenities at a Teaching Assistant. I called Stephie's class teacher who said she was deathly afraid of Mrs Osei.

"She always makes sure that there is at least one other person within earshot of the insults she rains down. The other day, she brought a three-tiered cake for Stephie's birthday and I told her this was not allowed. I asked her to see you in the office since I was only allowed to receive cupcakes. She refused and said no one had told her the policy. Then she left the cake and walked out."

I smiled. She probably hadn't read any of the welcome messages at the beginning of the school year, reminding parents of the rules and regulations.

"Was she given a parent handbook?"

"Yes, Ms Bannerman, she was."

I retreated to my office and tried to stop myself from feeling like I'd let her off easily. No doubt she'd be going above me right now, to the Principal, Mr Hoak.

III

The sun was high up in the sky but the breeze was unbelievable. The straw in my coconut wasn't working properly. I lazily shifted my body off the hammock so I could look towards the restaurant area of the resort to catch the eye of a waiter or other resort employee. Isaac, from last night – he went to buy me some phone credit – saw my raised hand and bounced towards me.

"Yes Madam?"

"Isaac – can you get me another Mojito?"

"Virgin again?"

"No, Isaac. I'm ready for a real Mojito. And another straw please."

He smiled and made off to the bar to get me a bit of a stiff one. Service in Africa is slow but honestly, it's good to be able to have all kinds of services in this place. I'm thinking of the simple stuff, you know. The kind I never got when I was in New York. The kind that costs too much for me to justify it on my surprisingly good salary, but here in Ghana, many things are cheap. And it's amazing how cheap you can get things for if you just smile and respect people.

IV

I scrolled through my messages as I sipped my loaded Mojito. With my minimal capacity for alcohol and the breeze kissing my face, I was sure I would soon fall sleep.

From: Ben Hoak <bhoak@ImperialDaySchool.com
To: Juliet Bannerman <jbannerman@ImperialDaySchool.com>

Good Afternoon Ms Bannerman
I hope the day has gone well for you and there were no serious incidents to speak of. I've just had a visit from one Mrs Osei, parent of Stephie Osei. She mentioned having met with you in what she described as a tense meeting. You accused her of ingratitude and basically insulted her when she asked for a paper report card.

Could you give me your perspective on this conversation before I invite her in for a follow up meeting? I mentioned to her that I'd be speaking with you.

As always, thank you for your hard work and diligence. I continue to have great confidence in your leadership.

Sincerely
Ben Hoak
Principal

From: Judith Bannerman <JBannerman@ImperialDaySchool.com>
To: Ben Hoak <bhoak@ImperialDaySchool.com>

Dear Mr Hoak,
Thank you for your email. Yes, I did meet with Mrs Osei earlier in the day and welcomed her concerns regarding the many emails she receives, as well as her need to have a paper report. I explained our management policy that you had so clearly outlined; that we are going electronic on many of our processes. However, I made it clear to her what services she would be opting out of if she took herself off the mailing list.

Re: Ingratitude. That may have been surmised from a comment I made regarding Ghanaians who don't give good international schools in Africa a chance to make tiny mistakes. She found us wanting in so many ways and it made me wonder why her daughter was still in the school. I stated as much, to her.

Kindly let me know if there's anything you'd like me to do.

Sincerely
Judith Bannerman
Vice Principal

From: Ben Hoak <bhoak@ImperialDaySchool.com
To: Juliet Bannerman <jbannerman@ImperialDaySchool.com>
Dear Ms Bannerman,
I appreciate your candour. Mrs Osei has had a difficult year of

adjusting to life in Ghana and I think her language and attitude perhaps reflected this. As a re-pat yourself, I'm sure you can appreciate some of the frustrations inherent in coming "back home" after several years outside Ghana.

I will have a chat with her and stress the school's intent to move forward with the technology initiative.

In the mean time, I hope you enjoy your "sanity day"!

Sincerely
Ben Hoak
Principal

From: Judith Bannerman <JBannerman@ImperialDaySchool.com>
To: Ben Hoak <bhoak@ImperialDaySchool.com>

Dear Mr Hoak,
Many thanks for the support. I can understand Mrs Osei's frustrations but find they are inappropriately placed. I trust you will convey the school's intent as you've done so masterfully over the past few years we've worked together.

You should take a sanity day too!

Best Wishes,
Judith Bannerman
Vice Principal

V

The sun was setting on the Atlantic coast and it was beautiful. I felt the warm wind on my face and heard the waves lapping the sand from just a few feet away. My mind kept going back to school and the amazing people I worked with on a daily basis. This would be my last year on the second of a two-year renewable contract and I'd avoided thinking of what next. Zambia sounded exciting and so did Botswana. Everyone seemed to "do" Kenya so I wasn't about to! Johannesburg wouldn't be too bad either, I thought.

Although my eyes were closed, I felt someone walk towards me. The person stopped right beside my hammock and I smelled the familiar scent of Brut by Faberge. I peeked with one eye open and made out a blurry face with a smile. I gave in and opened both eyes, smiling as I did so.

"You're here…" I murmured into his face.

"You did say I needed a sanity day didn't you?"

"Since when did the Principal do what the Vice-Principal asked, Mr Hoak?"

We both chuckled as he climbed into the roomy hammock with me.

"Your contract is ending too, this year isn't it?" I asked.

"Oh don't remind me. I love it here but… gotta move on. I was thinking Zambia or Botswana. Maybe even Johannesburg…"

EIGHT

Death of a Son

Njabulo S Ndebele

At last we got the body. Wednesday. Just enough time for a Saturday funeral. We were exhausted. Empty. The funeral still ahead of us. We had to find the strength to grieve. There had been no time for griefing really. Only much bewilderment and confusion.

Now grief. For isn't grief the awareness of loss?

That is why when we finally got the body, Buntu said, "Do you realize our son is dead?" I realised. Our awareness of the death of our first and only child had been displaced completely by the effort to get his body. Even the horrible events that caused the death, we did not think of them as such. Instead, the numbing drift of things took over our minds: the pleas, letters to be written, telephone calls to be made, telegrams to be dispatched, lawyers to consult, "influential" people to "get in touch with," undertakers to be contacted, so much walking and driving. That is what suddenly mattered: the irksome details that blur the goal (no matter how terrible it is) each detail becoming a door which, once unlocked, revealed yet another door. Without being aware of it, we were distracted by the smell of the skunk and not by what the skunk had done.

We realised. We realised something too, Buntu and I, that during the two-week effort to get our son's body, we had drifted apart. For the first time in our marriage, our presence to each other had become a matter of habit. He was there. He'll be there. And I'll be there. But when Bantu said: "Do you realize our son

113

is dead?" he uttered a thought that suddenly brought us together again. It was as if the return of the body of our son was also our coming together. For it was only at that moment that we really began to grieve; as if our lungs had suddenly begun to take in air when just before, we were beginning to suffocate. Something with meaning began to emerge.

We realised that something else had been happening to us, adding to the terrible events. Yes, we had drifted apart. Yet, our estrangement, just at that moment when we should have been together, seemed disturbingly comforting to me. I was comforted in a manner I did not quite understand.

The problem was that I had known all along that we would have to bury the body anyway. I had known all along. Things would end that day. And when things turned out that day, Buntu could not look me in the eye. For he had said, "Over my dead body! Over my dead body!" As soon as we knew we would be required to pay the police or the government for the release of the body of our child.

"Over my dead body! Over my dead body!" Buntu kept on saying.

Finally, we bought the body. We have the receipt. The police insisted we take it. That way, they would be "protected." It's the law, they said.

I suppose we could have got the body earlier. At first I was confused, for one is supposed to take in the heroism of one's man. Yet, inwardly, I could draw no comfort from his outburst. It seemed hasty. What sense was there to it when all I wanted was the body of my child? What would happen if, as events unfolded, it became clear that Buntu would not give up his life? What would happen? What would happen to him? To me?

For the greater part of two weeks, all of Buntu's efforts, together with friends, relatives, lawyers and newspapers, were to secure the release of the child's body without the humiliation of having to pay for it. A "fundamental principle."

Why was it difficult for me to see the wisdom of the principle? The worst thing, I suppose, was worrying about what the police may have been doing to the body of my child. How they may have been busy prying it open "to determine the cause of death?"

Would I want to look at the body when we finally got it? To see further mutilations in addition to the "cause of death?" What kind of mother would not want to look at the body of her child? People will ask. Some will say, "Its grief." She is too grief-stricken.

"But still…" they will say. And the elderly among them may say, "Young people are strange."

But how can they know? It was not that I would not want us to see the body of my child, but that I was too afraid to confront the horrors of my own imaginations. I was haunted by the thought of how useless it had been to have created something. What had been the point of it all? This body filling up with a child. The child steadily growing into something that could be seen and felt. Moving, as it always did, at that time of the day when I was all alone at home waiting for it. What had been the point of it all?

How can they know that the mutilation to determine "the cause of death" ripped my own body? Can they think of a womb feeling hunted? Disgorged?

And the milk that I still carried. What about it? What had been the point of it all?

Even Buntu did not seem to sense that that principle, the "fundamental principle," was something too intangible for me at that moment; something that I desperately wanted should assume the form of my child's body. He still seemed far from knowing.

I remember one Saturday morning early in our courtship, as Buntu and I walked hand-in hand through town, window-shopping. We cannot even be said to have been window-shopping, for we were aware of very little that was not ourselves. Everything in those windows was merely an excuse for words to pass between us.

We came across three girls sitting on the pavement, sharing a packet of fish and chips after they had just bought it from a nearby Portuguese café. Buntu said: "My man is greedy!" We laughed. I still remember how he tightened his grip on my hand. The strength of it!

Just before then, two white boys coming in the opposite direction suddenly rushed at the girls and without warning, one of them kicked the packet of fish and chips out of the hands of the girl who was holding it. The second boy kicked away the rest of what remained in the packet. The girl stood up, shaking her hand as if to throw off the pain. Then she pressed it under her armpit as if to squeeze the pain out of it. Meanwhile, the two boys went on their way laughing. The fish and chips lay scattered on the pavement and on the street like stranded boats on a river that had gone dry.

"Just let them do that to you!" said Buntu, tightening once more his grip on my hand as we passed on like sheep that had seen many of their own in the flock picked out for slaughter; we note the event and wait for our turn. I remember I looked at Buntu and saw his face was somewhat glum. There seemed no connection between that face and the words of reassuance just uttered. For a while, we went on quietly. It was then that I noticed his grip had grown somewhat limp. Somewhat reluctant. Having lost its self-assurance, it seemed to have been holding on because it had to, not because of a confident sense of possession.

It was not to be long before his words were tested. How could fate work this way, giving to words meanings and intentions they did not carry when they were uttered? I saw that day, how the language of love could easily be trampled underfoot, or scattered like fish and chips on the pavement and left stranded and abandoned like boats in a river that suddenly went dry. Never again was love to be confirmed with words. The world around us was too hostile for vows of love. At any moment, the vows could be subjected to the stress of proof. And love died. For words of love need not be tested.

On that day, Buntu and I began our silence. We talked and laughed, of course, but we stopped short of words that would demand proof of action. Buntu knew the vulnerability of words. And so he sought to obliterate words with acts that seemed to promise redemption.

On that day, as we continued with our walk in town, that Saturday morning, coming up towards us from the opposite direction, was a burly Boer walking with his wife and two children. They approached Buntu and me with an ominously determined advance. Buntu attempted to pull me out of the way, but I never had a chance. The Boer shoved me out of the way, as if clearing a path for his family. I remember, I almost crashed into a nearby fashion display window. I remember, I glanced at the family walking away, the mother and father each dragging a child. It was for one of those children that I had cleared the way. I remember, also that as my tears came out, blurring the Boer family and everything else, I saw and felt deeply what was inside of me: a desire to be avenged.

But nothing happened. All I heard was Buntu say: "The dog!" At that very moment, I felt my own hurt vanished like a wisp of smoke. And as my heart vanished, it was replaced, instead, by a tormenting desire to sacrifice myself for Buntu. Was it something about the powerlessness of the curse and the desperation with which it had been made? The filling of stunned silence with an utterance? Surely it ate into him, revealing how incapable he was of meeting the call of his words.

And so it was, that that afternoon, back in the township, left to ourselves at Buntu's home, I gave in to him for the first time. Or should I say I offered myself to him? Perhaps from some vague sense of wanting to heal something in him. Anyway, we were never to talk about that event. Never. We buried it alive inside of me that afternoon. Would it ever be exhumed? All I vaguely felt and knew was that I had the key to the vault. That was three years ago, a year before we married.

The cause of death? One evening I returned home from work, particularly tired after I had been covering more shootings by the police in the East Rand. Then I had hurried back to the office in Johannesburg to piece together on my typewriter the violent scenes of the day and then to file my report to meet the deadline. It was late when I returned home and when I got there, I found a crowd of people in the yard. They were those who could not get inside. I panicked. What had happened? I did not ask those who were outside, being desperate to get into the house. They gave way easily when they recognized me.

Then I heard my mother's voice. Her cry rose well above the noise. It turned into a scream when she saw me. "What is it, mother?" I asked, embracing her out of a vaguely despairing sense of terror. But she pushed me away with a hysterical violence that astounded me.

"What misery have I brought you, my child?" she cried. At that point, many women in the room began to cry too. Soon, there was much wailing in the room and then all over the house. The sound of it! The anguish! Understanding, yet for knowledge, I became desperate. I had to hold onto something. The desire to embrace my mother no longer had anything to do with comforting her; for whatever she had done, whatever its magnitude, had become inconsequential. I needed to embrace her for all the anguish that tied everyone in the house into a knot. I wanted to be part of that knot, yet I wanted to know what had brought it about.

Eventually, we found each other, my mother and I and clasped each other tightly. When I finally released her, I looked around at the neighbours and suddenly had a vision of how that anguish had to be turned into a simmering kind of indignation. The kind of indignation that had to be kept at bay only because there was a higher purpose at that moment: the sharing of concern.

Slowly and with a calmness that surprised me, I began to gather the details of what had happened. Instinctively, I seemed to have been gathering notes for a news report.

It happened during the day, when the soldiers and the police that had been patrolling the township in this Casspirs began to shoot in the streets at random. Need I describe what I did not see? How did the child come to die just at that moment when the police and the soldiers began to shoot at random, at any house, at any moving thing? That was how one of our windows was shattered by a bullet. And that was when my mother, who looked after her grandchild when we were away at work, panicked. She picked up the child and ran to the neighbours. It was when she entered the neighbour's house that she noticed the wetness of the blanket that covered the child she held to her chest as she ran for the sanctuary of neighbours. She had looked at her unaccountably bloody hand then, she noted the still bundle in her arms and began at that moment to blame herself for the death of her grandchild...

Later, the police on yet another round of shooting found people gathered at our home. They stormed in, saw what had happened. At first, they dragged my mother out, threatening to take her away unless she agreed not to say what had happened. But then they returned and instead, took the body of the child away. By what freak of logic did they hope that by this act their carnage would never be discovered?

That evening, I looked at Buntu closely. He appeared suddenly to have grown older. We stood alone in an embrace in our bedroom. I noticed, when I kissed his face, how his once lean face had grown suddenly puffy.

At that moment, I felt the familiar impulse come upon me once more, the impulse I always felt when I sensed that Buntu was in some kind of danger, the impulse to yield something of myself to him. He wore the look of someone struggling to gain control of something. Yet, it was clear he was far from controlling anything. I knew that look. Had seen it many times. It came at those times when I sensed that he faced a wave infinitely stronger than he and that it would certainly sweep him away, but that he had to seem to be struggling. I pressed myself tightly to him as if to vanish into him; as if only the two of us could stand up to the wave.

"Don't worry," he said. "Don't worry. I'll do everything in my power to right this wrong. Everything. Even if it means the police!" We went silent.

I knew that silence. But I knew something else at that moment: that I had to find a way of disengaging myself from the embrace.

Suing the police? I listened to Buntu outlining his plans. "Legal counsel. That's what we need," he said. "I know some people in Pretoria," he said. As he spoke, I felt the warmth of intimacy between us cooling. When he finished, it was cold. I disengaged from his embrace slowly, yet purposefully. Why had Buntu spoken?

Later, he was to speak again, when all his plans had failed to work: "Over my dead body! Over my dead body!"

He sealed my lips. I would wait for him to feel and yield one day to all the realities of misfortune.

Ours was a home, it could be said. It seemed a perfect life for a young couple: I, a reporter, Buntu, a Personnel Officer at an American factory manufacturing farming implements. He had

119

travelled to the United States and returned with a mind fired with dreams. We dreamed together. Much time was spent, Buntu and I, trying to make a perfect home. The occasions were numerous on which we paged through *Femina, Fair Lady, Cosmopolitan, Home Garden, Car*, as if somehow we were going to surround our lives with the glossiness in the magazine. Indeed, much of our time was spent window-shopping through magazines. This time, it was different from the window-shopping we did that Saturday when we courted. This time our minds were consumed by the things we saw and dreamed of owning: the furniture, the fridge, TV, video cassette recorders, washing machines, even a vacuum cleaner and every other imaginable thing that would ensure a comfortable modern life.

Especially when I was pregnant. What is it that Buntu did not buy then? And when the boy was born, Buntu changed the car. A family, he would say, must travel comfortably.

The boy became the centre of Buntu's life. Even before he was born, Buntu had already started making inquiries at white private schools. That was where he would send his son, the bearer of his name.

Dreams! It is amazing how the horrible findings of my newspaper reports often vanished before the glossy magazines of our dreams, how I easily forgot that the glossy images were concocted out of the keys of typewriters, made by writers whose business was to sell dreams at the very moment that death pervaded the land. So powerful are words and pictures that even their makers often believe in them.

Buntu's ordeal was long. So it seemed. He would get up early every morning to follow up the previous day's leads regarding the body of our son. I wanted to go with him, but each time I prepared to go he would shake his hand.

"It's my task," he would say. But every evening he returned, empty-handed, while each day passed and we did not know where the body of my child was; I grew restive and hostile in a manner that gave much pain. Yet Buntu always felt compelled to give a report on each day's events. I never asked for it. I suppose it was his way of dealing with my silence.

One day he would say, "The lawyers have issued a court order that the body be produced. The writ of *habeas corpus.*"

On another day he would say, "We have petitioned the Minister of Justice."

On yet another he would say, "The newspapers, especially yours, are raising the hue and cry. The government is bound to be embarrassed. It's a matter of time."

And so it went on. Every morning he got up and left. Sometimes alone, sometimes with friends. He always left to bear the failure alone.

How much did I care about lawyers, positions and chief security officers? A lot. The problem was that whenever Buntu spoke about his efforts, I heard only his words. I felt in him the disguised hesitancy of someone who wanted reassurance without asking for it. I saw someone who got up every morning and left not to look for results, but to search for something he could only have found with me.

And each time he returned, I gave my speech to my eyes. And he answered without my having parted my lips. As a result, I sensed, for the first time in my life, a terrible power in me that could make him do anything. And he would never ever be able to deal with that power as long as he did not silence my eyes and call for my voice.

And so, he had to prove himself. And while he left each morning, I learned to be brutally silent. Could he prove himself without me? Could he? Then I got to know, those days, what I'd always wanted from him. I got to know why I had always drawn him into me whenever I sensed his vulnerability.

I wanted him to be free to fear. Wasn't there greater strength that way? Had he ever lived with his own feeling? And the street of life that could only come from a humbling acceptance of fear and then, only then, the need to fight it.

Me? In a way, I have always been free to fear. The prerogative of being a girl. It has always been expected of me to scream when a spider crawled across the ceiling. It was known I would jump onto a chair whenever a mouse blundered into the room.

Then, once more, the Casspirs came. A few days before we got the body back, I was at home with my mother when we heard the great roar of truck engines. There was much running and shouting in the streets. I saw them, as I had always seen them on my assignments: the Casspirs. On five occasions they ran down our street at great speed, hurling tear-gas canisters at random. On the fourth occasion, they got our house. The canister shattered another window and filled the house with the terrible pungent choking smoke that I had got to know so well. We ran out of the house gasping for fresh air.

So, this was how my child was killed? Could they have been the same soldiers? Now hardened to their tasks? Or were they new ones being hardened to their tasks? Did they drive away laughing? Clearing the paths for their families? What paths?

And was this our home? It couldn't be. It had to be a little bird's nest waiting to be plundered by a predator bird. There seemed no sense to the wedding pictures on the walls, the graduation pictures, birthday pictures, pictures of relatives and painting of lush landscapes. There seemed no sense anymore to what seemed recognizably human in our house. It took only a random swoop to obliterate personal worth, to blot out any value there may have been to the past. In desperation, we began to live only for the moment. I do feel hunted.

It was on the night of the tear gas that Buntu came home, saw what had happened and broke down in tears. They had long been in the coming...

My own tears welled out too. How much did we have to cry to re-float stranded boats? I was sure they would float again.

A few nights later, on the night of the funeral, exhausted, I lay on my bed, listening to the last of the mourners leaving. Slowly, I became conscious of returning to the world. Something came back after it seemed not to have been for ages. It came as a surprise, as a reminder that we will always live around what will happen. The sun will rise and set and the ants will do their endless work, until one day the clouds turn gray and rain falls and even in the township, the ants will fly into the sky. Come what may.

My moon came, in a heavy surge of blood. And, after such a long time, I remembered the thing Buntu and I had buried in me.

I felt it as if it had just entered. I felt it again as it floated away on surge. I would be ready for another month. Ready as always, each and every month, for the new beginnings.

And Buntu? I' ll be with him, now. Always. Without our knowing, all the trying events had prepared us for a new beginning. Shall we not prevail?

NINE

The Proposal

Louise Umutoni

She could feel her nails digging into his sweaty palm. Her head was bent, unable to meet anyone's eyes. She willed herself to say something, anything, but the words had rebelliously formed a huge lump that was now lodged in her throat and made it difficult to breathe. She could feel her sweat soaking into the underarms of her dress. She worried it would leave a yellowish stain on the ivory coloured wedding gown she had hired for the day. She wondered if they would ask her to pay more for the damage or whether they would be sympathetic to the fact that most brides tend to sweat volumes when making this life-altering commitment.

She forced her mind back to the bare white walls of Alive In Christ Church, a church where she had served unreservedly in the choir for the past year and where she believed she had found a new family. And yet now she could not bring herself to look at any of them. She knew she would have to say something; she was expected to say something. She exhaled slowly and looked up, hoping that words would follow. She had promised the church committee an apology. A confession of her sins in front of the whole congregation, whose trust she was told she had betrayed. She had promised her family that she would do it. She had promised Yves she would do it for them. The evidence of her transgression kicked as if spurring her on. She took another deep breath and started.

II

Alice would never have gone back home if she thought it was a final move. She referred to it as a testing of the waters, something to allow her to get back in touch with her Rwandan roots (whatever that meant). She had spent the last eight years in Quebec struggling to carve out a space for herself in a society that still saw her as an outsider. Her accent had never been Quebecois enough, lacking the crassness that defined this bastardised version of French. She had always prided herself on being able to speak French like a Parisian and could recall the looks of jealousy on her classmates' faces at Ecole Secondaire Nyamata when Père François remarked on her perfect French accent. She was usually called upon to do readings during Mass to please the French clergy who saw her as a symbol of their great work to civilise the locals. Mama and Papa saw this as a testament to their good parenting and assumed they were to be thanked for her impeccable French. They ignored the fact that they sounded nothing like her, their tongues weighed down as they were by the Kinyarwanda dialect. It was as if their tongues were stuck to the roof of their mouths, over-pronouncing "r" sounds and being unable to produce the perfect guttural "h". And yet, they made it a point to speak to her in French when in public.

"Alice turva marngeraurujouridwi" or "Alice turvaoui."

She never corrected them. What would be the point? Alice knew that the real source of her accent was a French radio drama that her father listened to religiously every Saturday evening. She would listen intently and then repeat the words to herself over and over again until she thought it sounded right. She never told anyone and she never admitted it, but she basked in all the adulation.

She thought she would fit in when she moved to Quebec; everyone said she would. She remembered her first three years in Quebec: the initial offer of security and palpable sense of aspiration. A promise that if one worked hard enough, lived in the right places and went to the right schools, then all the benefits of a Quebecois identity were at their disposal. Alice had believed this for a while and spent eight years of her life chasing this obscure sense of belonging. During the first four years, she worked forty hours a week as a bank teller at Banque de Montreal and divided the rest of her time between evening lectures for a Politics Degree at McGill University and church activities. The church had remained an important aspect of her life and she made her way to St James United Church every Sunday without fail. The biting cold and several inches of snow during winter did very little to deter her.

She had managed to make the "right friends" starting with her choice of housemates. Samantha also attended McGill and her father, a wealthy plastic surgeon, made a habit of flying his family to private islands for surprise holidays. Alice had been on one of these trips to Angra Dos Reis and she remembered secretly thinking that she had really made it. Her other housemate Christine was from a less flashy background; both her parents were in the Canadian civil service, but sufficiently well-to-do that they could afford their daughter's tuition and living costs at the prestigious McGill.

The charming red brick house she shared with Samantha and Christine was in the exclusive neighbourhood of Westmount and rent chewed up 70 per cent of her monthly income. Alice convinced herself that this was a necessity and that rubbing shoulders with the right people was fundamental. This was her way to the top and her ticket to becoming a true Quebecois. That was until she met Yves.

III

She looked at the heart-shaped foam in her café latte placed before her by a young man with an incredibly wide smile. "Enjoy," he said. She imagined he had been trained to do that, told to go home every evening and practise his smile in front of the mirror and proclaim "enjoy!" She thought that on being presented with a smile, his bosses would prod, "wider", until it got too wide. How else would one's smile become so wide? She smiled at her train of thought and reached for her cup. She liked the fact that she could order her favourite caffeinated drink here and convinced herself that coming back to Kigali was the right choice; that Yves was right about moving back to Rwanda and joining the myriad of returnees eager to stake their claim in the constantly touted new Rwanda. Yves had insisted that her skills would be wasted in Montreal, that Rwanda needed her and that Rwanda was no longer the stiflingly poor country she remembered.

It rained the night he told her he was moving back to Rwanda. It was the icy kind of rain that turned every sidewalk into a skating rink. His exact words were, "I'm going back home." Alice had initially thought he meant that he was moving back to his parents' house. Why else would he call this place he had never set foot in "home"? She almost dismissed his words as mere chatter but was stopped by the set look of determination on his face. Alice had seen that look before. She immediately knew that he would leave Quebec. He would leave everything he had ever known in search of this "home" and she knew that she would follow him. She would forget the life she had worked tirelessly to forge for herself and go back to one she had desperately tried to escape.

She got up to go to the bathroom but after looking around and seeing no bathroom sign she walked up to one of the waitresses clad in a black micro-skirt and asked where the bathroom was? The waitress, looking a bit bored by the question, pointed to the exit, "toilette irihanze" she said. Alice quickly walked outside and scanned around for the toilet, but she didn't have to look further as a whiff of stale urine assailed her nostrils. She walked to the light blue painted door with the sign for women and was greeted by a cracked toilet seat and no toilet paper. She immediately started to question her decision to come home. She wondered whether she had come too early; whether if she had waited a few years she would be just in time for the squeaky clean bathrooms she had become accustomed to in Canada.

She could imagine her peers chiding her about how much she had changed, how quickly she had forgotten about her friend Sandrine's latrine in Gikondo, the one that looked like it was about to collapse, every step on the muddy floor as though walking on a mountain of faeces, walls caked with different shades of excrement. And yet, Sandrine's small room and its accompanying bathroom had become a favoured weekend destination for Alice and her friends. What it provided was a safe haven away from home and their parents' watchful eyes. At Sandrine's there was no curfew, no rules about who dropped you off at 4am in the morning. "Paradise," they sometimes called it and sometimes just Sandrine's ghetto. Alice could never forget the one night she spent in the nauseating latrine, her bowels on fire, sweating profusely, the Indian curry she had for dinner, putting up a tireless fight. That suffocating, narrow room had never felt more welcoming.

She walked to the waitress, at first hesitating before asking for toilet paper. The waitress was unfazed, as though this was a regular ordeal. She walked briskly to the men's bathroom, took the only toilet roll and handed it to Alice.

She wondered what Yves would say in this situation. She imagined he would make a funny remark and laugh his throaty laugh as though thoroughly enjoying his own joke. Nothing seemed to surprise or faze him. She imagined he had some mental depository of wisecracks or quick responses for the most awkward situations. Oh Yves, why did he always make it seem so easy!

IV

He was laughing rather loudly with a group of four men when she first saw him. He had the confident air of a man safe in his own skin. His hands were in the pockets of the well-fitting dark blue jeans he had on and he stood inches taller than all the men in the room. His white teeth, which contrasted against his rather dark gums, accentuated his smile. Alice couldn't stop staring and he looked in her direction as if aware that he was being intensely observed. He caught her gaze, smiled and started making his way towards her. She thought she should either look away or walk towards the large wooden doors of Eglise St Joseph as though making an attempt to leave. Before deciding between the two, he was right in front of her, hands stretched out.

"Ça va? Je m'appelle Yves," he said going in for the customary greeting of three kisses on the cheek.

"Alice," she heard herself say.

"Enchanté," he smiled back.

For a moment, she just stared at his smile, her tongue retreating to the back of her mouth. She swallowed and prepared to say something, but he quickly rescued the situation and inquired about where she lived. He whistled when she said Westmount.

"Les bourgeois de Montreal," he said.

She immediately protested appealing to her humble background in Nyanza. His eyes widened and asked, "Where exactly in Nyanza?"

"Mayaga," she responded.

"Unbelievable! My mother was born and raised in Mayaga."

He looked at her with renewed interest and insisted that she meets his mother.

"She lives right here in Montreal. She would love to meet someone from her hometown. I think she is tired of having to explain every detail when telling stories from her childhood."

Alice reluctantly agreed and Yves offered his hand to seal the deal, as though this would force her to keep her promise. She extended her cold hand only for it to be swallowed up in the warmth of his rather large hand. His hand should have burned her then, seared the skin right off her bone. Maybe then would she have known the true meaning of this encounter, that her life would be completely altered by that one handshake?

V

She remembers the day she told him she was pregnant. She used her most matter-of-fact voice as though steeling herself to whatever response might follow. Looking straight at him she muttered those two words that she had spent hours practising. A palpable fear engulfed her as the words left her mouth, leaving a bitter taste in their wake. She worried that he might see how desperately she needed him in that moment. That his eyes would peer into her heart and unearth the decision she had already made. And yet, she refused to look away, even when the initial look of confusion on his face turned into worry lines on his forehead.

"You are what?" he blurted out without thinking.

"I'm pregnant," she calmly responded.

"But how, how, we did…"

She let him ponder this at his own pace. There was no point giving him a biology lesson and there was too much at stake to waste time on this. She understood that he would be shocked. It had taken her some time to get used to the idea that she was pregnant.

They had been holding hands across the table and he immediately tightened his grip on her hands as if resolving to deal with the issue. Alice felt a wave of relief as she realised that she would not be alone. He did not smile or reach across to hug her as she had secretly hoped he would. He immediately went into problem-solving mode as if not a second could be wasted.

Furrowing his eyebrows, he looked at her.

"We have to get married."

TEN

Recipe for an Escape

Lionel Ntasano

The day begins like any other summers day for Seki as the radio
turns on automatically waking him from his deep sleep. A jazzy
Herbie Hancock tune plays as the deejay mentions that the
legendary musician will be performing live at the Montreux Jazz
Festival later in the week. Seki takes a mental note not to forget
to grab some tickets; the festival is fifteen minutes walk from his
large apartment. He gets out of bed as the aroma of coffee from
the timer-operated percolator lures him towards the kitchen. Curls
of steam rise from the bowl of instant oatmeal; the microwave
had produced predictably perfect results in perfect cadence with
his thirty-five minute wake-up schedule. After wolfing down his
power breakfast, he enters the bathroom, splashes some cold
water on his face and glances at himself in the mirror. His tired
and sluggish look turns into a determined one. He unhooks a pair
of sweat pants from the bathroom door; a grey *H&M* sweater
over his white T-shirt. His digital Casio watch reads 5:19. The sun
is about to rise and Seki is going sailing on his private boat on
Lake Geneva.

Getting away from shore, Seki feels a link to those ancient
mariners who set off for undiscovered lands. He is harnessing the
same forces of nature that powered the early explorers.

"Sailing is harnessing the power of Mother Nature," Seki always
answers whenever he is asked why he loves sailing so much. There
is nothing, absolutely nothing, worth doing as much as simply

messing about in a boat. Any kind of boat is exhilarating. The escape of the stress and anxieties of everyday life, conveyed on a craft powered solely by the force of nature is enlivening. Perhaps the most enlightening part is when his mind goes to places he has never been, promising experiences yet untold. President Kennedy pointed it out best when he said that all of us have in our veins, in our blood, in our tears, in our sweat the exact same percentage of salt that exists in the ocean. We are tied to the ocean and when we go back to the sea, whether it is to sail or to watch it, we are going back from where we came.

II

Seki's day officially begins after his habitual two hours of summer sailing. It is now about eight in the morning. Apart from the night porter and the kitchen brigade, no one else is awake at Seki's popular restaurant *Domaine-de-la-Bastide*. The kitchen is ubiquitously calm in the morning: the stainless vinegar induced glimmers off the chef pass, steel pots and pans sit neatly in their places, split evenly between stations. Columns of polished milky china run on shelves beneath the shiny tabletops. The floors are mopped and dry. Most of the equipment is switched off, most significantly the intake hoods. Without the insistently loud clamour of the hoods, serenity engulfs the place. The only sounds are the purr of proofing boxes, the occasional burble of a thermal immersion circulator and the hum of refrigeration. The garbage cans are empty. They smell of nothing. The place might even seem abandoned if it weren't for the prep lists dangling from the ticked racks above each station.

Seki is chef-patron of this fine dining establishment. Graced with a natural poised nature, a large smile, clean hands, a well-groomed beard, and a calm voice with a sincere tone to it, Seki is a star. He is humble enough to get behind the wheel of the delivery van and hit the road to the Montreux *Riviera Market* for the local, fresh produce — artisan oil, cheese, jam, honey, liqueur or local wine. He loves talking to people and farmers at the market; he is sort of a local celebrity with his tamed African accent when he speaks French. He regales them with stories from his gastronomic world of fine ingredients, excellent recipes and valued guests. People love his common-sense approach to life, his charm, good nature and seemingly unselfconscious ability to have fun no matter the circumstance. Feeling good, having a moment to think less about the daily stress and sharing a moment of joy with one's neighbour are simple pleasures that he does not take for granted. He could fool the most astute psychologist or detective because Seki hails from one of the grittiest slums of Bujumbura, Buyenzi. He grew up in a neighbourhood where most homes are modest mud-wall structure shacks, rusting corrugated tin roofs, rocks and dirt floors. Buyenzi is typically crowded with displaced relatives from other parts of the country, barefooted kids careening at full speed between food stalls, chickens and many dogs.

III

It is now nine o'clock and the deliveries have begun to arrive at Seki's restaurant. American Linden crates of produce lie in heaps in front of the back kitchen doorway: Turkish pistachios, Manni extra virgin oil, balsamic vinegar, Brinata cheese and top-drawer saffron. These are the samples Seki has requested from the dry goods purveyor. He takes hold of the box, tiptoes past the rest of the deliveries and heads to the office. He places the box on top of the compact refrigerator designated for chef use only. It holds safe the chefs' supply of expensive perishables: white truffles, rare cheese like *Bitto Storico*, *Strottarga Bianco* caviar and fine wines like *1986 Chateau Mouton Rothschild*. Suddenly, the phone rings and Seki answers quickly.

"*Cuisine – Domaine de la Bastide!*" Seki answers.

"Yes. Hello? May I speak to Seki?" A familiar man's voice answers back. Seki is rather surprised to hear French with a Burundian accent.

"Who am I speaking to? This is Chef Seki on the line," he replies feeling tense for no reason.

"This is Kagenza! Seki, how are you?" In spite of the lightness of his words, Seki detects worry in his interlocutor's voice. Rather quickly Kagenza adds, "What are you doing? Do you have a minute? I would like to speak with you!"

Seki sits down in his revolving chair to brace himself. This is his oldest brother probably calling from home. They have barely spoken since he moved to Switzerland twenty years ago. Understanding family is always complicated.

"How are you doing Kagenza? How did you get this number?" Seki asks trying to diffuse the rough air.

Kagenza answers, "It was actually easy finding you now that you are a big time chef. I have something to tell you though."

Already, Seki feels alarmed. He tenses up because he feels how hard Kagenza is working to normalize the conversation. Seki then speaks from inside a numb fog, "I'm listening!"

Into the silence, Kagenza says, "There was an accident. Dad has passed away." Flashes of lightening go off behind Seki's eyes. His breathing speeds up, yet he is suffocating. Immediately he asks, "When?"

Kagenza answers, "Yesterday morning."

"How did it happen?"

"He fell in the bathtub."

It painfully gets silent. It seems as if the problems Seki worries himself sick about never materialize; it is the ones he never sees coming that usually knock him off sideways.

"Does Ciza know?" Seki asks about their other brother.

"He has already booked a flight." Kagenza answers calmly.

"How was Dad doing these last years?" Seki asks with no emotions.

"Well you know how quiet he became once Mother passed away." Kagenza answers candidly.

"How are you feeling?" Seki asks, trying to keep his cool now that Kagenza has mentioned their mother.

"For some reason, I always thought he would always be around, you know?" Kagenza answers sounding disappointed and hurt.

"Yeah, umm, Kagenza!"

"Yeah!"

"I will have to call you back, I need to process this."

"Yeah, okay! Take your time."

Click!

Now, alone in his office, in shock, adrenalin rushing through his body, numb on the outside, Seki tumbles slowly through blank space. "Please, God, no," he hears himself moaning deeply from his gut. Vincent, Seki's sous-chef comes into the office with the day's guest list and notices Seki's face fraught with agony. Vincent asks if he is feeling well. A flash of commiseration and guilt crosses Seki's face as he shares the news with Vincent. His sous-chef remains silent, for one seldom knows what to say in these kinds of situations. Seki stands up aggressively, irritated and lost as he opens one of the fine wines, pouring himself and Vincent a glass.

Seki gulps down his glass of wine as if it is a dose of medicine. It gives him the sensation of being hit on the back of the head with a rubber club. The burning in his belly dies down and the world begins to look more cheerful. Seki pours himself another glass and gazes out the window. The world outside begins to dissolve, melting into images from another time, another place. His eyes stare blanking out his immediate surroundings, blinded by his memories as he begins to hark back to his time in the slums. A broad, affectionate smile of reminiscence lights up his bearded visage as he savours the memory of himself at the age of seventeen.

Seki had already quit school when his mother knowing he could use spending money of his own, got him a job washing dishes in Bujumbura's most popular restaurant at the time. Last born child of a family of three boys, Seki spent a lot of time at home with his mother. Kagenza, the oldest was more like a caring and dependable uncle than a brother. Ten years older, Kagenza worked closely with their father maintaining their small business of repairing cars and trucks. Ciza, the middle child, lived in perpetual motion and the youthful air of a guy who had managed to escape the normal adult responsibilities and emotions. Graced with natural athletic talent, Ciza played professional soccer for a second division league team.

In order to let his mom rest, Seki would do the shopping of groceries, cleaning up, washing and cooking. Occasionally, he would also do the stitching and sewing. This type of work didn't scare him. Their mother, a stay-home matriarch was the kind of cook who would heap up a plate with such food as sweet potatoes, plantain, bananas, red kidney beans, finger-licking Mukeke fish and cassava. The more you put away the better she felt. They could afford to eat meat only a few times a month, but she always spoiled them with snacks such as groundnuts, sugar cane and fruits.

She passed this love and ability to cook and care to Seki and he intuitively respected food and cooking, especially the power it possesses in bringing people together. Seki worked out at her kitchen table like there was no tomorrow. Inevitably, all this annoyed their father down to his core. This brought so much grief and despair to his father because deep down, he knew Seki was different from all other boys. He could see the disappointment in his father's eyes when he looked at him.

His father would always comment on Kagenza's diligence and Ciza's dexterity, but there were no words of love, no words of pride when it came to Seki. Maybe it was his father's way of acting out of love, maybe it was his beliefs, but, if you notice closely, reality often possesses its own kind of power. Seki's way of being was a challenge to the integrity and moral fabric of his family and Burundian society: – men have their roles and women theirs. Regardless, Seki's way of being should have been respected. His way of being was not the totality of his identity; it surely didn't make him a bad person. However, this reality kept his father awake at night and sadly, it influenced all of his reactions towards his last-born son. He even went to seek advice from religious leaders, and they told him that homosexuality is a grave sin. He had difficulty loving his son.

Seki found refuge in his job and new-found trade thanks to his mother. Chef Marc, Seki's boss was an all round fair Belgian man. It was fire working there; labouring impossible hours for next to no pay, but learning a thousand tricks of the trade. It was a fabulous experience for it opened his mind. He had the luck to see every aspect of the business. The restaurant was called *Hotel Restaurant Tanganyika*. Located by the shores of the Lake, it got flooded from 1963 to 1967 and abandoned until the early 70s.

Chef Marc's family, remnants of colonial Belgians, purchased the place in 1972 and restored it as it became the most popular place in the city of Bujumbura. Marc, the heir of the family, took over in 1982 after winning culinary prizes at his hospitality school in Liege in Belgium. Not only was he a visionary, he was a clear-eyed businessman who knew how to count. He was a master saucier in the art of French cuisine and the restaurant was respected for their delicious fish from Lake Tanganyika. Soon word went round the foodie grapevine of Burundi's expats, politicians and wealthy individuals that extraordinary things were happening at *Hotel Restaurant Tanganyika.*

Seki had spent almost seven years working there; it was like an apprenticeship of life. He spent his youthful hours doing the dishes and then was promoted onto prepping everything for the chefs – salt, oil, vinegar, all the basic stuff and then he began cutting the herbs: chives, tarragon, garlic and the rest and dicing shallots for the rib steaks, then prep the *beurre Cancalais.*

"Whip the butter, salt and pepper it and add lemon and tarragon. It's still the best sauce there is for seafood," Seki would say. It went on the grilled lobster just before it was sent out into the dining room. It was quite evident that Seki was made for this work. He had the physique for it, he was very agile with his hands, he had the ambition and he wanted to be recognized.

They would serve exquisite dishes that were *a la mode* at the time – dishes like thrush pâté. Chef Marc would finely grind the bird meat in the robot mixer, mix it with chicken livers, juniper berries and goose fat, and slowly cook it in the *pâtissier's* oven, reposing in the gentle luxury of a *bain marie.* When it had softened to the texture of a thick puree, he would pass it through a fine sieve to free it of the last bits of bone and beak or any other hard matter likely to distract a client's attention from its enjoyment.

At the end of the day, before going back home, Seki would usually cross the narrow street separating the restaurant from the lake to share a drink with some of the other cooks and dishwashers. Common Burundians hung out there – drinking, dancing to music and experimenting with various drugs. They basically indulged in activities that soothed their feelings of inferiority and sadness.

One night, during their habitual after work drink by the lakeside,

Seki and his colleagues stumbled upon a half-naked woman holding a large beer bottle, drunk out of her mind, venting her frustration about how she lost her husband to two fishermen who usually fished with him. She lamented on how one fateful day the three of them went on a fishing trip together as they always did. At the end of that day, only two of them came back. Her husband was missing. At that particular time, there was a shortage of fish and fishermen did not manage to reach their normal quotas; anxiety was rampant as their catch basically meant their livelihood. She accused them of having thrown him into the lake. She explained how they did so as a form of sacrifice to whatever creature or mermaid god, which ruled the deep waters, in order to appease it so that it could release the flow of fish. It sounded absurd and Seki could not believe what he was hearing. She further explained how she had never been the same since. She searched and went to the police, but all to no avail. She went to see pastors, gurus and witch doctors to get justice, but nothing worked. Frustrated, she started drinking to alleviate her trauma. It destroyed her. It annihilated her energy. It confused her, making her hallucinate.

Seki walked away after hearing enough as he perched under a palm tree, slowly sipping on the local brew and started thinking about happiness. He wondered what made it so fleeting; he did not even know what it meant. Was it love? Was it the ability to love? Was it the sensation of being loved unconditionally? Could it be security? Peace? What about the stillness of the mind? These philosophical thoughts got interrupted by an old bum playing beautiful music on a dingy home-made guitar. The music was hypnotizing and soothing, but let out feelings of despair, hurt and disappointment. The small waves smashing on the reef mixed with the complex guitar riffs made it sound like a symphony of life – a life of sadness counterbalanced with a consoling promise of hope.

After the drinks, Seki would have to go back to the slums. Conditions were more crowded than elsewhere; people with all kinds of different psychologies were constantly in your face. People would verbally say that they were not into politics, but rather into prayers and business. Nevertheless, any power one had depended on their ability to know everything that was going on around them, but mostly, to be sensitive to changes.

Unequivocally, there was no time or room to escape to some inner dreamland. This intuitive sense of urgency to stay connected to the environment and the people around was somewhat imperative for survival. If you acted like a child in the slums, you were not going to last long. Seki had to quickly understand his world – a nation that lived in social ghettos. The insecure generally congregated around other power hungry individuals and the religious and spiritual lot were ecclesiastically cloistered in their world because people like to associate with those of their kind. Even though the very air was so disturbed by a myriad of tongues blabbing about ethnic relations, Seki had resolved to stay still and worked harder. He had the opportunity to live in between these narrow worlds; he had the privilege to be an observer of another way of life.

In 1994, Burundi was standing on the brink of genocide. Seki, aged twenty-four, would never forget the day he heard the story of how the Zaire-based guerrillas attacked the King Khaled Hospital as they tried to overthrow the government. Windows in the hospital maternity ward had been shattered by rifle butts. On the floor in one room was dried blood where a patient had been shot by the guerrillas. In the courtyard was a charred area where another patient had been set on fire on her mattress. Many Burundians were fleeing the country, running away from danger, escaping their reality.

Seki decided to flee Burundi in order to survive and also, perhaps, find a kind of love that was forbidden. He had to get to a country that was safe, accepting and understanding. He then fled to the closest safe country, Tanzania. He walked a lot and caught numerous buses. Plagued with worry, distracted by nostalgic memories of home and busy with the red tape involved with migration organizations, he failed to notice time pass by as he spent two years in a refugee camp. Life was reduced to basic needs and physical protection.

The talented oral folklorists present in the camp blissfully created passing but powerful illusions that life had remained the same. It was accepted that, in conditions of exile, nostalgic feelings were nourished by altered memories of past life. All forms of divisions were discarded, while peaceful everyday life was praised and venerated. This was quite ironic as the history of their nation made it difficult to romanticize past life. The devolution of culture can be traced directly to broken men. Nonetheless, through the solidarity of certain upright individuals, Seki found himself boarding a plane destined for Geneva in Switzerland. He was granted asylum on a humanitarian visa.

Here he was, in Europe, feeling like a hayseed and he rather looked like one as he fumbled and wandered around the Geneva metro system in his shiny new shoes, smelling of misery and trying to locate a restaurant called, *Brasserie du Grand Chêne*. Seki had nothing except a pair of knives and a thick skin – he was used to being treated like he was a piece of dung on someone's shoe. Reaching at the entrance of the restaurant, a skinny, businesslike man of fifty or so approached, wearing a cook's apron and a sardonic smile. His face bore the characteristic flush of the wine-drinking bon vivant as he welcomed Seki in letting the immigrant know that he would start work the next day. All Seki wanted was a chance, a promise of recognition – respect. All he wanted was to prove to his father that he was worthy.

IV

It is now ten o'clock. The restaurant is two hours away from opening its doors to its guests. Seki is inebriated after having finished a whole bottle of wine with his sous-chef, Vincent. Looking back at everything he has gone through in his journey up to this day, Seki has never shed a single tear. For some unknown reason, he lets out tears like never before. Things have come full circle because all roads lead to the past.

ELEVEN

Grasshopper Redness

Monica Arac de Nyeko

Oola. He owns a law firm in Bugolobi. He is choirmaster of the Bugolobi Anglican Church just around the corner after the charcoal market where the women traders sit under the sun. They sit there till they don't feel its sharpness burn upon their skin like the flames of an angry bushfire. When he meets me today, in between a brisk walk and graying hair still uncombed, Oola is almost startled. He wants to look at me but for a moment he is unsure if he should. Like always, he speaks quickly. Almost breaking into a slight stammer and constantly pulling at his beard with his teeth biting at his lower lips. He bites his lips now.

"Atek! You are growing up like a weed. Only yesterday, you were a little girl!"

He lifts and drops his hands in unison like the one two, two one, beat to the tune of *Amazing Grace How Sweet The Sound*. He has this smile, which cracks upon his face and vanishes sooner than expected. He pushes forward his hand and waits for mine. He does not look at me, but at my hands.

"Do you like it at university?"

His eyes are still on my hands. He is always searching for the words behind my hands as I slowly take my right hand out of my pocket and extend it to him. I withdraw soon after. I have it rehearsed. I always let my hand brush his and withdraw soon after. I have to. If I let him hold on, then he starts pleading. I can't bear to see his eyes like that. He always has that same look. Not

141

exactly a sad one. Not even a sorry one. Just insistent. As if he is demanding me to open myself up and unravel his wounds. I have tried to say this to him, always through the flapping of my eyelids as I avoid his own. That his past is bound with his own, not mine. I have a future to quest after. I can't help him heal. The wounds he caused me are too deep.

"You don't talk much these days? Well, you have never spoken much really! Is your Ma okay? Does she still have trouble with that piece of land?"

I nod my head left and right. Standing on the road like this will get us knocked by these bicycle men who pay no attention to anyone. They are hurrying past Bugolobi church and towards the market, which sits in the valley, below where we stand now. Without making a huge effort, you can hear market vendors calling out to buyers to come finish their merchandise so they look into another day and earn more shillings. Things do not always work that way. There are always the unsold tomatoes, so red on the stalls and almost daring to stain the wooden stands to a deeper red! The drying pepper is almost as red as the oil paint on the stalls. Everything is so red. Sometimes I want to wrap a bandage around my eyes to avoid this redness which lacks tenderness I can sniff.

"I should be on my way now," I say.

My voice is still. I can barely hear myself. Oola has not heard me. I try to look at him again. I can't hold onto a long gaze. Not with his eyes, as red as meat and beamy with the residue of *waragi*, maybe from the last night, or the night before. Everyone in Bugolobi church knows. They pretend they don't notice, after all the man is a good choirmaster. Today, when the sun shows up its rays, Oola will be at Mama Damali's place, asking for a tot. Now I must be on my way, to see Ma.

"I dreamt of meat last night."

"Meat? Meat is bad! Bad! Terrible." Ma always says. Ma wishes my recurrent dream was about water. You see, according to Ma, although water steals from us, water also extends the night into the day with promises of birth or life. Meat?

Meat is bad! Bad! When Uncle Giwa joined the army 12 years

ago, Ma always dreamt of big chunks of meat in big pots. She was always stirring into the meat with the big *ogwec*; the one Uncle Giwa carved out of the guava tree in Grandpa's compound; the same one he crushed upon Ma's back when Ma tried to block him from taking the army recruit bus to become a cadet. He became a cadet. He even came home with his friend Oola the first day we ever saw him in his new uniform. It was a green one and Ma pulled my ears for saying it was very beautiful like Mother Nature.

"Mother Nature? What do you know about Mother Nature, you Atek? You think you are so good about colours that we should all listen to you now? Eh! You open that no good mouth of yours again and I will pull your ears till you fart like Mother Nature itself!"

Ma does not speak like that often. When she does, its because she has been looking into her cowries. Ma likes to cast them on the floor. She searches for hidden tongues, patterns and revelations. She casts them on the floor. She cast her cowries on the floor the day Uncle Giwa and Oola came home. She said she could see a storm forming in the skies. The lines on her face grew deeper. Ma stood behind the house and held her hands across her face searching for some clearing in the clouds. Then she held her hands upon her breast and muttered.

"I don't like this. This is not good."

Grandpa used to say – after some of Ma's revelations – holding his stick and pointing at nothing in particular.

"Taking your Ma's cowries too seriously is as good as throwing oneself in the river, Atek, do you hear me? Do you?"

When he spoke like that, his eyes focused on a particular spot and he seemed transfixed there for a long time. Grandpa liked to hum songs. For some reason, his songs always bore a certain brunt of sadness that matched the pace of his greying hair. It did not matter if it was the happiest song I had heard the women or girls in the church choir sing with so much mirth the day before at so and so's wedding. When Grandpa picked it up and started to hum, slowly tapping his walking stick on the ground or scribbling unreadable symbols and letters on the ground, it seemed, he was struggling to calm some thoughts laying deep with him, throbbing or tossing and rendering him in this constant state of melancholy.

It was hard to imagine the way Ma described him. Grandpa with stooped back and knees which seemed hardly able to carry his weight is not exactly easy to see as the leader of the rogue village boys who took matters into their own hands and constantly terrorized men who made a habit of beating up their wives. Ma said, at the time before she was born – and before Grandpa lost his young wife, who one day fell in the middle of the large compound and never got up again – Grandpa had made a name, as the de facto head of that gang which for a long time, had most men scared of even lifting a finger to hiss at any woman. Ma knew I laughed when she told these stories about Grandpa which I hardly took to heart. How could I, when Grandpa constantly grumpy, chewing at his tobacco in the middle of a hot afternoon, never did hesitate to swing his stick at the chickens in the compound, which innocently quaking and searching for left-over nuts in the dust, did not anticipate even the possibility of a stick always aiming at their feet. It seemed ours was the only compound with no short supply of limping chickens.

Ma tried to look into her cowries to ask about Grandpa and the chickens despite Grandpa's mantra which he often uttered in between clenched teeth, saying:

"There is absolutely, no point in asking for answers from the dead when they always obscure the world of the living with stains and worry. When I get my hands on those cowries I will throw them in a blazing flame!!!"

I am not sure what Grandpa says now, especially when Ma sometimes throws cowries upon the compound on which he once sat and aimed at the chicken's feet. Ma likes to evoke his name and conjure his presence seeking answers to the questions Grandpa never got to answer. Did Grandpa blame Ma for Grandma's death? Why did Grandpa stop believing in Ma's cowries? What harm had any chicken ever done him?

Everyone knows Grandpa liked everyone to believe he was never in Ma's cowries and "that kind of thing," the way he referred to whatever Ma did. Ma says the old man liked to think he was too rational for his daughter's unexplainable complexities. That is why he let Uncle Giwa's friend Oola spend the night with us, although Ma had told him there was something not quite right about the man.

He Grandpa was tired of listening to Ma and being called names for it. Ma never did tell me this but the day Grandma died was the day Ma started to see the future in cowries. That's when everyone started to tell Grandpa that there was something not quite right about this. People said the cowries had gained power by sucking out the life from someone, as dear to Grandpa as Grandma; that only Grandpa did not see anything wrong with Ma because he was only happy to let his wife go so that his daughter could terrorize everyone by seeing things that no normal person ever saw.

Grandpa used to say:

"I can't stand those fingers pointing in my direction when I go to drink some *Liralira* in the evening like everyone else. Do you know that no one wants to sit with me?"

Grandpa wanted the whispers and accusations to stop. Perhaps that is why he aimed at the chickens so much and had over the years perfected his little sport. It was not just the chickens, as I learnt afterwards watching him closely one evening. Grandpa's stick seemed sharp and on spot when he prepared his target at the hens particularly. Even still, it was not just any hens. They were Ma's hens.

I told Ma. She said:

"You talk like that again and I will feed you with cow dung till you go to search for your good-for-nothing father in Kenya! You hear me?"

That was when I was little. I learnt to keep my thoughts to myself. If it was not for cow dung and Ma's threat to send me to search for a father I had never known, I would have pointed out to Ma that it seemed a little strange that Grandpa always encouraged her to go to the river at the height of every flood season. Mudfish were known for swimming far off the banks of the river and hiding too deep in the mud. If one was not careful with the business of catching them, their feet could stick in the mud and at such moments, the river tide always claimed its offering.

"Strange, how these things happen."

That is how Grandpa would have spoken. Grandpa said that when Grandma died and everyone except himself seemed to know what had happened to her. Yes, it was strange and so were lots of things. A strangeness that Ma had learnt to live with I suppose, because, this river, to which Grandpa always sent Ma, never claimed her. It took Grandma instead. I heard Ma say in passing the other day that it was what Grandpa wished and chose. He wanted to go, at the time when the river, confused if it should rise or fall, remained static and took on a falling offering rather reluctantly.

Sometimes I think of Oola like that. Even as he walks, his strides are reluctant to admit he is falling. Yet, the days come and take him with them. No one will sit near him at Mama Damali's place. The sores on his body declare their presence too willingly and proclaim a pattern even Ma's cowries cannot comprehend. He does not need to go for a test. People know these things by just looking. Each day that comes and goes, leaves him with a thinness that is almost hard to bear. His lips are so red and raw with sores that are hard to lay eyes upon even for a second. And that terrible cough he has; so sharp like his chest is cracking open!

"If Oola just goes, then he will not haunt everyone else. Maybe the wounds he created will start to heal."

Ma likes to say that. But Ma's wounds are not about to heal. Even if Oola with his awkward tallness and knock-knees, was taken today by the water demon riding on the river wave, to the land beyond the first death and the second death, Ma would still bleed. Ma would carry her spear into the realm of the gone and departed to demand that Oola be denied entry into the kraal of redemption.

Perhaps Ma thinks that way of Grandpa too. He started it after all. Ma saw the dark clouds in Oola's eyes, even when he smiled shyly, wore his hair and moustache neatly and carried a transistor radio which matched the greyness of his khaki shorts. All Grandpa had to do was believe Ma. Perhaps Grandpa believed Ma and chose to ignore her, like he had often done. Grandpa was tired of everything. He wanted a normal life, with a normal daughter and family like everyone else. Uncle Giwa however did not believe Ma one bit. He shouted in her face that she was extending her hatred for his uniform a bit too far.

"I have known Oola for three years. You and your cowries should be cast away. How dare you say, you see darkness in my friend's eyes. A man who helped me like a brother. A man who sat by me when I was sick in cadet school and wiped my direst parts! A man who knew I had you for a sister and chose to be my friend."

But there was something perhaps Uncle Giwa did not know about Oola. Maybe that's what Ma saw that day. There was a thirst for innocence untouched by lust. A virgin perhaps? During that time the rumours had just started. Those rumours about the blood test for which Oola's wife had died, but "it was cancer." That's what Oola told him. Yet every rumour knew it was far from being cancer. What cancer made one suffer from incurable bouts of green diarrhoea that left one skinned to the bone? As it goes, someone had told Oola, that all he needed to cure himself was a virgin. That was after he had taken the tests, which turned out positive positive positive… and the fear of death started to mount upon him and he thought he would lose his mind.

Meanwhile, the dark clouds Ma saw in her cowries, started when Oola and Uncle Giwa came to visit Grandma for a day. The next day, they would go back to cadet school. It was the grasshopper season. The moon was high. Every ray of light enchanted the insects as young kids got ready with their plastic containers to storm into the night, like their fathers and those before them had done; the grasshoppers, each of them, flying towards light, without any knowledge they would be on dinner plates the next day. Oola, not knowing he was the object of any family discussion and me getting impatient that Uncle Giwa, Ma and Grandma would not stop their argument, hurried into the night, with this kind stranger who is also my uncle Giwa's friend and had offered to walk me to the spot, somewhere near the main road, where all the kids, who were going to trap grasshoppers that night, had agreed to meet.

"If only he had listened to me."

147

Ma says that often. When she talks like that you know she is talking of Grandpa. She blames Grandpa for the red stains on my cream skirt that night. She never says it, but I know when she stares into her cowries sometimes, she is asking Grandpa if the stains drove him into the river. Or if perhaps by some strange inclination of thought he had gone to the river to ask the waves, why after all this time, they had never let Ma stick her feet in the mud.

Ma still goes to the river, to search for Grandpa. Perhaps the river will. Who knows? Perhaps the river also knows, where she can find her brother Giwa, whose face she can't trace in the cowries and whose decades of absence haunts Ma, because she can't find him anymore. Not in her dreams of meat, or in mine.

I met Oola today. When I meet him sometimes, it's hard to believe it had been almost ten years, since that grasshopper night and the red stains. I can't tell Ma I just met Oola going towards Mama Damali's place on my way to come see Ma this morning. She cannot stand his name. It breaks her every nerve till she is weak and drained and her wrinkles draw in deeper. Ma will not show me she is crying. But she does. Often. Her eyes stare blankly into my eyes, not sure why after all this time, I will not let my pain bleed like her own. The stains are mine. Not hers. Ma thinks that's even the more reason why I should let the pain bleed out of me more. When she searches into my heart, Ma cannot understand why there is no sign of rage. How can I even offer him my hand to shake? Don't his sores bother me? Do I know what they mean? Do I know?

Ma. My Ma!

Every time I see her I think she has aged. She is sitting on a *toktok* stool today. Her head is wrapped in a *kanga* head scarf with bits and pieces of Swahili words fading into the fabric whose colours were bright like her smile. The patterning of the textile which carried images of several birds in flight has also disappeared and lost themselves around the folding of material around her head. Ma is watching her garden with *sukuma wiki* sprouting out of the ground. The vegetables planted in this front garden of hers have become a rich dark green since I last saw them about a month ago. I like the way they light up her front yard and flap their large leaves about. Ma attends to them everyday. She knows it will not be long before they are ready to leave her garden. That means she should not put too much energy in them for they have their own destiny. But Ma attends to each and every plant as if persuading it to stay a bit longer.

Sometimes I catch her whisper:

"Please deliver me that promise. Please!"

As I approach the short steps leading up to the verandah on which she sits, Ma lifts her eyes and smiles. It's the same smile she had when she started to look into her cowries after the river and Grandma. I stopped by Bougolobi market to buy her some tomatoes from a man who offered me a good price. I hand them over to her in the *kaveera* and make my way inside. The sun is mild today and the verandah gets a light breeze from the direction of the mango tree standing at the end of the garden. I have come to see Ma this early morning. I have had this dream of meat several times. Why does it bother me so, this time? Sometimes I think Ma can read my thoughts. Can't she?

"Why have you come when you are about to write exams?"

Ma asks me as she rises and follows me into the cowry house. There is animal skin over the floor, which Ma says, belonged to her Ma. She sits in the corner of the house where she would usually position herself when she has guests with requests for cowry services.

"I just wanted to come home. I say to Ma."

I want to talk about my meat dream. But I know surely that even if I did not talk about that, the smell of her animal skin will calm me. I will feel Ma's walls enclose me with a reassurance I feel only when I am inside this space, which belongs to my Ma and her Ma before her.

"Can I make you some porridge?"

"No Ma. I am not hungry."

My answer is quick. Ma stops just as she is about to rise and settles back into her position. She rests her back upon the wall. She is humming a song. It sounds like one of Grandpa's melancholic tunes. Of ummmmm… um…

149

Water has taken
Water has taken
My friend
Water has taken
Water has taken
My friend…

Ma stops. She is smiling. That same smile she had when she saw me come through the gate. The smile she has when she tends her *sukuma wiki*.

"You need to let go of the pain. You need to bleed, Atek." She begins.

This is not the first time Ma says this. There is firmness about her tone today and a kind of certainty that has been absent from her voice since Grandpa and Uncle Giwa. Very often I want to stop fighting battles. I do not want to see her lose herself fighting both the living and the dead. She needs to learn to look into cowries again without seeking the lost or those she will lose. She needs to know when to stop. She has lost interest in everything but tending her *suskuma wiki* which she is terrified of losing. The same vegetables she refuses to harvest. The women in her neighbourhood will not let such good food go to waste. They pluck the leaves every time Ma leaves her verandah. This has made Ma want to sit at the verandah all the time. But she cannot be a prisoner watching over the stems every minute. The night is there and the night always takes away, even if you are watching.

"Ma, the meat dream again."

She pays me attention without seeming to search for signs of pain and the bleeding behind my eyes, when I go silent.

"Was it the same dream?"

"Exactly. Except that this time, the meat smelt of grasshoppers and I could not resist it, so I took a bit. And it was strange as well, because the grasshoppers were red, not green," I say.

"You ate them?"

"It's what I just said, Ma."

"I see."

"What does this mean?"

Ma is quiet. She sends her hands to fetch her bag of cowries. Then she changes her mind and looks at me intently."

"Not good? What does the dream mean?"

"I am not sure."

She is avoiding my eyes now in the same way she was the other day when I told her that I was tired of searching in the darkness and always guessing, worrying, if I was... if I could be... Or if it was just a matter of time before I would be like Oola, with the sores and that terrible thinness and the cough. That day I told Ma I would take the test. When? I was not sure. But last night, I lay facing the ceiling. The uncertainty of not knowing and guessing seemed even harder to bear. I made up my mind to take the test today.

"I am not sure." Ma repeats.

"How can you not be sure Ma, how?"

Ma is quiet. Her quietness terrifies me. She will not even try to look at me. What does the dream mean? Why does it bother me so this time?

Somewhere in the folds of Ma's silence, I start to get a sense that Ma knows what this dream means. That she just refuses to untangle it for me, because it goes back to that grasshopper night and the stains on my cream skirt. That same grasshopper redness which returns to haunt me in my dreams!

In this silence, I find myself thinking of Grandpa who went at the time when the waters, confused if they should rise or fall, remained just static. Yet, without Ma having to tell me what my dreams meant, I know it is okay if I let myself start to fall. I should. I am sitting on Ma's animal skin, feeling the claws of the leopard to which this skin belonged. The proximity to such strength loosens my muscles and the weight of these tears fermented over a decade old start to tear me down. Ma rushes forward. She lets me fall upon her chest; her breasts firm like the day I suckled them, hold me before I crash. Slowly I pulled away from her. Ma lets go of me, humming...

Water has taken
Water has taken
My friend

Water has taken
Water has taken
My friend…

Pacing to Ma's hum, my feet carried me out of Ma's cowry house, off the verandah and into the compound, past Ma's vegetables and off the path that leads to Mama Damali's house.

TWELVE

In the House of Mitego

Bwesigye Bwa Mwesigire

We are at home. This two-roomed house in the police barracks. It is not fair to call this house two-roomed. The house has four rooms, according to Mama. She makes what looks like a single bedroom become two bedrooms, with the help of a curtain. The living room is cut into a living room and a kitchen. Outside, there are many similar houses, maybe a hundred or so.

Mitego is lost in his world, collecting half-bricks, spoiled ones from the nearby construction site. He has a structure of his own that he is putting up. A miniature structure, but one that will lead to a third world war if tampered with. Just ask Kandebe, someone his age from the neighbourhood, she got a bloody nose sometime last week for merely touching the edifice. Mitego plays no games when it comes to his structures.

He must be planning to rest now. He enters the house, looks around and settles underneath the table. Mama is away, at work. Underneath the table is this box in which Mama's *Panasonic* radio cassette came. The box is now a shop, complete with shelves and goods. The now empty Kiwi shoe polish tins, the various empty matchboxes, expired Tiger head batteries, used up *BIC* pens, Colgate toothpaste boxes and many more things are neatly arranged in the radio cassette box.

"Oragambakyi?" he says.

"Nimarungyi," he responds to himself, softening his voice.

"Do you have matchboxes?"

"Yes, just kikumi for each"

"Eh – that is expensive, no discount?"

"But surely, one hundred shillings is not too much. What better price can I make?"

"Okay, give me two of them."

His left hand places two of the empty matchboxes in his right hand.

"Thank you and come again."

Kandebe is standing near the table. Mitego did not see her entering.

"Who are you talking with?" she asks.

He turns, disturbed, gives her one long stare and turns back to his shop. But she does not go. She bends and joins him under the table.

"Mitego, come we go and play," she says touching his shoulder.

"I am busy; can't you see?" he is barking, almost.

She stays there, sitting beside him, maybe to see if he can soften and come and play. But he ignores her. His hands continue twiddling around his shop. She touches him again, with some faint firmness, but she gets more than she bargained for. He pushes her away and starts to really bark, "Do not disturb me. Do you ever see me disturbing you? Now stop putting a stick on an army of ants." There is finality in his voice. He did not even face her rather, he sat still staring at the wall, under the table and put what should be a stop to her shenanigans.

"But, but – " she does not give up, this girl.

"But what?" This time he faces her and the venom in his eyes is blinding. It swallows whatever she was saying. But it is the sight of his coiling fingers, almost completing a twin-shape of fists that propels her to her feet, forgetting to first bend, in the process knocking her head on the table roof. There is no room for feeling the pain, she bends and emerges from his territory. She is not ready for a war.

Kandebe, Mitego and warfare are not strangers. Their latest engagement was during the recent national elections. Mama had hosted the children of the barracks to a popcorn and *Coca Cola* session in preparation for the announcement of the electoral results when the war began. Mitego was absent from the party, in their own courtyard. He was in his own world, at the verandah chanting slogans, clapping, cheering and whistling. He was holding pencil-drawn posters of his candidates, taking time to drop one bundle and pick another as he changed voices and support for the two rival political camps and ruptured in applause time and again as the candidates spoke, through his voice changes.

Kandebe nudged his arm slightly, to try and see what was written on one of the posters and the war-sirens went off.

"Police! Police! Come and arrest her," Mitego shouted. "She is disrupting the rally."

All the children who had ignored Mitego more than he had now turned to the verandah. Mitego went on, in a funny forged bass. "Madam, you are under arrest; whatever you say shall be used against you in court." He dropped the posters and stood to attention with his arm curved to touch his forehead in a salute.

Kandebe laughed and some in the small crowd in the courtyard joined her.

"Do you think we are joking? *Beba bibie huyo*" Mitego bent down, to lift her and as he touched her legs, she firmly pushed him away. She had answered the call to war.

"She is resisting arrest. Who do you think you are?"

Slaps in the air, kicks doing the rounds. She tried to hold him, as they do in wrestling, to bite him, but he was a little stronger. He threw her down and continued to rain heavy blows on her back.

Until Mama returned from the neighbours', the crowd of children looked on helplessly. Kandebe was crying for help; Mitego was spitting police law enforcement lingo. He was doing his job, keeping law and order in his world. Mama shouted his small frame off Kandebe and started consoling her in the same breath cursing Mitego.

"He is a bad boy," she was saying. I will beat him. He will not touch you again.

The policeman in Mitego was still hissing like a cobra. The crowd had forgotten about the party. They huddled behind Mama and a crying Kandebe, opposite the charged Mitego. Kandebe did not have to wipe her own tears, Mama was all over her. She started promising supermarkets – chocolate and biscuits and everything else and soon Kandebe was sparkling with laughter as her ribs responded to Mama's tickles. The party could resume. Kandebe joined the huddled crowd and like a ripple of water in a lake, the sparkle spread to the other children. Sure that the party was safe from Mitego, Mama turned and caught him unawares, dragged him into the house and locked the door from inside.

The two of them in the small living room. Mitego instantly knew what would follow and what had been hisses turned into sobs. Tucked away from the crowd, he could sob as loud as he could, but he could not save himself from the bite of Kanyafu, the cane now in Mama's hands and looking menacingly at his buttocks. He did not require any instruction; he lay on his stomach and the cane started eating away at his buttocks and occasionally strayed to his back and legs.

The intensity of the landings of Kanyafu was increasing with the gaudiness of his wails. His wails seemed to grease Mama's hand. Soon enough, he started punctuating his wails with desperate pleas and threats. "You are killing me. You will bury me yourself. You are killing your son. They will take you to prison. You are an evil mother. You are not my mother. Who kills her own child?"

Mama did not stop. Neither did Mitego. He cried on. He pleaded. He threatened. He wailed. He appealed. He attempted all the blackmail his tongue could muster. Mama suddenly stopped and as soon as the next landing did not happen, Mitego tried to stand, but his body was half-suspended in space as it met Mama's Kanyafu pointing; "I gave birth to you, let me kill you myself, you shall not kill other people's children in my house."

She had not stopped whipping, it was a verbal break – his frame was beaten back to the floor.

The crowd had in the meantime caught the waves of his wailing and were tiptoeing as tall as they could, to catch a glimpse of the massacre of Kandebe's nemesis through the window and some through the cracks in the door.

She continued to whip.

"There is fire on my *kibunu*. Ayii ayii ayii," he cried.

The crowd outside started wailing with him, Kandebe in the

lead. They hit the door, the walls as they tried to reach the window. It was, as if the pain had suddenly passed through Mitego and the walls, the door and window to all of them. They wailed and wailed.

"Say sorry to her," Mama said. He remained still. "Say sorry or I give you more," Mama was oblivious or playing oblivious to the anger-filled stares from the children. He lurched to his feet finally, looked around and opened his mouth, as if to say something and in a blink of an eye bolted, to the cheers of the crowd. Mama tried to run after him, but he was a tad too fast and egged on by the crowd's cheers, Mitego disappeared at the corner of the third row of barracks homes.

Wars with Mitego end with sympathy. Kandebe is not in the mood for another pity-party. She leaves Mitego to concentrate on his world.

Outside it is threatening to rain. The clouds are gloomy and promise not to disappoint.

II

The roofs of the houses in the police barracks are old. When seen from far, they look brownish. As the rain gathers momentum, each raindrop starts fighting for attention. The raindrops hit the roof more intensely and one can hear them chattering against it, outshouting themselves. Mitego listens to the uncoordinated loud beating of the raindrops on the roof until it dawns on him that his school uniform is still out on the line.

He picks the wet uniform, *khaki* shorts and a *kapere* shirt of green squares on white background.

With clean hands, he returns to his uniform. He squeezes the water out of it by rolling the shorts and shirt in between his hands.

"Those bastards!" he mutters to himself. He knows them and their voices are so familiar. Samwiri, Yozefaati and Kandebe – their excited noises keep ringing in his mind. But did he think he was in the world alone, just because it was raining? They saw his fruit. Kandebe paid him back for his own notorious antics of throwing small stones at her own fruit whenever she sits with her legs apart. He feels like tearing a part of his skin from himself. How had it happened? What were those bastards doing in the rain? Or were they standing on their verandahs?

He picks the clothes from the chair, places them in the basin and bends to push it under his bed. As he rises from pushing the basin, lightning strikes. Mama is standing in front of him, with a look that speaks more than it sees. The only thing that he sees is Kanyafu eating his buttocks as soon as the look is done with saying its many angry and harsh words. How did she enter the house? How come the door did not screech? He does not know where to look. His mind is neither here nor there. He is thinking from his buttocks. He has never felt as exposed as now. He has never felt there was anything to hide from Mama but right now there is everything to hide.

III

The whole evening, Mitego waits for Kanyafu to eat his buttocks. Everything Mama does becomes a sign of Kanyafu's arrival. She sends him to fetch his report card for last term and he imagines she is looking for a poor grade to combine with spreading mud on the floor and administer the punishment. He performed quite well last term that he knows, but the Maths grade was not impressive. It is the reason he did not top the class. Kandebe, who got her numbers and calculations correct utilized the gap and for the first time beat Mitego. Not that he was unbeatable, he had not been the regular number one in class, but Kandebe had never beaten him. This time, she did not just beat him, but she also topped the class. He cried all the way home. Mama consoled him, saying it was not as bad to be beaten by a girl in class, as it would be were it to be a boy. He did not see the logic; it was perhaps worse for him to be beaten by a girl, but he allowed himself to be consoled.

As he hands the report card to Mama, he is careful not to knock anything, not to add a reason to the already pregnant ones, not to incite Mama into pulling Kanyafu from its storage place.

"Do we have enough paraffin in the lamp?" she asks.

Silence. He does not know, but thinks they should have enough, because it is a long time since they lit the lamp, so the paraffin could not have gone anywhere. But he does not want to give an answer he is not sure of. He wants to say No, just in case, but that would be telling a lie.

"Let me check," he says simultaneously as Mama barks.

"Do you not have ears at the sides of your ball for a head?"

"I am going to check," he repeats and enters the bedroom. He reaches, shakes the lamp and finds out that in fact there is a drop or two of paraffin left in its tank.

"There is so little left."

"Pick money from the top of the sideboard and go to *Kobil* and buy a litre," he is told.

As he bolts out of the room, Mama asks if he will bring the paraffin in his hands. He returns and picks the faded yellow two-litre jerry can from the bedroom and heads to the oil and gas station.

He still knows that Kanyafu will 'eat' him tonight. He knows that it is not forgivable to spread mud all over the floor the way he did in the afternoon. He knows that Mama cannot mop his mess out of gratitude. He knows that there is a storm brewing, that he will have to pay a price for the mess. In many ways, he is sure that there is nothing he can do to survive the fate of Kanyafu sprinkling pain on his body.

It would not be the first time a prayer is disappointing him. He had prayed that God would help him never to lose the first position in class. He had not just prayed, he had taken to fasting as well. He had prayed most of that term when Kandebe beat him. When he poured his heart to Samwiri, on how the prayer had disappointed him, Samwiri laughed and advised that he should read more than pray the next time; that God helps those who help themselves.

How can he help himself now? He can't clean the house; Mama would have done that already. What else can he do to erase the wrong committed and survive Kanyafu?

As he approaches *Kobil*, he hears someone whistling at him, but decides to walk faster and ignore any distraction. He knows that it is Samwiri calling him, probably for a ball-juggling contest but he is not ready to risk.

The pump attendant is unbothered that there is a customer waiting at the pump. She takes her time doing nothing, just staring at the road and the cars snaking slowly in a traffic jam that is losing momentum near the station. Mitego stands on the step where the pump is placed to attract the attendant's attention but fails. He walks towards the attendant.

"You talk to me, an elder like that?" she keeps asking him. He wants to tell her that elders are women and men who are older than herself but he was fearful of doing that. When she gives him the jerry can with the paraffin, he turns to leave but she grabs his small arm and asks him to thank her.

IV

There are strange shoes at the door. They are masculine shoes. Who is visiting the Mitegos this late? He tiptoes pricking his ears as much as he can to tap into the conversation in the house. He puts the jerry can with the paraffin on the side and sits so close to the door to hear what the voices inside are saying. But he does not hear much. His ears can only catch the voices, not the words. His ears tell him the stranger's voice is masculine, like the shoes. He does not know how to announce his arrival.

Mitego is not used to hosting visitors; he always does his best to avoid them when they come, by going to play ball-juggling with his friends or losing himself in his world. That is when the visitors come during the day but this is night time. He knocks on the door and then wishes he had not knocked thinking it is weird to knock on their own door. But how can he just walk in when there is a conversation going on? That is what he does when he gets no response to his knock anyway.

He avoids the face of the stranger, sitting on a chair facing his mother who is sorting rice grains. He goes straight to the bedroom with the jerry can of paraffin. The stranger and his mother laugh at him.

"He is shy," the stranger says.

"He is just pretending; he is very stubborn," Mama says.

"Are you going to hide there the whole night?" Mama asks.

"Come and greet your father," the man says.

Father? Could he be? He tells himself that he remembers his father and he is not as short as this stranger. He does not wear shoes, as small as this stranger's. His father did not leave his shoes outside the door the last time he visited. But when was this last time? Mitego had not even begun school. Unsure and aware that Kanyafu could still visit his world, he comes out of the bedroom with his face downcast. He stretches his hand to greet the stranger who, standing up stretches his hands and lifts Mitego's frame into the air.

"*Eh, noyenda kutooru omushaija mukuru?*" Mama asks.

"He is indeed grown," he says as he puts him down.

When he asks for his report, Mitego starts thinking that maybe it is true, that this is his father. He goes into the bedroom and picks the report from the table. He was not top of the class. Kandebe beat him. But will Father Stranger, Stranger Father ask? He gives him the report and readies himself to answer any questions. But he tells himself that there will be no questions. Father obviously does not know that his son is sad for having come second to Kandebe in class.

"This is very good," he says and Mama wipes the happiness off Mitego's face by revealing that he has declined, that his Maths performance is worsening. Mitego wishes to have some time with his father without Mama spoiling the moment.

"What do you want to be in future?" Father, to Mitego's disappointment, asks.

He hesitates. He does not know what answer to give but Neil Armstrong comes to mind and he says at once that he wants to be an astronaut when he grows up.

"Impressive," Father says and asks him why he has changed his ambitions.

"I have not changed," the son says, easing into the conversation.

"But last time you told me that you wanted to be a pilot when you grow up."

He tries to remember exactly when that was, the last time

Father came home. He tries to remember how old he was, how many years have passed. Then he thinks to himself, doesn't one have to be a pilot first before becoming an astronaut? Is there any difference then, from being a pilot and an astronaut? He does not remember exactly if he told Father what he is alleging. There is no difference, he argues.

Father claps for him. "Brilliant. You can make a lawyer too. You know how to argue."

"But he fails Maths," Mama says.

"The reason Law should also be in his sight, as Maths is more essential for astronauts than it is for lawyers," Father repels the spoiling.

"He is good with the arts and social studies," Mama says.

"He is good enough for anything, as bright as his father," Father says and Mitego wants to voice his agreement with him loudly but fears Mama.

V

As he lies in bed, waiting for sleep, Mitego admires Father's speaking back to Mama, arguing against her and winning the arguments. But he does not like Father for his absence. He knows that tonight, he may have survived Kanyafu because Father is around, but all the years he is away, Kanyafu eats him. When sleep comes, it takes him away, far away from the barracks. In this place, there is Father, there are uncles, there are brothers and sisters and there is another Mama. A Mama who does not beat him and a Mama who does not encourage other children to disturb him. The dream is nice but in the morning when he wakes up, it is all blurry and not even Father's announcement that he is taking him to the village for the holiday can replay the details of the dream in his mind.

THIRTEEN

The Lady, the Dreamer and the Blesser

Mukuka Chipanta

Inonge felt his stale breath brushing against the side of her face – a day old beer mixed with the remnants of last night's dinner and how shamelessly he had devoured it, like a wild animal let loose on a carcass. She turned away from him and looked up at the room. Threadbare curtains yielded golden streaks of early morning sunshine into the tiny space. An old wooden dresser with an oval mirror sat against the wall a few feet away from the bed. She had noticed how it rocked unsteadily when they tried to lean against it the night before, yes, the night before, when his impatient hands foraged over her youthful curves as soon as they entered the room. He had tried to take her right there against the dresser but its uneven legs persuaded him to take to the bed.

He gave a guttural groan that made Inonge turn to face him again. He shuffled his body from side to side before slowly caressing his midriff and finally scratching at his crotch. Grey curly tufts of hair lined the causeway of his expansive belly. He sickened her. Keeping her eyes firmly fixed on him she inched away and slid to the side of the bed. She sat up. The soles of her bare feet felt the coldness of the tiled floor. Her eyes searched for her clothing near the foot of the bed. A laced brassiere and an errant stiletto were immediately in sight.

"You want to leave?" he said in his stodgy voice. She felt his sandpaper palms stroke the small of her back. She was rankled by his touch.

"No, I just need to pee." She turned her head to face him again. At this angle his nostrils seemed even broader than usual and the cleft in his chin merged seamlessly into his thick neck. She felt her stomach churn as her late mother's words fleeted through the corridors of her mind. "The worth of a woman is in her dignity," she had said. "Once a woman loses that, she has no value, none at all." The words stung. They left her to feel alone in the nakedness of her shame. He stroked her back again but this time she retracted and got up from the bed.

"Last night was amazing as usual!" he said triumphantly as she opened the door to the bathroom. "You're a good gal – eh, a good, good gal!"

II

Inonge didn't think much of Lunsemfwa Guest House. It was for the most part a drab place but he always brought her here, most likely because it was safely tucked away in a nondescript *cul-de-sac* far from the tittle-tattle of wives and neighbours. The dining room was empty but for two men in suits sitting at a table in the far corner. They looked like businessmen deep in conversation. She imagined they were striking some type of nefarious deal. Why else would they be in a place like this?

"What do you want to eat, *Mammie*?" he asked, breaking Inonge out of her reverie. Before she could respond, he looked up in the direction of the bar and waved for one of the waiters to come over. She shifted uncomfortably in her seat trying as much as possible to keep a distance between them.

Much as she hated it, he insisted they sit next to each other; never face to face like normal people. It was as if he needed to mark his territory and show her off—"Look here, I own this!"

A young waiter hurried to the table. She immediately recognized him; she had seen him once before. He was the one with the kind eyes – eyes that sloped ever so slightly to his temples as if always on the cusp of shedding sorrowful tears. A week ago she had caught him staring at her as she walked to the restroom, but it was not like most people. Most people poked her with judgmental stares and often quick to write her off as one of "*those*" girls. She could tell what most people thought of her, how they either reviled her or desired her like some inanimate object. She felt as though his eyes saw through her outward appearance in search of something more.

"I want your sausage and chips, with that omelet you do so well – eh," he commanded, stabbing his finger in the face of the young man. He then rubbed his chin as if fighting the urge to order more for himself. "Ah – okay, that will do for now. Bring me the newspaper as well … *The Post*, okay?"

"Yes, Sir," the waiter nodded. "And what will the lady have today?"

He called her "Lady" – the word flowed earnestly out of his mouth – no malice, no double meaning. The word lifted her spirit, if even for just a moment. She stroked a loose braid away from her face and looked up at the young man. He wore a white starched uniform with a necktie that hung around an unbuttoned collar. Her eyes lingered on him for a few seconds too many before she looked past his shoulder in the direction of the bar behind him.

"I'll just have some tea with milk," she said.

"Sure, Madam. Will there be anything else for you – eggs, toast, perhaps?"

She shook her head. "No, just tea will be fine." She ran her fingers over the small purse nestled in her lap underneath the table. It was now markedly chunkier than the night before. She glanced at him filling the seat next to her, with his pudgy fingers and the overstretched buttons on his shirt. "Two more semesters to go, just two more," she thought.

The mini bus shuddered to a stop right in front of the red Coca-Cola kiosk at the mouth of the *cul-de-sac*. Samuel jumped out and carefully straddled the ditch in front of him.

"*Allo, ze biggie!*" a young man yelled from inside the kiosk. It was early in the morning, but his newspapers were already stacked high above his window and a wad of cell phone scratch cards were sitting at the ready.

"*Ati* how *mudala wandi!*" Samuel shouted in response to the crusty-eyed peddler. This was his third week since starting work at Lunsemfwa Guest House and each morning he received the same full-hearted salutation. He hurried past the fence with the overgrown shrubbery to his right and four houses later he was knocking on the gate to the Guest House. Old man *shikulu* Banda cracked the metal gate open and let him inside.

Lunsemfwa Guest House had two cooks. Mama Harriet Mwelo prepared the evening meals while Joe Zulu took care of breakfast and lunch. Samuel had only ever encountered Mama Harriet once, but her surly demeanour was enough to make him glad that he only worked the day shift.

"My man – Sam the man! You're here!" the effervescent Joe Zulu shouted. He was already dicing onions on a chopping board while a huge pot of something stood bubbling on the stove behind him. "Bright and early as usual, I love your style!" Joe was something of a renaissance man. He had travelled all around the world – from Russia to Australia and many places in between. He claimed to have received tutelage from a famous Louisiana chef named Mamou. It was rumoured that Joe once helped prepare a meal for none other than the President himself, who was entertaining a foreign diplomat in his countryside residence. It was hard for Samuel to separate truth from fiction, but what was undeniably true was that Joe was an excellent cook and his talents seemed wasted in a tawdry place like Lunsemfwa.

Samuel put on his uniform. The starched shirt was tight around his neck so he undid the topmost button and made his way to the bar area. Cleaning the bar and restocking alcohol from the night before was always his first chore of the day. Today, like on most days, the management had scheduled two waiters per shift, so he was expecting Chungu to show up anytime now. He wiped the countertop clean with a moist rag and carefully rubbed away circular smudges left behind by coaster-less tumblers and beer bottles.

Chungu, who had been hired eight months before Samuel, finally walked in. "You're in early again?" Chungu asked, tucking in his shirt. "Just who are you trying to impress eh? I always tell you, easy does it...!

Are you trying to make some of us look bad or what?" His

disapproval was only thinly veiled in a cloak of humour. Being several years older than Samuel, Chungu viewed himself as wilier than his younger underling. This meant that he was frequently the purveyor of unsolicited brotherly advice.

Samuel mustered a tepid smile. "Ah-*ba* Chungu, no, that's not my intention. I just wanted to get a head start – it's not a problem. *No vundu bakamba.*" Chungu shook his head. "At this rate you'll have us all out of work. *Ni pa easy che!*" He slid a crate of beer along the floor and crouched to the floor. Picking one bottle at a time he began to restock the half-empty refrigerator. "So, did you hear what happened last night in Buyantanshi?"

"No. What happened?"

"Ha, this world, *ni* drama *che*! I tell you." Chungu paused to look up at Samuel before continuing. "So apparently *ma* cops arrested a woman last night for pouring hot cooking oil on her husband. Burnt him pretty bad but he survived. Oh *ni* drama so!" He gave a rueful chuckle. A bottle slid out of place but he caught it before it reached the floor. "Hmmm, *ati yali* bad, I tell you!"

"*Ah-ah* for what? Why did she do it? Did she find him with another woman?"Samuel scanned the room ahead of him. Two gentlemen in suits sat down at a table in the corner. They were in the throes of a conversation, one of them seemingly attempting to put his hands around an invisible elephant.

Chungu continued with his story. "Ha-ha, that's the thing. *Ati* she discovered he was cheating on her with a *kama* student and it was posted all over social media. The girl made a video and posted it on Facebook! Can you imagine?" He stopped to clap his hands. "Hey – *kaya* – this world of today? There's no hiding with this internet ..."

A couple walked into the dining room. Samuel recognized them from the previous week. He was sure it was the same couple. How could he forget beauty and the beast? She had an unforgettable face. Something about her had drawn him in. He couldn't explain it, but there was an enigmatic quality about her that had left him fixing together would-be storylines of her past. Samuel was a writer at heart. His passion was to take what he saw in the physical realm and weave it into words on paper. Just a few nights ago, he crafted a poem about this mystery woman on the little notepad that contained his innermost thoughts. He pictured her in his arms while he breathed her in, her sweet flowery scent filling his nostrils. Despite his proclivity to daydream, he was not naïve and he could read what was happening. But a part of him hoped in the face of the obvious that the man next to her was merely a doting uncle.

The clatter of bottles made Samuel turn around to face Chungu who was now standing at his shoulder. "Just like that couple over there," Chungu said with a cheeky smile. "They're clearly not husband and wife. Don't be surprised to see them all over the internet one of these days!"

III

Samuel walked into the kitchen. Joe was bent over with his nose in the refrigerator. Ever the perfectionist, he was most probably rearranging condiments of the day before. "We have one order of sausage and chips with the chef's special omelet and one tea with milk," Samuel announced. He felt at once lifted by the thought that his mystery lady had graced him with a look of acknowledgement.

"Sausage and chips with an omelet?" Joe parroted back Samuel's words.

"Yes, I'm sure you can handle that one in no time!"

"That one I can with my eyes closed … if only they would allow me to experiment more in this kitchen! All I do here are the same boring dishes… You have a champagne maker brewing beer!"

Samuel chuckled before returning to the bar. Just as he reached the door, Chungu walked in with a glib smile. He raised his index finger and wagged it from side to side.

"What?"

"What? – You know what."

"No, what's up?"

Chungu placed his hand on Samuel's shoulder. "I've seen you, my young brother. I saw how you were eyeing Miss Sweet *Mbalala* out there." Samuel didn't need to explain himself to anyone, but Chungu's astute observation left him feeling exposed.

"I-I don't know what …"

"No need to explain, sonny. All I can tell you is that she's not your type, *mwana*, believe me. Stay away from that one. Those ones need real *blessers* who can shower them with money and expensive gifts – her kind are not for the likes of you and me!"

IV

The silver Mercedes Benz floated underneath the raised walkway and stopped in front of a block of student hostels adjacent to the university bookstore. He kept the engine idling in neutral. It was indicative of his impatience to get rid of her once he had had his fill.

"I'm late for a very important meeting – eh," he said, looking down at her exposed thigh. "I wish I could stay longer, but ... you know."

Inonge pulled at the hem of her skirt before gathering her purse. She knew the deal – *quid pro quo*: he got what he wanted and she received what she needed. She surely didn't want to spend any more time with him than was absolutely necessary. She pulled at the door handle. It was locked. He pressed a button on his armrest to unlock it.

"Wait!" He placed his hirsute hand on her knee. "I really enjoyed it – eh. You're the best, *mammie*, until next time. If you need anything, anything at all, you call me, okay?"

She couldn't figure out what irritated her more: his awful attempt at affection or his presumption that there would be a next time!

She entered her room just before 10 am. Her roommate, Bwalya, was out most likely attending a lecture. She kicked off her high heels and undressed to take a shower. She always felt as if she had to scrub extra hard after every encounter with him. Standing underneath the drip-drab of cold water from a naked pipe, she thought about her life over the past three years. The sudden news of her mother's death from a car accident on the road back from Lusaka had devastated their family. Their father had been inconsolable. It drove him to drink and to ultimately lose his job as a sales and marketing manager at Jambo Milling. Mother dead, father drunk and out of work, Inonge's world collapsed under the weight of her problems. After receiving a final notice from the university that she would be kicked out if she didn't pay her fees, she did what any strong woman would do – she found a way to survive. She was now in her final year, two more semesters to go and she would be graduating.

Inonge gathered her books together in her satchel and raced down the corridor, past the library, to the first lecture hall on her left. She sat down in an empty seat towards the middle of the room. Professor Amon Chisote was at the far end handing out papers. She looked around, Mwanda and Irene sat next to each other a few rows ahead of her. The two vixens gave her disapproving looks from the corners of their eyes. She ignored them and thought they could burn in hell for all she cared. Who were they to pass judgment upon her? She felt a gentle tap on her left shoulder. It was Kondwani, one of the few people she spoke to in the class.

"How are you? Didn't see you yesterday," he whispered. She nodded. "He's handing out results from the mid-term paper – it's forty per cent of the final score."

"Yeah, I know." She felt confident about it. She had studied fastidiously before taking the test and she was certain her hard work had paid off. Everyone knew that you needed to get at least a passing grade on the mid-term paper to stand any chance of clearing the class. Relying on the final exam was a fool's wager, for the final was infamous for shattering hopes.

There were audible sighs of relief as well as a few gasps of anguish in Professor Chisote's walk as he made his way through the neat rows of desks. Finally, he reached Inonge and laid a few stapled sheets of paper face down on top of her desk. She hesitated a moment before picking them up.

V

"But Sir, please explain why …" Inonge implored. The lecture hall was now empty; her shrill voice echoed against the tall ceiling.

Professor Chisote pushed the bridge of his spectacles up his nose. "That is the grade this paper deserves." His tone was devoid of compassion.

"But, but I worked so hard. I-I ..."

"It's not about how hard you work. It's what's written on that piece of paper when it is handed in. I cannot award marks where there are none."

"Professor Chisote, I need to pass this class if I am to graduate this year ... I have to graduate this year." Her upper lip began to quiver as dollops of tears welled up in her eyes. "Sir, I need to pass this class, I-I just have to."

Professor Chisote removed his spectacles and rubbed his eyes. He leaned back in his chair before carefully completing his face again with his silver frames. "So what do you think we should do about it?"

Inonge at first did not catch the inner lining of his multilayered question. "Well, perhaps you could relook at ..." she began to answer but stopped in mid-sentence when her eyes met his and she understood. The muscles in her back tightened at the thought of him breathing on her. No, there had to be another way.

VI

His cell phone rang just as he parked his car in his dedicated parking spot underneath a green-and-blue-striped awning. The sign at the front of the parking space read **SUPPLY CHAIN MANAGER** in bold cursive letters.

"Hello?"

"Daddy, it's me ..."

"Inonge?"

"Something's come up, I need some money."

"Wait, why are you calling from this number and not your phone?"

"This is my friend's phone. I don't have credit on my phone."

He clutched his phone a little more tightly in his hand. It was so typical of her, always needing more money. He was a self-made man. In his day he had no one to turn to, no rich daddy or benevolent uncle to help him. When he needed something he had to struggle and fight for it. He took a deep breath. "What about the money I gave you just last night?"

"I have an emergency. It's my cousin, she needed transport money so I gave what I had but now I'm short for the books I needed."

He sighed. "How much do you need?"

"Mmmm … two thousand?"

"Two thousand? …What kind of books are these?" Silence. "Okay, okay, I'll tell Mildred to send something."

"Thank you, Daddy, you're the best!" She hung up.

He walked straight into his office, ignoring the "*Morning, Sirs*" that were being hurled at him from left and right. Once inside, he shut the door behind him and sank into his swivel chair. He sighed once more. There were so many demands on him these days; his wife at home, his two ex-wives, Inonge, his two spoilt daughters at college in Lusaka and a wayward son who seemed to be in and out of police custody for one reason or another. Lately the willingness of suppliers to give him backhanders on deals had diminished considerably after this new Head of the Anti-Corruption Committee had taken office. "That bloody Mwendapole with all his investigations!" he cursed under his breath.

He reached into a drawer, pulled out a little white container and placed it on top of his desk. "Mildred!" he shouted. His deep voice easily carried through the thin walls of his office.

Always impeccably dressed, Mildred entered the office. Her tight pencil-skirt made his heart do a little jig. "Eh, my dear, I need you to withdraw some money for me, okay?"

"Yes, Sir, of course. How much would you like?"

"Two thousand," he said straightening his back. "And I want you to make arrangements to give it to Inonge. You know her number."

"Yes Sir." Mildred averted her eyes. Being his secretary made her privy to personal information she would rather not have known.

"Eh, but first, be a good gal and get me some water, will you?"

"Of course Sir, I'll be right back."

His eyes chased lustfully after her as she made her way out of the room. He then looked down at the little white container again and sighed. If it weren't for these little pills that he now had to take every day for the rest of his life, he would have been gone a long time ago. He remembered what the nurse had told him: "This virus is not a death sentence anymore. Nowadays the stigma surrounding HIV has been removed. It's a disease just like any other. The important thing is that you now know your status. You just need to manage it and you'll be fine."

VII

After knocking repeatedly without a response, Mildred walked into her boss' office. She shrieked at the sight of him keeled over the side of his chair with his eyes rolled back into his head.

"*Eish!* Sir, are you okay?" She slowly stepped closer and noticed the stiffness in his face and a long thread of spittle dripping from the corner of his open mouth. She screamed!

At the hospital the doctors said that he suffered a stroke. They said he had high blood pressure amongst other ailments. If he had been taken to the hospital sooner, perhaps he would have survived. Mildred sat at a distance as she watched members of her boss' family trickle into the ward wailing and gesticulating wildly. The memory of him leaning lifelessly in his chair was still vivid. She knew he was a flawed man with his playboy lifestyle, but what man wasn't? She thought back to their last conversation. He had wanted her to give Inonge some money. Who was she to deny the last wishes of a dying man?

The news of his sudden passing hit Inonge like a heavy-laden sack. She didn't quite know what to feel; sadness for the loss of a life, or relief that she wouldn't have to feel his crusty hands on her skin again?

As she listened intently to the voice on her phone, she scribbled down the instructions of where to collect the money and then rushed out of her dorm room.

The queue to see the teller in Standard Charted Bank was long. It stretched past the little make shift barriers almost reaching the main entrance. It was the end of the month, which meant that a host of people were in line to cash their salary cheques. Inonge squeezed her purse tightly underneath her arm as she looked at the people ahead of her. A well-dressed woman about her age had identified herself as Mildred – his secretary. She had handed over an envelope of cash as they sat across each other in a restaurant booth. Now Inonge was determined to deposit the money into her account for her school fees.

She finally reached the counter. The cashier was a pimple-faced woman with far too much makeup. They exchanged perfunctory greetings before Inonge asked for a statement of her account balance. After several keying strokes into her computer, the cashier scribbled a number onto a notepad and slid it forward. Inonge's heart sank. It had been a while since she checked it but even then she had hoped there would be more money in the account. She hesitated for a moment as the gravity of her situation began to really sink in. She had lost her source of income and she didn't have enough money to settle her school fees and pay off Professor Chisote!

Inonge sat quietly on the bus ride back to her university campus. The constant banter of men and women sitting around her seemed to blend into one indistinguishable white noise. As she stepped out of the bus onto the well-beaten dirt path to the main gate, she knew what had to be done even though she reviled the thought. She slowly dug into her purse and pulled out her cell phone.

"Hello?" sounded a male voice on the other end of the line.

"It's me, Inonge, from your class."

"Ah yes. Do you have something good to tell me?"

She bristled at his glib tone. "Let's meet tonight at Lunsemfwa Guest House ... Twenty one hours." In that moment she remembered the young waiter with the kind eyes. Would those eyes remain kind once he saw her again with yet another man?

VIII

The air in the stuffy living room was thick with plumes of tension. Samuel's mother held her sides, rocking slowly back and forth at the edge of her seat. "Sit down, my son. Your father and I have something very important to discuss with you."

Samuel circled the wooden coffee table in the centre of the room, bumping his shins in the process. He took a seat on the sofa, facing his parents. When his mother raised her head to the light he could see the tight knots of worry strewn across her face.

"Your father and I are concerned, very concerned about your future." She paused as if struggling to find the right words to convey the depth of her consternation. "It's about your future, my son. We are worried – so worried." She clasped the sides of her face with her palms and shook her head slowly from side to side. His father sat quietly, staring blankly at a spot on the coffee table.

"My son," she continued, "it's been three years since you finished secondary school and yet we see no seriousness in you. We have not seen you applying to any colleges to do a course that will allow you to get a good position in a company somewhere. *Bushe,* what is wrong with you? Please tell us. Maybe you are waiting for something we don't know about?"

Samuel felt the weight of their disappointment in him. It pierced him like a lance to his gut. "But Mama, I'm trying … I – I have a job, I'm working –"

"Hey-yah!" his mother exclaimed, raising her hands up towards the ceiling.

His father could not maintain his silence any longer. "A job? You call *that* a job?" The old man shook his head. "No son of mine will go around cleaning up after people for a living! No! Never!" He clutched the arms of his chair, digging his fingers into the worn velvet upholstery. "Why did I struggle – working all those years in the council, buying you school uniforms and paying your school fees, eh? For what?"

"But Papa, you know … I didn't mean it like that … This work that I'm doing is only temporary. You know my passion is to become a writer, but it takes time and …"

His mother clapped her hands in resignation. "A writer? – A writer? *Uhm.* Oh, it is my fault, it is my fault – I should not have breast-fed you for so long. Look at what it has done to you."

"Listen to me, my son. We are men and a man must find a respectable job, a job that will allow him to hold his head up high in society. You need to find a career, Samuel, one that will ensure that you can get married, have children and provide for those children. Forget this nonsense about writing. Will your family eat your little poems?"

Samuel sank deeper into his seat. Trying to convince his parents that he was a writer and an artist at his core was a futile proposition. They would never understand.

Later that evening, Samuel lay shirtless on top of his bed and stared at a crack in the ceiling above. There were concentric rings following the length of the crack where water had seeped through during past rainy seasons. Twisting his head to the side, the rings looked like the top of an undulating hillside. His thoughts drifted effortlessly into a world of dreams. He imagined himself lying on the slopes of one of those hills next to his mystery lady from the guesthouse. He wondered where she was at this very moment and whether she too, was thinking of him.

FOURTEEN

A Woman is her Hands

Wame Molefhe

These words are recited to you before you are allowed to boil water on the primus stove; before you have learnt how to arrange cups and saucers on a tray so you can serve guests tea; when you are still too young to be entrusted with money to buy at the corner shop. Still learning how to sweep the yard – under your mother's eagle eye, you try your very best to copy the fine, even swirls she leaves in the sand with her grass broom. You have not yet mastered how to balance a bucket of water on your head and walk hands-free. Matches are off-limits, so lighting the candles at sunset is a duty strictly for your older sisters.

But you sparkle at shining the special cutlery that the family uses for Sunday lunch. You follow your grandmother's step by step instructions: a drop of *silvo* on a scrap of fabric; vigorously rub the fork or knife or spoon; examine the utensil for smudges by holding it up to sunlight; repeat the process, if necessary; rinse in clean water and dry with a dishcloth. You fold your sheets into tight envelope corners when you make your bed. Like all clean girls do, you wash your panties every day and hang them out to dry in the sun. You know never to walk barefoot in winter because the cold will penetrate your soles, snake past your ankles and calves and thighs. It will reach your womb, damage it, and prevent you from receiving God's gifts.

When the *kgeru-sized* lumps sprout in your chest, your grandmother brushes them with a grass broom: up, down, down

177

up, over and over again. Once, twice, she succeeds in flattening them, but her third attempt fails. Your breasts harden, then soften and fill out. On the morning your menses start, she calls you to her room and closes the door behind her. On her face settles an expression you recognise. It is the one she wears after receiving Holy Communion, when she feels most sanctified, replenished. You watch her cross her ankles and study her hands as she irons the creases out of her dress. Wrinkled, as if they have soaked too long in water, blue veins showing through the surface of the speckled brown skin, her nails always clipped straight across the top. She furls her fingers, unfurls them. She rotates her thumbs. Round and round. The indentation above her nose, on her brow, deepens. Finally, after taking a deep breath, she speaks. "Run away from boys. They will make you a mother before you are ready… and keep your name out of boys' mouths and never, ever allow yourself to become a girl of the boys."

When she is done lecturing, you extract your favourite book from under your pillow. It is the one you chose from the big boxes that the Church in America send to you. You stroll to your favourite spot where you sit in the shade of the huge blue gum trees and disappear into the words of Beth, Jo, Amy and Meg and their world of snowy Christmases. Every time you read Little Women, you promise yourself that one day you will escape your home to live in a place far away where you will become more than your hands.

It is only when you hear mothers' voices urging children to return to their homes that you realise that daylight has crept away. You run all the way home, but your grandmother is already stationed at the gate when you arrive. She points to the sky and asks: "*le kaeletsatsi?*" You cannot find the sun that she is demanding from you, because it has dipped out of sight already. The moon has risen. When she spies the book you have clamped against your ribs, she cautions you again that girls who read too much and think too much are inviting trouble.

It is early one summer Saturday morning when the blue, black and white plumaged birds are singing as if to coax the sun from behind the hills. Your mother's friends and other female relatives have gathered to thrash out the details of your big sister's wedding. Each suggestion is full-stopped with "Ilililili! Ililili! And a light-footed jig.

With a plastic basin held in one hand, a jug of water in the other and a towel slung over your shoulders, you pour water on to the women's outstretched hands before serving them *magwinya* you kneaded yourself. Your ears steal snippets of conversations as you pour them tea. They chorus that your sister is a good woman. She has made them proud. She will make a good wife. How can she not raised as she was by a mother whose hands are known the village over? On this day, the line between your mother's eyes is not visible − not until her sister arrives, stooping slightly in the way people do when they are trying to be inconspicuous. Your grandmother has already opened the meeting by thanking God for the many blessings He has bestowed on them. She presses her lips together at the sight of her daughter.

Unlike the thirty women there, your aunt does not hide her hair under a headscarf; she has coiled her braids into a bun. A few beaded strands slide over her shoulders. She does not wear the uniform that has been specially designed for the day: a German print fabric dress, apron-like with frilly pockets, matching shawl held together with a safety pin. Although your mother has never actually said so, you suspect that Aunt Beauty − who wears her pants so tight they sculpt her buttocks and struts across the village in heels that sink into the sand, who smokes cigarettes and drinks hot stuff at the local spot, was probably a girl of the boys. You suspect that many mouths have spat out Beauty's name − all over Botswana and beyond. When the final Amens are murmured and the closing,"Thanks to God, there is no one like Him" hymn is sung, she beckons you to her side and pulls out a bottle of nail polish from her handbag. She places it in your palm and curls your fingers over it and touches her index finger to her lips. In that instant, she becomes your favourite aunty. You slip your secret into your apron pocket and press your lips together to keep your smile tucked away.

When a letter arrives from the Ministry of Education, informing you that you have won a scholarship to study in America, for a moment you cannot move. You feel your heartbeat in your head. Excitement tingles in your fingers and the letter falls to the ground. You pick it up and read it again.

"I'm going to America," you scream. "I'm going to America." You believe America is everything.

The night before you leave your grandmother calls you to her side. Her words are a warning, an amber robot: "Do not be fast. Always listen to your teachers. Do not forget the good manners you were raised on. Always be humble. It is what makes us human." You hold her words sacred. On the bus ride to the capital city, you do not complain when the man sitting next to you opens a box of Hungry Lion and crunches the bones. You surreptitiously push the window a little wider when he cracks the first of three boiled eggs. And you do not refuse when a young woman asks to put her toddler on your lap – for just a little while – so she can rest a bit, she explains. It is well, you think. You will soon board an aeroplane to America.

But America is too much everything for you. On the day you arrive you are taken to a restaurant where you are served a hamburger so huge you need to grab it with both hands and open your mouth so wide hippopotamus-like to take a bite of it. On the streets, food-turned-garbage, overflows from bins. The apartment in which you lodge gives you no respite. All night traffic roars past your door. The *mabele* your mother had snuck into your suitcase finishes and you fail to find it in the ethnic section of the grocery store. You hear your grandmother saying the reason for her good health is a bowl of *mabele* every morning.

How you ache for your mother who speaks in whispered tones, whose strength shows in how she carries herself upright – just as she did when she balanced a bucketful of water on her head. Her back was strong from carrying you and your sisters on her back as she worked. All you want is to complete your studies and return to the home you have been raised in. You nod and smile the kind of smile that tires your facial muscles when your landlady asks you, for the umpteenth time, eyebrows raised, if you are really sure you want to return to Africa?

You are savouring the last shreds of the Air Botswana biltong snack as the aeroplane prepares to land in Gaborone. Forehead pressed to the window; you scan the ground for familiar landmarks: the Notwane dam is there – at least the wall is visible but it holds no water; the once shiny Onion Tower is rusted; Capitol Cinema – razed to the ground.

When you arrive back in the home you grew up in, wood smoke from the outside fire meets you. The aroma of *seswaa* and *phaleche* and *magwinya* that your mother has cooked for you the old-fashioned way reaches you and you clean your plate. But out of the corner of your older, more-seeing eyes, you sometimes catch her resting her hands on the table as she inhales deeply. You feel the weight of her exhaustion bearing down on her. You wonder if it is sadness that has creased the corners of her eyes. The callousness on her hands scratch against your cheeks when she cups your face.

It strikes you how much of your mother there is in you: teeth that jostle for space in your mouth, shoving some out of alignment; how you tilt your head when you do not agree with something that is said, but cannot find gentle words with which to say no. And many times, people who telephone her tell you how your voice deceives them when you say hello.

But you want to be different from them.

Standing in front of the mirror, you think how blessed you are to have inherited your mother's blemish-free skin and smile as you tint your lips red. You run an emery board across your nails and shape the ends into crescents. And then you paint berry-coloured polish on them. Your eyes meet your mother's as she looks at you and that worry line furrows between her eyes. You hear impatience in her voice as she hurries you up because she says you're taking far too long in the bathroom and she chides you for your vanity. But you wonder if you do not detect the slightest hint of a smile as you say goodbye as you strut out of the door.

You vow that when you have a daughter of your own, she will not become you, or your mother or your mother's mother. You will bestow upon her a great name, a name that you would have given to yourself if you had had the choice: Toro – so that she dreams – big dreams. And like Setswana says, *leinalebeseromo*, she will become her name and shatter the mould that has been cemented in the language of tradition. And though you will repeat to her, the words that were said to you when you were just a little girl: *mosaditshweneojewamabogo* – that the beauty of a woman must show through her deeds – in how well she kneads the dough for the *magwinya* she fries and how smooth and without lumps her *phaleche* must be and in the fine lines her grass broom leaves in the sand when she sweeps the yard and you will say to her, her name should never fall carelessly from people's mouths, you will also tell her that she must be more than her hands – that you did not try to walk a different path for her to simply be her hands.

You will make sure that she becomes more than her hands.

FIFTEEN

The Desolate Altar

Kafula Mwila

Luombe ran her hand over the well-spread double bed. The cover was a beautiful deep blue nylon that matched the floral curtains that dropped majestically onto the aqua green-carpeted floor. The combination of this deco made the room come alive to a very colourful and beautiful image that contradicted the icy and empty feelings that the owners had for each other. The bed was stone cold. It was in the middle of winter and on this particular night Luombe knew that she was in for a very chilly time. She pulled the covers back and carefully took off her soft pink slippers pushing them aside with her left foot and drew her maroon silk dressing gown closer. Underneath the gown she wore a matching nightdress that clung to her curves softly. She snuggled into bed propping herself on the huge pillows that made the bed look larger than it really was. When she was comfortable enough, she turned the bedside lamp on.

Luombe was a beautiful middle-aged woman, in her early forties. She was the only child of Chileshe Bwalya. Luombe had received a good education that had seen her through secondary school and university. Luombe was also the Director of Marketing in one of the biggest telecommunication companies in the country with a good salary but not good enough to afford the luxurious delights that she unreservedly indulged in. Her husband of fifteen years was the provider of the superfluous wealth that comprised a large house, cars and trips abroad and she had travelled extensively.

She picked a book from the side table and started to read. This was her way of whiling away the lonely nights that she usually spent in this mansion. She thought about her absentee husband Shadreck who spent almost all his time with his long-standing girlfriend, Felicia. Their relationship had been forever, long before Luombe got married to Shadreck. She had been aware but her strong love for him had hoodwinked her into this loveless marriage that started on a good note. She had since lost all energy and courage to get out of it or was it the rich life that kept her glued to a man who could not even mention her name.

The title of the book was *Desolate Altars*. Luombe was at chapter eight, which took her way back to the early sixteenth century; a time when a man's life much depended on the dictates of his surroundings. The setting was Sensela village, which was well-known for its great hunters and medicine men. Their reputation had spanned the entire region in the north and stories about the mighty men who hunted in the most dangerous forests had been passed on for generations by their oral traditions.

In Sensela, there was one warrior by the name of Bwalya, a mighty man with prowess, who had killed both large and small animals. His family was one of the largest. Being famous and rich, Bwalya attracted every beautiful maiden who crossed his path. Parents of young girls offered their daughters for Bwalya to marry and as a result, his compound sprawled with many huts that housed his large extended family. Bwalya had ten wives and countless number of children, some of them born to concubines he had met on his numerous adventures.

But how had Bwalya waxed so great? Many people asked without getting answers. Some said that it was because of his large family that the spirits of his ancestors were obliged to bless him. Others resolved that it was just plain luck. Deep in the enigmatic forest, on untrodden paths was an altar that received sacrifice full moon after full moon. His wealth also received blessings from the profound furtive charm that he kept close to his heart. It was a piece of dried human flesh that had been wrapped on a dry piece of leaf from the Mubanga tree. The fetish came from the heart of a virgin. At full moon in winter and it was always winter,

Bwalya disappeared for days on the pretext of going hunting, but his concealed activities that led him on a path of murder and immense sacrifice, what he called, "the renewal of a covenant." He kidnapped and killed virgins, whose hearts he ripped out and would rush to the most dreaded medicine man, who lived in the middle of the thick forest, for a sacrifice that took place at midnight. For this ominous sacrifice to the gods and his ancestors, Bwalya was made proficient in hunting and given much wealth. A piece of this heart would be wrapped afresh for Bwalya to carry around until the next ritual. This dreaded medicine man, feared by many in the surrounding villages made incantations in Bwalya's favour.

Bwalya was the fourth generation to enjoy the power of the covenant that his great grandfather had made with the witch who dwelt deep in the forest many miles away from Sensela village. The initiator of this covenant, Bwalya Mukali, was his great-grandfather. He had been born into a very poor family.

"It is a curse," the old witch had said when Bwalya Mukali had gone for the consultation.

"But how could it have happened?" Bwalya's great grandfather had asked, very perplexed.

"Well, your forefathers caused this misfortune when they failed to appease their forefathers before that. The potent of the curse becomes stronger in every generation. You are the fourth in line and the worst has happened."

"How can I put a stop to this thing?" Bwalya Mukali was desperate.

The solution that the old witch gave to Bwalya Mukali is what turned out to be the generational wealth that the Bwalyas had enjoyed for a long time, bringing marked success in Bwalya's lineage. But the witch had been quick to caution, "It needs to be passed on to the eldest male in every generation, who should continually offer sacrifice at the altar. Otherwise, the curse will return and worse things may happen. Never leave the altar desolate." With the finality of his word, the witch had handed Mukali the initial ingredients of the pact.

When Bwalya's great-grandfather emerged from the witch's

den, he did not look back. Within a short period, he grew great to the amazement of those around him. His prosperity mushroomed from nowhere and he faithfully passed it on to his son at his death. This went on until Bwalya who was the fourth in line received the mantle from his father.

Luombe was jolted back to reality when she heard the key turn in the lock. She looked at the clock on the wall opposite her bed. It was four in the morning. Shadreck had returned from his "other home." She put the book down and turned off the light. She pulled the cover over her head and pretended to sleep. It had been two years now and her husband had not spoken a word to her, making it pointless to welcome him.

Shadreck's routine was the same. When he reached their bedroom, he would throw his clothes all over the floor, take a shower and get into bed with his back towards his wife. On other nights, like he had developed the habit lately, he would go and sleep in one of the other spare rooms. The pain that his actions caused in Luombe's heart was immeasurable.

She had talked in vain with her mother Chileshe and her best friend Patricia but that is how far she could go. Both Patricia and Chileshe were not married. They did not really care about having the same man permanently fixed in their lives. Therefore, they did not see the reason why Luombe remained stuck to Shadreck.

Luombe had discussed the possibility of witchcraft, as the cause of the impasse. "You know," she had told Patricia, "this is why I can't have children with him. Are you aware that he has not spoken to me for..." Luombe was never allowed to finish because Patricia had grown weary by her friend's immense sorrows.

"Please Luo, I don't believe that stuff, it's weird," her friend Patricia had answered.

"Pat, my husband has not spoken to me for the past fifty-two weeks. He has two sons with his concubine. How can you tell me that there is nothing spooky about all this?"

Patricia, who was visiting Luombe that weekend had stood up to leave and said, "This mess is your own creation; what is so

special about this guy anyway? Men are toys; you play with them
and dump them when you get tired of the game."

Patricia was unbelievable.

Well on this particular night Shadreck went to the spare
room to sleep. When Luombe tried to sleep, she was troubled
by nightmares throughout. There were creatures eating out of
her womb, snakes waiting for her to birth a child and then the
creatures would swallow it immediately. It was one of the worst
nights that she could remember. When she woke up with a start,
it was eight in the morning. She was already late for work. She
took a quick shower and sped off in her Mercedes. Shadreck
had already left. The morning routine in their house was void
of activity. There were no children to make ready for school;
Shadreck never ate food cooked by Luombe and his wife hardly
had the stomach for food from a house that was so desolate that
it felt like a mortuary.

Once in the office, she attended to one or two issues that needed
her immediate attention but she could not keep her mind off her
story. She picked up her book again and continued reading.

It was a cold night in Sensela village. The moon was at its fullest.
Bwalya had braved the low temperatures and sneaked out to the
border of the next village. He had only one mission this time of the
year. But there was a strange phenomenon; virgins were nowhere
in sight. Not even around the river where they came to draw water;
he knew that some had the habit of coming very late as they took
the opportunity to chat with friends or exchange glances with
would-be suitors. He had waited three days and all Bwalya saw
were elderly women trekking to and from the water source. "Have
people noticed his criminal activities and were being cautious?"

On the evening of the third day when he was just about to give
up, his luck changed. Bwalya saw a group of women with young
girls in their company who had beads around their waists. He
could tell that they had just come of age. He also knew that this
group was making this trek to conclude the period of isolation
accorded to initiates according to the tradition.

Carefully calculating his chances Bwalya pounced on the
unsuspecting crowd. He was desperate and had run out of time;

the moon would soon disappear behind the clouds. To Bwalya's astonishment, the people he was dealing with were resilient. When he finally got away, he dragged the girl deep into the forest, cut her chest open and pulled her heart out. He ran the whole evening in order to make it for the sacrifice.

"You are late," the medicine man said as Bwalya handed over the heart, which was still warm.

"I had to deal with some complications," was all Bwalya could muster, panting.

"We shall try," the medicine man said and shook his head slowly in gross despair. When the ritual was completed, Bwalya made his way to the exit of the cave but just as he was leaving, the medicine man stopped him.

"Come back for a moment."

"There is going to be a problem," he began, "the owners of the girl you abducted today…" he shook his head again. "Come back in three days and I will have consulted, perhaps there could be a solution."

When Bwalya arrived home the following day at noon, he found a crowd had gathered in his compound. He thrust the duiker he was carrying to the ground. His eldest wife took all that he was carrying and placed them carefully in his hut and returned to join the others. There were strange faces.

As soon as Bwalya had settled, the one who seemed to be the eldest in the delegation spoke, "We have come to take our daughter back."

"What are you talking about?" Bwalya feigned ignorance. He remembered the witch's words, "There is going to be trouble." Bwalya was not worried. All he needed to do was to turn the people away till the third day.

"We saw you that day when we were headed to the river. We have also consulted our powerful men and they have confirmed that it was you. You will surely not get away with this! You have been doing this…"

Bwalya raised his hand. He was not going to allow the women to jeopardise him – the audience was now growing beyond the borders of his compound.

"Leave!" Bwalya shouted on top of his lungs. "Leave immediately!" he repeated.

The visitors rose but before they left, they had poured curses on Bwalya and his descendants up to the fourth and fifth generation.

"Yes, we shall leave, for we know what you have done. We are going back empty handed; without our daughter but listen to this very, very carefully. You are cursed; you shall not live for a long time. Just as you shortened the life of our own child, so will the life of your children and their children after them be shortened. Our daughter would have given us strong, handsome and beautiful children but they have died in her womb. In the same way, your daughters and their daughters after them shall not know marriage and neither will they bear children. Those who will ever get married or indeed succeed to childbirth shall suffer the worst in the process; their wombs are cursed. What comes forth shall reproduce the curse."

For Bwalya's family, this was a big blow. Fear had gripped them, from the oldest to the youngest. For a brief period, they could not rise from where they were seated, each one of them deep in thoughts. Then they all returned to their chores, slowly and quietly.

When Kaemba, Bwalya's favourite wife finally decided to confront her husband about what had transpired, she was stopped in her tracks. One of the children screamed from the direction of Bwalya's hut. Bwalya had suddenly become ill. By now the sun was already setting and the rest of Sensela Village was retiring indoors.

"It is a strange sickness," the local herbalist said when he arrived. There was an aura of uncertainty on the gloomy company that had gathered around him. They all looked on as the local healer administered several potions to Bwalya, who now lay helpless, on the reed mat in his hut. In the early hours of the next day, Bwalya died taking his secret to his grave. He did not go back to the medicine man. In fact no one ever went back to offer sacrifices after that and from that time the altar lay desolate. With time, the medicine man who knew about the pact also died and the place where sacrifices were made was covered with thick foliage.

The new curse however, started its course in the first line of Bwalya's children. Out of his twenty-five daughters, only fifteen found suitors. Very few successfully in bearing children and only gave birth to daughters born from one generation to another. Over time, the family did not really expand and there was no one to carry the name, apart from a few who continually used the name, "Bwalya."

Luombe closed the book and for the first time paid particular attention to the middle name of the author, Elizabeth Moloshi Chikwama. The author's background showed that she had been educated by the missionaries in the early twentieth century. Her parents had been committed members of the early missionary church that had first established a mission in Sensela village.

As Luombe went back to read the epilogue, she was captivated by the words, "Unless it is broken, the curse will continue to wield its power over the descendants of Bwalya. I have tried in vain to break the power of the curse that was pronounced five centuries back. I hope that someone, somewhere in the future will succeed."

Luombe looked at her watch. It was just about knocking off time. She decided to visit her mother. Her mother's house was a mere twenty minutes drive from her office but with the traffic congestion at that hour it took her a good forty minutes.

"Hi Mum," Luombe said as she alighted from her car.

Chileshe was in the garden. "Luombe baby," Chileshe said as she put the garden fork she was working with down and pulled off her gloves. She had never stopped calling her only daughter "baby." The birth of Luombe had nearly taken her life. Chileshe was educated, had had a very good job that had paid her well. She was now retired comfortably enough to sustain a little business that kept her going. "At least I can pay the bills," she always told herself. Single-handed she had managed to give her daughter a moderate education, but good enough to give Luombe a great start in life. Although Luombe was married to Shadreck, Chileshe did not really approve.

"Any woman can do just fine by herself," she had said when Luombe had introduced her fiancé.

Luombe didn't really know who her father was. There had been many men in her mother's life. Each one was introduced to her as her uncle. So from Uncle Allan to Uncle Zachary, there was no telling who had actually fathered her.

"I want to do this Mum," Luombe had insisted.

"I hope that you will not regret this decision my baby," Chileshe had emphasised.

Her mother had put up a front at the plush wedding that had been hosted in a five-star hotel. With guests from high-class society, the ceremony had earned gossip. That was fifteen years ago. Had Luombe regretted marrying the son of a tycoon despite her mother's warning? The man had everything every woman dreamed about.

Chileshe called for some drinks, which were brought in immediately.

"You look tired," she said staring at her daughter.

"Just pressure at work," her daughter lied.

"Or is it insomnia?" Chileshe gave her daughter a quizzical look. When her daughter didn't answer Chileshe suggested, "Luo, what do you want to prove? Anyway I've spoken; the rest is up to you."

"Oh Mum..." Luombe said. She didn't want to get into an argument with her mother.

Luombe had resigned herself to sticking it out, stay on in a marriage that had proved to be a nightmare from the first day, for Shadreck had not even spent his wedding night with his wife. He had gone to be with Felicia who was also among the invited guests.

Luombe knew that if she left Shadreck she would still make it on her own but how was she to sustain the sybaritic lifestyle that Shadreck gave her on a "silver plate?" She was now addicted to it; the fancy cars that she changed practically every month. The spacious mansion that sat on a ten-acre plot was well tended by five maids, three ground workers and twenty-four hour security. The furniture had been well-picked from as far as Italy. Luombe was given a huge allowance that she could spend throughout the month. She had travelled the world and could go on holiday to any part of the universe. The house was filled with the latest hi-tech equipment.

"No I can't leave all that," she thought and changed the subject.

"I've been reading this book entitled, *Desolate Altars* by Elizabeth…"

"Moloshi Chikwama," her mother finished for her.

"You know her? You've read the book?" Luombe asked excited.

"She was my great grandmother, well she was the cousin of my great grandmother," answered Chileshe.

"I read the story it was so…"

"Captivating?" Chileshe asked.

"Mum, is the story true?" Luombe asked leaning forward.

Chileshe stared at her daughter, "Fiction will never be gospel truth Luo."

"What if it is true, Mum?" Luombe asked.

Chileshe did not want to go into an argument with her daughter so she too changed the topic.

When the two women had talked for about an hour, the younger one looked at her watch and bid her mother farewell.

Chileshe did not go back to her gardening. She sat briefly thinking about what her daughter had started. She remembered her own mother's warning against treading carefully with matters concerning the covenant that their forefathers had started. But Chileshe had dismissed it as mere speculation by an old lady.

However, as Luombe drove home, she made up her mind to do something about her predicament. She was now very convinced that her marriage was under some sort of spell that she needed to deal with.

"I will make a trip to Sensela Village and try to find this altar," she thought.

When she arrived, back at her house, Shadreck was out as usual. Felicia's cooking was more palatable. He had blatantly told his wife over and over again. After a shower she went down to see what her chef had prepared for dinner. She sat at the huge ten-sitter dining table and practically pushed food down her throat. It was delicious but she did not really recognise any taste. Her mind was elsewhere fixed on the journey she intended to undertake to the north of the country.

"Surely someone would have a clue as to the location of Sensela Village, it must have existed."

After lingering on in front of the huge flat screen television for most of the evening, Luombe decided to retire to bed. As soon as she fell asleep, dreamland transported her to a place that she had never visited before, yet it felt and looked very familiar. The sun was just setting and she was standing on the bank of a river. She looked around and across she saw a group of young girls. They were naked apart from the loose raffia skirts that covered their waists. They wore beads around their necks and across the chest. Just as she was about to beckon for their attention, someone tapped her on the shoulder. She turned only to face one of the girls that she had seen across the river. How had she crossed? The girl was very pretty; her breathing rhythmically caused her soft breasts, which were covered scantily with beads, to rise and fall. Her dark, smooth skin glowed in the light of the setting sun. She had some kind of tribal markings on her cheeks.

After staring at Luombe for a while, she said, "You are Luombe, daughter of Chileshe."

Luombe nodded her head and asked, "May I know who you are?"

"If I were you, I would just listen," the girl continued, "you're not supposed to be here. Leave right away." It was an order.

"Who are you and what right do..."

"You are not welcome here," the girl interjected. "We know what you are looking for."

Then the girl broke out into laughter. It was evil, loud and deep like a man's – just then she was transformed into a grown man, her eyes, blood shot with deformed teeth.

"You see, your forefathers should have thought about the consequences of their actions, the pain and the suffering that their greed would bring to their descendants, to you." The man roared again, his voice reverberating across the river to the girls who also joined in the laughter.

Luombe, now on her knees, shook her head violently, "B...b... but I'm innocent, I ..." No one was listening.

"Do you think I was happy to lose my life at a young age?" The man was back in the form of a girl, bearing a very innocent countenance.

Luombe was shivering to the core; she could not sum up the strength to run. She remained fixed to her spot as if she was held in place with a huge peg. Just when she thought it was over, Luombe heard the sound of many babies crying. She looked in the direction of the noise and saw, on the river, many infants floating on the water.

The girl laughed a little longer and said, "Those are the children that you should have had; you, your mother, her mother and all the women before you."

Luombe was stunned into silence. When she turned to face the girl again, she was gone. So Luombe started to scream.

Just then she felt someone waking her up. It was Shadreck; she had not heard him come in. She looked at the clock; it was three in the morning. She sat up and looked at him, still confused by her dream. Shadreck stood in front of his wife, gazing at her expressionless. From the look of things, he was just arriving or had been standing there for a while?

He threw some papers at her and said, "I don't expect you to contest that. He hesitated and then added, "I want you out of my life; you are like an obnoxious weed. Felicia and the kids will be moving in soon. Don't do anything to delay the process." With that he walked out of the room, without giving Luombe an opportunity to respond.

Luombe stared at the door her husband had just closed and then looked down at the papers that were now on her lap. She was confused by everything that had happened; the dream and now a divorce? Shadreck could not have picked a better time. She sat in bed for a very long time, thinking. She thought about how life would be after leaving Shadreck. She wanted her marriage to work badly, more than anything in the world. Was she going to stand seeing Felicia with him? Was she going to allow another woman enjoy all the luxuries that were rightfully hers?

Just before dawn, Luombe rose from her bed and walked to the study, opened the safe, picked an item that Shadreck always kept locked away. She walked to the spare bedroom, where her husband was sleeping. After letting herself in quietly, she looked at him for a moment. He looked peaceful in his sleep, very handsome. Then she pulled the trigger, killing him before she turned the gun on herself.

The Desolate Altar still cries out today; cries out for a sacrifice that it has been denied for over five hundred years.

SIXTEEN

A Labour of Love and Hate

Richard Ali A Mutu

It was raining. Raining hard and harder. At the time, the two of you just kept on running. Running harder and harder. You had been running for days and nights. Indeed, running for survival, running towards the dark unknown. Running, running, running. What a macabre music, the sound of bullets rattling around in a mad rush towards death! You were all gasping for breath, collapsing on the ground. The forest was deep, the paths wet and muddy, but you had to run. You couldn't dance that morbid dance, not with death lurking in the shadows. Dancing! Yes, from beyond over there they were dancing too! They were dancing themselves into a sweat-drenched frenzy. Getting drunk. Cracking jokes. Drinking. Stuffing themselves with food. You had a hard time picturing it all. Yes, I know that too. You never wanted to run, nor dance to the cadence of death stalking you at each and every step. You were just born into the world then, just breathing the fresh air from the hills and the blue lakes. You kept saying yes to life with a smile. How beautiful life is in its pure state! The school was a few kilometers away from the house. Akili was running with you. You both loved to run, run, run. You both left the house running and came back home running. A curvy, banana-shaped smile on both your lips, your innocence warmly embraced the day and sang the joy of living.

Do you still remember that day, Furaha, when you did all you could to keep your white blouse clean? "Stop running, Akili! Stop it! You are going to mess up your uniform!" Akili was hard to wean away from his carelessness. He kept on running. Life is so much fun when children get all messy and dirty. Akili did not have to understand that Mummy toiled every day to wash both your clothes. On the other side, Aristide was playing too. He was running in the park. Aristide liked to play on the lawn so much. He was all covered in dirt, but never mind that: the babysitter will take care of everything. The washing machine was there, spinning around the clock. After all, Aristide was the "Little Prince" of the villa. He needed to grow up happily, the better to fulfill himself more completely.

The grasshoppers! You were so fond of them. You taught Akili how to wet forefinger and thumb with spit in order to catch dragonflies. It was so hilarious. Akili couldn't manage to catch a single dragonfly. You were making fun of him. He was quite annoyed and sometimes he cried. Ever the considerate sister, you calmed him down, took him in your arms, wiped his infant tears. To please him, you agreed to go for a run. Off you went then, running. Akili loved to run. The sun was smiling, watching the two of you run. Birds were chirping and waltzing in the scented atmosphere.

By then Akili had a sizeable lead. Indeed, he was outrunning you. That's when you decided to catch up with him. But he was getting away, further and further away. Akili ran just too fast, with his small legs. "He always runs so fast, my brother!" you once confided to the Maths teacher. Mr. Majaliwa told you it was normal, because he was a boy. Akili could run for hours and still not feel tired. He must have been born with steel lungs, the little kid who had been around for only a few years in this ancient land of hills and mountains.

You were racing after him when you suddenly realized he had vanished into the forest. "Akili! Come out my dear, stop playing hide-and-seek! Mummy is going to be upset if we go home late!" There was no use screaming so loud and so hard, only the sound of your own beautiful voice echoed back. Only the wind-swept foliage and the birds singing in its midst bothered to tell you where your little brother was hiding, but alas you were not yet schooled in the art of decoding the sounds of nature. Then you remembered Grandma Acha who, every night around the fire, used to tell you old stories, telling you that Mother Nature, too, speaks. She told you how lake waters spoke, how birds sang, how tree leaves whispered stories into the passing wind, how the bush palavered no end. Grandma Acha had grown very old, long before life started to flow out of her body. The day she died, it was you who found her agonizing on her reclining chair. Her pipe had fallen to the ground. She was struggling to keep the last breath of life from leaving her body, pressing both arms against her chest, as if to hold it in. You? You were standing there, all in tears and speechless, watching her. It was alright, you couldn't do anything about it. It was just time for her to depart this world.

Then you told yourself if only you could listen to the sounds of Nature for a few minutes like Grandma Acha knew how to. Alas, Nature left you as cold as a stone. She was still speaking loud and clear and yet you didn't hear anything. Akili too was still hiding. He so loved this game of hide-and-seek you had taught him. It was noon and the weather was so hot you began to blow your cool. You shouted Akili's name, really loud, but he didn't respond. Now his carelessness was really getting under your skin. "Akili, will you come out, please? It's time to go home." Nothing came of it. What if Akili had lost his way in the forest? What if some wild beast had attacked him? What if he had fallen in a ditch or got caught in an animal trap? Intimations of fear and fright started to run riot in your little head. It was then you remembered your mother always insisted that you two don't go play in the forest alone and unsupervised. When you started to think seriously about it, dripping with sweat... you heard a snap, followed by a shrill voice that could only be Akili's screaming for help.

It was still raining. The rain was pouring heavy and thick, crisscrossing all over the misty air. You were still running. You started to run out of breath. You fell awkwardly, your face smack against the ground, covered in mud from head to toe. You cried hard, feeling the pangs of labour. Nyota had noticed the sinewy tears already surfacing on the skin. With the help of two men, they brought you to rest under a tree. There was water flowing everywhere. Nyota realized that something had to be done right there and then, or else they would lose you. So she took swift action. You had to push hard. "Push!" she was screaming hard into your face, so you would hear it loud and clear. You felt weak, you couldn't even feel your body anymore. Already so drained of life, exhausted. "Push, Furaha, come on, push hard!"

Over there too, they were pushing. "Shake it! Move it! *Tindika! Tekinik!*" They were feverishly pushing and grinding to the timeless tune of Ya'Jossart's *danse du moellon*, at a party hosted by the super-famous "Bana-Kin." It was raining outside, but everybody was soaked in sweat from dancing nonstop. That's how they do it on weekends in Kin City. They were all there, sleeves rolled up, blood-red ties loosened, jackets tossed all over the place, eyeglasses set aside, cars parked and "hood locked..." Yes, they were dancing frantically, breathtakingly. You too, you were running low on breath, little by little, like it happened for Grandma Acha. Nyota was fighting tooth and nail to keep you from blowing your last pipe and quitting on life.

The government was offering free drinks to all passersby. Everybody could come and drink their fill. The bill had been tallied and settled in advance for all who would be stopping by tonight. As for you, you kept suffocating, labouring to push all you could, hard and harder. Every now and then, you would drink that filthy water...

"Push!" Nyota was screaming with more vigour, almost yelling now.

You had found Akili dying, all sprawled on the ground that was tinged in red with his own blood, a rusty machete stuck in his thorax. As you emitted a scream, you realized the shock had left you voiceless. The bastards! All they needed was five minutes to despoil your graceful body, do their dirty business. You were crying, on and on. Then you ran out of tears and your voice died out.

"Push!" They were slapping you in the face, hitting you in the stomach...

"Push!" They were shoving wooden sticks into your desecrated womb, each time harder and bigger...

"Push!" They had all met and decided to do everything in their power to make justice prevail, to achieve something, anything. "Enough is enough," they were saying wherever they went, to whomever cared to listen. "This must stop now! This guy must go!"

"Push!" They sounded so determined that nobody could doubt their courage and the ultimate outcome: the end of this ordeal, the end of this century-old disgrace…

"Push!" As if they were in a stage play or a real-life comedy, they started to discuss a replacement for the man-with-the-red-tie and to think of who would keep an eye on the ballots, finances, budgets and all that government crap they needed to bloat their bellies and strut like peacocks around the streets of the capital and across the world.

"Push!" Since to speak was in the order of nature, they got a conversation going… until they congratulated themselves on replacing the man-with-the-red-tie, then they moved on to another topic… He who wasn't supposed to have a single day of the office left was still there, his ass glued to the throne. As he watched them trample each other for a few crumbs of stale bread, he could be heard thundering loud smelly farts from the heights of his presidential orifice…

"Push!" The dancing went on and on, while the torrential rain would not let up. As you lay dying, you had to push your guts to get it all out, labour hard to give birth to what was malignantly planted deep in your entrails, without love. You had to push and push again, for the sake of someone or something you still do not know whether you should love or hate.

Was it an angel or a zombie that I harboured in my womb?

SEVENTEEN

Damn the Receipt

Maliya Mzyece Sililo

I always avoid that crossing because of the confusion that goes on there ... especially on Fridays after the Islamic prayers! It is a horrible crossing with four lanes on three sides and two lanes on one side. That is confusing enough, but let me make it clearer; there is Marble Road which is a four lane road. It crosses Independence Road, which has four lanes, two coming from the Lusaka central business centre and two lanes going into the same business centre. When Marble Road crosses Independence Road, it changes its name and status to Shamba, a two -lane road. This crossing is manned by traffic lights. Matters are made even more complicated by the filter lanes that add an extra lane on each side just as you are approaching the crossing itself.

The congestion on Marble Road was already bad and it was being worsened by the traffic from the mosque, it being a Friday. I jostled for space and was determined not to be pushed away from the middle lane, which is the one that crosses Independence Road, to join Shamba Road. But the jostling of cars for the middle lane was too much for me. Partly because of fear of getting my car scratched, I was rather forced into the far right lane, which gave me a chance to watch only cars on my left. I soon realised I was in trouble as the lane I was in was turning right. My thoughts were to move back to the middle lane before I got to the traffic lights, but horror of horrors, the traffic lights were upon me before I could manoeuvre my car back to the middle lane and they were green!

The wise thing to have done would have been to go with the flow and turn right hoping to turn left at the nearest turning from Independence Road so that I would have ended up in Shamba Road somehow. In my panic I didn't. Instead, a quick glance in the mirror showed me that I could cross Independence Road without anybody hitting me from behind and I put my foot down, swerved left into the middle lane before the on-coming car could block the space and I was in the single lane on Shamba Road. Then I saw them standing by the roadside.

Too late. One of them jumped on to the middle of the road stopping the car in front of me. I hoped against hope that they hadn't seen me and that they were after the man in front of me, but no. They were after me. The man in front of me was waved on and I was directed to park on the side of the road by a short fat police woman who looked as if she would burst out of her uniform.

She had a pretty round face and looked friendly enough. The bright red lips parted, *"A mai,* you could have killed somebody today."* She looked me up and down. Why did I feel like she was sizing me up? She swept her eyes on the contents of the car as her stare came up to my hands on the steering wheel to my face. She noticed my real wax chitenje suit. It was a birthday present from one of my sons. My well-styled hundred per cent human hair wig gave me that expensive old lady look. I vowed to myself that whatever happens, I would get a receipt for any payment I would make. I had heard too many stories about how people paid for traffic offences on the road and never got government receipts for it. I was determined not to encourage such vices and my body language must have shown the fact to all who cared to interpret it.

"I am sorry Madam." There was another pause as she inspected my face once more.

"What were you thinking, driving like that?"

"I am sorry Officer. I realise my mistake. I was wrong." I did not reach for my leather handbag that was lying between me and the passenger's seat. My eyes fell on the bag and so did hers.

"Mmmm. Just wait here!" With that she hurried away for other unfortunate motorists.

It was a hot afternoon. I was left to roast in the car for about thirty minutes when another officer came. She was bigger and taller with a painted mask for a face. All her emotions were hidden behind a thick layer of foundation. I recognised her as the one who had been keeping an eagle's eye on the flow of traffic and warned the other cop when she noticed an anomaly. They were well placed and a motorist could only notice them after crossing Independence Road. She peered at me through the window of my Mini Morris.

"So you are the crazy driver who almost caused a very serious accident?"

"I am sorry Ma'am."

"Do you know how many offences you have committed?" I decided not to answer that one.

"Three offences," she answered her own question. "Three offences;" she repeated for emphasis, "dangerous driving, failure to obey traffic rules and failure to keep to your own lane." I looked at her and wondered whether all these offences did not mean one and the same thing but I thought it wiser to keep my mouth shut. She peered inside the car ending with a long severe look at me and then she walked away to net in more offenders.

It was getting unbearably hot in the car. So I decided to get out and stand outside until I was told what my fate would be. I was now quite flustered by the heat when the short police woman with a pleasant face came back. The red lips parted to show a set of beautiful white teeth. "So where were you hurrying to *Amai*?"

"To work."

"Mmmm, sorry *Amai*. But do you know that the offences you have committed are very serious? You could have caused a very serious accident you know?"

"I know and I am sorry."

"Suppose a truck was coming your way, what were you going to do?" I looked down.

"Mmmm." She walked away and I found myself staring at her behind which was fully packed in her uniform. I wondered how she would run after a criminal in that tight skirt and with that weight.

At that moment, I thought of calling my grandson who was in

the Special Forces of the Zed Security Wing. I told him what had transpired.

"Which police station are the cops from?"

How, in the name of all that is sacred, does he expect me to know which police station these young cops were from? "I don't know."

"Find out?"

Honestly, he expects me to go to these ladies and ask them where they were from. What if they asked me why I wanted to know? What would I say to that? "I can't."

"Well *Ambuya*, all those police officers want is money. You know our officers *niba njala*. Give them a small amount and they will release you."

"They look well-fed to me."

"No, *Ambuya*. What I mean is that they want a cut."

"A cut of what?"

"Honestly, *Ambuya*, it is hard to speak with you, but if you want to get out of there soon, do the right thing."

"And what is the right thing?"

"Simple, give them money. Any amount will do…"

That struck a bell. "But how do I do that?"

"*Ambuya,* do I have to teach you how to do that? Look, granny, just do it."

I thought he still hadn't answered my question but I detected a note of impatience in his voice, so I said, "Okay."

"Okay. Just let me know how it goes."

"Okay." The line went dead.

I put my phone in my bag and looked at my watch. I have been standing in the hot sun for an hour. My feet were killing me. I wished I had used sandals and not these full leather shoes. The thought of getting back into the hot car was out of the question. I started exchanging which foot to put my weight on just to get some relief.

There was a queue of people going into a parked Toyota Noah just a few metres away from where I was standing. A young man emerged from there and was heading towards the car that was parked in front of mine. He took one look at me and I could read pity on his face. "You can be out of here quickly you know," he advised.

"How?" I asked.

"By doing the right thing." I looked at him, uncertainty written all over my face. "They will tell you what to do when you enter the Noah. Wear an amiable face and do as you are told and then you are home and dry."

"Have you, emmm... done the right thing?" He gave a flippant laugh, walked to his car and drove off.

I was more confused than before. I have never offered a cop a bribe. The closest I have been to doing that was when I offered a policeman a token of appreciation and even that was an idea that came from a clever Dick in the group I was in. We had organised a sponsored walk and we were given two police officers to escort us. We were told that we had to give the two officers lunch which they accepted with grace. The problem was with the two brown envelopes, each loaded with some money. We had been advised that it was standard practice to offer the police a token of appreciation after such a job. This we did even against my better judgement. One police officer refused to accept the money and told us that he was just doing his job and he was paid for it. I was so embarrassed that I wished the earth could open up and swallow me. The other policeman accepted it without batting an eyelid.

The situation was different now. From the stories doing the rounds in Lusaka, the police give you a hint that they expect you to do the "right thing," but no one has given me any hint yet; and if anybody dares, I would ask for a receipt.

"*Amai,* do you know that you will have to pay a lot of money for the three offences?" The voice brought me back to reality.

"I don't know."

"*Muza ona kusogolo.*" Pretty face was in front of me again. Her voice was as sweet as ever. Some of the netted vehicles were driving off and I was wondering if they had all done the "right thing" or were driving away with government receipts in their hands. I noticed that there were still people in the queue. I wondered when I will be finally sent to the Noah.

The heat was suffocating and I felt like someone had covered me with a thick blanket. I pushed the wig away from my face exposing some grey hairs on the hairline, but that wasn't enough to cool me. My neck was burning and sweaty. I pushed the wig up from my neck so that it perched on my head like an eagle's nest on an old gnarled tree.

I wondered why I was not being told the amount so that we could get it over with. My friend had told me that she was told right there and then when she was caught exceeding the speed limit. She got out the four hundred kwacha she had been told to pay for dangerous driving and gave it to the policewoman who in turn, took one hundred from the amount and gave her back three hundred. My friend was livid. She is one of those who takes pride in being upright in all her dealings. "I don't do such things!" "She had barked at the surprised police officer. "Just give me my receipt." The officer was so taken aback that she gave my friend back all the money and told her to go.

I admired my friend's courage. I had also made a vow that I would never offer a bribe to any police officer. So far luck had been on my side. Once when I was pulled over for driving at 65 kilometres an hour in a 60 kilometres per hour area on Kafue Road, my grey hairs or my little three-year-old grandson at the back seat of the car had saved me. A young policeman told me to go and see the *Bwana* that was in a police car parked by the side of the road. Beside the police car was a BMW which I assumed belonged to the *Bwana*. The young lady took one look at me and asked me where I was rushing to in such a hurry. I told her that I hadn't realised I had exceeded the speed limit, it being a Sunday and Kafue Road being very empty which was a rare thing. She reprimanded me but let me go after making me promise not to drive so dangerously. I drove at 50 kilometres an hour all the way home for fear of being caught again. It was my lucky day because our police are not that amiable. I have been told that if everything appears perfect on the car, they would ask you if you have a spare engine!

It seems I would not be that lucky with these two. My grey hairs did not move them. The time now was almost 16:30 hours. I was very frustrated. I had missed my appointment, my shoes were killing me and I felt like throwing the wig into the back seat of my car. Just then, mask face came towards me. She told me to get into the car and she would direct me where to go. I got all my faculties ready to rebuff all attempts at soliciting money from me.

It didn't get to that, dear reader. After turning right, then left, then left again, we turned into Sodom and Gomorra Police Station. All this way, I think we exchanged about three sentences, with the police officer. She was surprised that my Mini Morris' engine sounded so good. I told her that the secret to good performance of any car is regular servicing. As if scared that she was becoming too personal, she concentrated on barking out directions until we got to our destination and I was told to park my car behind the main building after which both of us got out.

I was directed to a crowded room. There were many Moslems of Somali origin. I could tell from their dressing; there were about four ladies covered from head to toe and about five men dressed in long white Islamic shirts. I realised it was a good day for catching out moslems, it being a Friday and they were coming from the mosque which was very close to the crossing.

In the midst of all these people was a young man, who I could tell was a native by his language. He caught my attention as I proceeded to a bench that had seen better days. He was the one being attended to by one of the three officers manning the office. I noticed that the young man looked agitated. The policeman did not seem to care in the least.

"Do not waste my time, give me the car keys," said the officer.

"I can't. I have to take the children home first. I will come back later." I took it the young man was a driver. Either he was employed or he was running his own taxi.

"That's not my business. You committed an offence and if you can't pay, you leave the car until you pay."

"Please *Bwana*, what do I tell my boss? She will be worried if she gets home and the children are not yet there…"

"*Iwe,* bring the keys here," said mask face joining in the argument. "*Mulongeni ngati acitathota.* How can you be wasting time on him? Lock him up." As if on cue, the young man was roughed up and pushed away from the room. The next thing I heard were a few hard blows landing on someone's body. I shuddered, as a pain shot through my back as if I were in labour. My palms felt damp and there was a fluttering movement in my tummy.

I was the next one on the other desk. It was just as worn out as the bench I had sat on earlier. The chair behind the desk was rickety and with my heart in my mouth I faced another police officer. She must have been given the offences I had committed for she just produced a piece of paper with all the offences on it. The list read as follows:

Failure to obey traffic rules: K300
Dangerous driving: K450
Failure to keep to a lane: K200
Total: K950.

Now that I had been told the amount, I found I didn't have the money. I blinked at the young lady behind the desk. "Madam, hand over your car key if you can't pay."

I did not dare to argue; removing the car key from the batch of keys, I handed it to the officer, I walked out of the office very disheartened and worried about the fate of the young man and that of my car. But I was so tired and just wanted to get home, take a bath and rest my aching feet. Then I saw an ATM machine across the road. It seemed a good idea to solve the problem and take home my old faithful. So I walked to the ATM machine only to find there was a queue.

It wasn't my day. We say in the local language that the day you are unfortunate, even a cold meal would burn your tongue. So I queued up for the money being the sixth in the line. I stood with my back against the wall so that I could push my heels against the wall to release the toes from the sharp pointed part of the shoe. The temptation was so great to take the shoes off.

After withdrawing the money, I hurried back to the police station. I found the room had been cleared and there was only the policewoman who had given me the bill. She was busy counting some money and seemed surprised when I walked in. I told her that I had brought the money so that I could take my car. She told me that the one with the receipt book was outside and that I should go and find her. I wondered what a receipt book was doing outside but I did as I was told. I could not see any uniformed person outside the police station but I heard voices in a make-shift building nearby. I followed the voices.

The make-shift building looked decent enough inside. It was a restaurant and the two ladies who had impounded my vehicle were having a meal.

"*Amai*, you are back?" said pleasant face in her usual sweet voice.

"Yes Ma'am. I would like to take my vehicle."

"You have brought the money?"

"Yes, Ma'am."

"All of it?"

"Yes Ma'am." I pulled out a chair and flopped down on it without waiting for an invitation. Meanwhile, mask face was quietly eating her meal without showing any emotion. They exchanged glances. I was so tired and fed up that I didn't care any more. All I wanted was for the whole thing to come to an end and I could go home with my car.

"*Amai*, you have been very good. Let me see if I can get my boss to reduce the charges. I feel sorry for you. You are remorseful and I feel, you did not do this deliberately." I didn't know what to say to that. So she went ahead and made a call using a humble apologetic voice.

"Yes, it's the old lady who has three offences... Well she is remorseful and I think she has learnt her lesson... We can drop the two charges and only leave dangerous driving. We can? Thank you Madam... Thank you Madam..."

She then cut the line and turned to me.

"*Amai*. You are very lucky. The boss has agreed to drop two of the charges. You can pay K450 for dangerous driving."

"I have no change. I have only 100 kwacha notes."

"Okay, give me the four hundred kwacha. I shall explain to the boss."

I counted four hundred kwacha into her hand and waited for the receipt.

"Unfortunately, the receipt book is far from here." Decisively,

"Thank you *Amai*. Here is the key to your car." She fished the key from her pocket and dropped it on to my outstretched hand totally ignoring the surprise that was registered on my face. What was my car key doing in her pocket? My mind switched to the receipt. What was she saying? …I should wait for the receipt while she was busy enjoying a meal; and what had happened to the receipt book that was supposed to be with her outside? Didn't she care that I was hungry, tired and sweaty and that my shoes were pinching me?

Damn the receipt.

Contributors' Biographies

Wole Soyinka – Professor of English Literature, playwright, poet and novelist is also a human rights activist who was awarded the Nobel Prize in Literature in 1986. From 1958, when he wrote *The Swamp Dwellers* to date, he has written over forty books that include plays, poetry, novels, autobiographical accounts and essays. He has two novels: *The Interpreters* and *Season of Anomy* and several plays: *The Lion and the Jewel*, *The Trials of Brother Jero*, *Jero's Metamorphosis*, *A Dance of the Forests*, *Kongi's Harvest*, *Madmen and Specialists*, *Death and the King's Horseman* and *From Zia with Love*. His poetry collections include: *Mandela's Earth and Other Poems*, *Samarkand and Other Markets I Have Known*.

Soyinka has been President of The International Theatre Institute in Paris, President of International Parliament of Writers and UNESCO's Ambassador for the Promotion of African Culture, Human Rights and Freedom of Expression. He has taught and given lectures at many universities around the world including Obafemi Awolowo, Ibadan, University of Ghana, Legon, Cambridge, Cornell, Harvard, Princeton, Yale, Columbia, Emory and Loyola Marymount in Los Angeles.

Baroness Valerie Amos – Joined the School of Oriental and African Studies, SOAS, University of London as its Director in September 2015. From 2010, she served as Under-Secretary General for Humanitarian Affairs and Emergency Relief Coordinator at the United Nations. She also served in a number of roles in the public sector including in local government and as Chief Executive of the Equal Opportunities Commission of Britain. Amos was an adviser to the Mandela Government on Leadership, Change, Management and Strategy issues between 1994 and 1998. She was appointed a Labour Life Peer in 1997 and became a member of the Government in 1998. She has been a Foreign Office Minister, Secretary of State for International Development, Leader of the House of Lords and Lord President of the Council. She also served as UK High Commissioner to Australia before joining the United Nations. In June 2016, she was made a Companion of Honour in the Queen's Birthday Honours list.

Pinkie Mekgwe – Executive Director of Internationalisation at the University of Johannesburg in South Africa. Prior to that, she was Deputy Director for International Education and Partnerships at the University of Botswana. Mekgwe previously worked in the Research Department of the Council for the Development of Social Science Research (CODESIRA) based in Dakar, Senegal, where she directed research on gender and the humanities and was responsible for growing multi-disciplinary research networks across African countries, between southern countries and trans-nationally. She also worked with the Universities of Sussex (Britain), Malmo (Sweden), Botswana and the Witwaterstand. Mekgwe's scholarly contributions have been in the areas of creative writing and literary studies, gender politics and media.

In public policy, she has also worked in other parts of Africa and Asia. A past Board Chairperson of the Botswana Media Regulatory Body, she currently sits on the Board of Gender Links, a southern Africa gender and media organization.

She holds a BA from the University of Botswana, an MA (Critical Theory) and a DPhil (Gender and Literary Studies) from the University of Sussex.

Kofi Awoonor – (late) A distinguished Ghanaian poet and for years Professor of Comparative Literature at the University of Cape Coast, the University of Ghana and in universities in the United States. Awoonor died tragically in Kenya during the Al

Shabab attack on the Westgate Mall in Nairobi whilst attending The Storymoja Festival in 2013. Author of several volumes of poetry including, *Night of My Blood*; *Ride Me, Memory*; *The House by the Sea, Until The Morning After, The Latin American and Caribbean Note Book*, his last collection published posthumously and edited by Kofi Anyidoho is *The Promise of Hope* (2014) which publication also served as the inaugural work of The African Poetry Book Series. He wrote the allegorical novel, *This Earth, My Brother.* In public policy and service spheres, he served as Managing Director of the Ghana Films Industry and for years was Ghana's Ambassador to Brazil and later a Permanent Ambassador to the United Nations in New York. He became a Minister of State under President Jerry John Rawlings and was the Chairman of the Council of State during the Presidency of President John Evans Atta Mills in Ghana.

Ama Ata Aidoo – Best known as an international award-winning playwright, novelist, poet and University Professor. She was from 2004 – 2010 Professor in Africana Studies at Brown University and before then, from 1993–1999 served as Visiting Professor, Department of English at Hamilton College. She has been Distinguished Visiting Professor, Department of English, Oberlin College, The Madeleine Haas Russell Visiting Professor of Non-Western and Comparative Studies, Brandeis University, Visiting Professor, English and Theatre Departments, Smith College, among several other positions. She has also taught at the University of Cape Coast and started her teaching career at the University of Ghana where she had earlier graduated.

Her famous works include: *The Dilemma of a Ghost* (1965); *Anowa* (1970); *No Sweetness Here* (1970); *Our Sister Killjoy* (1977); *Someone Talking to Sometime* (1985) which won the Nelson Mandela Prize for Poetry; *Changes: A Love Story* (1991), winner of the Commonwealth Writers Prize for Africa; *An Angry Letter in January* (1992); *The Girl Who Can and Other Stories* (1997); *Diplomatic Pounds and Other Stories* (2012). She is the Editor of *African Love Stories: An Anthology* (2006). In 2012, scholars from around the world honoured her with a Festschrift titled; *Essays in Honour of Ama Ata Aidoo at 70:*

A Reader in African Cultural Studies edited by Anne V. Adams and in 2014 a film, *The Art of Ama Ata Aidoo* produced by Yaba Badoe.

Sefi Atta – Was born in Lagos, Nigeria, in 1964 and currently divides her time between the United States, England and Nigeria. She qualified as a Chartered Accountant in England, a Certified Public Accountant in the United States and she holds a Master of Fine Arts in Creative Writing degree from Antioch University in Los Angeles. She is the author of *Everything Good Will Come, Swallow, News from Home* and *A Bit of Difference.* Atta was a Juror for the 2010 Neustadt International Prize for Literature and has received several literary awards, including the 2006 Wole Soyinka Prize for Literature in Africa and the 2009 NOMA Award for Publishing in Africa. In 2015, a critical study of her novels and short stories, *Writing Contemporary Nigeria: How Sefi Atta Illuminates African Culture and Tradition,* was published by Cambria Press. Also a playwright, her radio plays have been featured by the BBC and her stage plays have been performed and published internationally. Her collection of plays, *Sefi Atta: Selected Plays,* is forthcoming in 2017. "The Conference" is an excerpt from her unpublished novel titled *Made in Nigeria.*

Ogochukwu Promise – Director of The Lumina Foundation, Administrators of the Wole Soyinka Prize for Literature in Africa, received the 1999 Cadbury Prize for poetry with her collection, *My Mother's Eyes Speak Volumes,* while her novel, *Surveyor of Dreams* got the 1999 Spectrum Prize for prose, also in the same year. In 2000, she was awarded the Okigbo Poetry Prize for *Canals in Paradox* and she again won the Spectrum Prize for prose in 2000 for her novel, *Deep Blue Woman.* In 2002, she earned the maiden ANA/NDDC Prize with *Half of Memories* as well as The Matatu Prize for Children's Literature the same year with *The Street Beggars.* In November 2003, she won the Flora Nwapa Prize for prose with *Fumes and Cymbals* whilst her 2004 *In the Middle of the Night* won the first Pat Utomi Book Prize. Again, *Swollen and Rotten Spaces* and *Naked Among These Hills* were selected for the Flora Nwapa Prize for Literature as one of the three best poetry books in Nigeria respectively. Promise is an

Azikiwe Fellow in Communication as well as a Fellow of Stiftung Kulturfonds. She has enjoyed fellowships in the US, Italy and Germany and travelled extensively in Europe, Africa and Asia as a scholar, playwright and a poet. She is also an essayist and wrote, *Creative Writing and the Muse, The Writer as God, Dreams, Shadows and Reality* and *Wild Letters in Harmattan*. She does abstract painting and has exhibited in Nigeria. She holds a PhD in Communication and Language Arts from the University of Ibadan.

Ivor Agyeman-Duah – A Centenary Research Associate at the School of Oriental and African Studies at the University of London is the Development Policy Advisor to The Lumina Foundation in Lagos, which awards The Wole Soyinka Prize for Literature in Africa and from 2014–15 was Chairman of the Literature Jury of the Millennium Excellence Foundation. Agyeman-Duah was part of the production team for the BBC and PBS-*Into Africa* and *Wonders of the African World* presented by Henry Louis Gates, Jnr. He wrote and produced the acclaimed television documentary, *Yaa Asantewaa: The Heroism of an African Queen* and its sequel, *The Return of a King to Seychelles*. He was Chief Advisor to the Arts Council of England and Ford Foundation – supported theatrical production, *Yaa Asantewaa Warrior Queen* as well as Co-editor, with Peggy Appiah and Kwame Anthony Appiah of *Bu Me Be: Proverbs of the Akans* (2007); with Ogochukwu Promise he was co-editor *Essays in Honour of Wole Soyinka at 80* (2014). Agyeman-Duah has received fifteen awards, fellowships and grants from around the world including Distinguished Friend of Oxford Award from the University of Oxford and is a Member of the Order of Volta, Republic of Ghana, Fellow of the Phi Beta Delta International Society of the College of Arts and Letters, California State University, Pomona, US State Department International Visitor, the Commonwealth's Thomson Foundation Award, among others. Agyeman-Duah has held fellowships at the WEB Du Bois Institute for African and African American Research at Harvard University and been a Hilary and Trinity Resident Scholar at Exeter College, Oxford. From 2014–2015 was a Research Associate at the African Studies Centre, Oxford. He holds graduate degrees from the London School of Economics, the School of Oriental and African Studies, London and the University of Wales.

Boubacar Boris Diop – One of the most prominent African writers of his generation. He writes novels, drama and essays and is currently a Visiting Professor at the American University in Nigeria and before then was a Visiting Professor at the Gaston Berger University in Saint-Louis, the ETH University of Zurich and at Rutgers University in New Jersey. He has held seminars on Senegalese literature in Wolof, novel-writing and remembrance. Diop is a former Editor-in-Chief for *Le Matin*, an independent Senegelese daily and has for years collaborated with the Zurich-based daily *Neue Zürcher Zeitung* and the Italian weekly, *Internazionale*. He is currently a columnist of the *New African* in London. His works have been translated from Wolof into French and English and include *Murambi: The Book of Bones; Kaveena* (Indianan University Press), *The Knight and His Shadow; Doomi Golo: The Hidden Notebooks* (Michigan University Press) and *Africa Beyond the Mirror* (Ayebia Clarke Publishing Limited, Oxfordshire). His most celebrated novel, *Murambi: The Book of Bones* was listed as one of Africa's 100 Best Books of the 20th Century by the Zimbabwe International Book Fair in 2002 – the book was inspired at a writer's house in 1998 in Kigali during the Duty of Memory Project. *Doomi Golo,* originally published in Wolof in Dakar has been translated into French, English and Spanish. He has created at the Editions Zulma in Paris, Céytu, a literary collection named after Cheikh Anta Diop's birthplace and is translating into Wolof literary masterpieces from other languages.

El Hadji Moustapha Diop – A literary translator with a PhD in French from Western University in Canada (2016) and an MA in Comparative Literature from Brown University in the US (2010), translated Boubacar Boris Diop's contribution in this anthology originally written in French as *La Nuitde l'Imoko* and published here as "Good Night, Prince Koroma!" He also translated Richard Ali's contribution in this collection, "Labour of Love and Hate." Diop has done several translation projects in English, including the first biography of Sembene Ousmane, *Ousmane Sembene: The Making of a Militant-Artist* (Indiana University Press, 2010), short fiction from contemporary West African writers, essays and books by French and Francophone scholars. He recently co-translated Boris Diop's novel, *Doomi Golo: The Hidden Notebooks* (Michigan State University Press, 2016).

Zukiswa Wanner – A South African born in Zambia and currently living in Kenya was the 2015 winner of the K. Sello Duiker Award for her fourth novel, *London Cape Town Joburg* (2014). Her third novel *Men of the South* (2010) was shortlisted for the Commonwealth Best Book (Africa region) and the Herman Charles Bosman awards. Until September 2016, she was on the Board of the Pan African literary initiative, Writivism and is on the Advisory Board of the Ake Literary Festival. Wanner was one of the three jurors for the 2015 Etisalat Prize for Fiction and is the African Juror for the Commonwealth Short Story Prize 2017. She has facilitated writing workshops in Ghana, Tanzania, Kenya, Uganda, South Africa and Zimbabwe. She is a columnist for the continental publication from London, *New African and Saturday Nation* in Kenya and has been a guest-host for the monthly BBC Africa Book Club with Audrey Brown. In 2014, Wanner was selected as one of the top 39 African writers under 40 likely to change African Literature. She was also a 2016 Danish International Visiting Artist (DIVA).

Mary Ashun – Was born and raised in Ghana. Her father served in the diplomatic corps and for three years the family lived in London, beginning when she was six. After completing pre-tertiary education, she left for university in England, eventually immigrating to Canada in 1994. She earned her BSc from the University of East London, UK, her BEd from the University of Toronto and her PhD in Biochemistry from the University of Buffalo, New York. After several years of teaching at the primary, secondary and university levels, Mary now lives back in Ghana. In 2008 she won an African Canadian Women's Achievement Award for her work in education and her first novel, *Rain On My Leopard Spots* was a quarter-finalist in the 2010 Amazon/Penguin contest and later published as *Tuesday's Child*. She is the author of eight other novels for children and adults and also writes under pseudonyms Asabea Ashun and Abena Apea.

Njabulo S Ndebele – Chairman of The Nelson Mandela Foundation and the Mandela Rhodes Foundation, Chancellor of the University of Johannesburg and before then, Vice-Chancellor of the University of Cape Town. A Professor in creative writing and the First President of the Congress of South African Writers, he was for years, Visiting Scholar to universities and institutions in and outside Africa. His fiction includes: *"Fools" and Other Stories* which was awarded in 1984 the NOMA Prize for Publishing in Africa, *The Prophetess, Bonolo and the Peach Tree* and *The Cry of Winnie Mandela*. Non-fiction works include, *Rediscovery of the Ordinary: Essays on South Africa Literature and Culture (1991–2006)*; *Fine Lines from the Box: Further Thoughts About Our Country*. Ndebele has received many awards and fellowships including a Rockefeller Foundation Residency, honorary degrees from South Africa, United Kingdom, The Netherlands, Japan, United States and a Fellowship at Churchill College, Cambridge University (where he had previously studied for a Master of Arts degree in English Literature); Cape 300 Foundation Molteno Gold Medal for Services to Literature and Education in 2015. He holds a PhD in Creative Writing from the University of Denver.

Louise Umutoni – Writes short stories and poetry. She has published in anthologies including *Boda Boda*. She is also a media consultant who recently established the Rwanda based publishing house, Huza Press and is running its first short story prize. Umutoni has worked as a regular reporter and contributor for several newspapers and magazines including *The Gazette* and *Ottawa Citizen* in Canada, *The New Times of Rwanda, Rwanda Focus* and *Enterprise Magazine*. She is also a scriptwriter and radio presenter. In 2008, Umutoni won the award for Best Arts and Culture Journalist at the Rwanda Golden Pen Awards. Umutoni graduated from the University of Oxford with an MSc in African Studies where she researched on National Liberation Movements in Africa and Women's Political Inclusion which was selected for the Winihin-Jemide grant. She is currently working on a book that looks at the role of women in National Liberation Movements in Rwanda, Eritrea, Ethiopia, Uganda and Kenya and is passionate about narratives from Africa and the importance of having African voices as part of conversations about the continent.

Lionel Ntasano – Was born in Burundi and raised in Zambia but currently lives in Bujumbura. He attended university in the United States, Switzerland and Kenya earning a Bachelor's Degree in Management and a Masters in International Business. He runs the Nonara Beach Resort in Bujumbura. As a voracious reader since childhood and an avid follower of the philosophical school of Stoicism, he decided on writing as a therapy and wrote his first novel, *Greener on the Other Side* to great reception.

Monica Arac de Nyeko – A member of the 2017 Judging Panel of the Caine Prize of African Writing is a Ugandan writer currently based in Jordan in the Middle East. She won the Caine Prize (2007) for her story, *Jambula Tree* published in the anthology, *African Love Stories* (Ayebia Clarke, 2006). In 2004, she was shortlisted for the prize for her story, *Strange Fruit*. Nyeko is a Member of the Uganda Women Writers Association (FEMRITE). Her works have appeared in several anthologies including, *Words From a Granary* (FEMRITE Publication 2003), *Memories of Sun* (Green Willow Books 2004) *Seventh Street Alchemy* (Jacana Media 2005), *All the Good Things Around Us* (Ayebia Clarke Publishers Oxfordshire 2016).

Bwesigye Bwa Mwesigire – A Ugandan lawyer and writer whose short stories have appeared in *Africa Roar 2013*, *New Black Magazine*, *Kalahari Review* and others. He co-founded the Pan African Writivism Literary Initiative and directed its activities between 2012 and 2015. He was awarded the Harry Frank Guggenheim Foundation Young African Scholar Grant in 2015 and in the same year enrolled in the African Leadership Centre's Peace, Security and Development Fellowship.

Mukuka Chipanta – An aerospace engineer and author currently living in the Washington DC metro area. Born in Zambia, he spent his formative years in the mineral rich Copperbelt Province near the border with the Democratic Republic of Congo. Chipanta has several degrees in engineering and business from the United Kingdom and the United States. Chipanta was part of the integral team that designed the Boeing 787 Dreamliner airplane and has travelled widely across North America, Europe, Africa and Asia. His published debut and well-received novel was *A Casualty of Power* (Weaver Press 2016).

Wame Molefhe – A writer from Botswana, her fiction has been published in local and international journals, anthologies and online. *Just Once* (Medi Publishing 2009), a children's collection of short stories is her first book. *Go Tell the Sun* (Modjaji 2011) is her second short story collection. *Blood of Mine*, a story from this book was recently adapted into an opera and performed in Cape Town at Artscape. Molefhe has written a column for the *New Internationalist* of London and travel writings for television and radio.

Kafula Mwila – Born in 1969 in Zambia, her writing has been partly inspired through travelling. Her two published novels, *Deflowered* and *Shorn Lambs of the City* were in 2009 and 2012 respectively. Mwila has taken part in many writers' residencies including the 2012 Uganda African Women Writers Residency organized by Femrite, and in 2016 the Caine Prize Writers Workshop. Among her published stories are: "Tighten Your Belts" and "77 Steps."

Richard Ali A Mutu – Better known as Richard Ali – is a Congolese writer living in Kinshasa. He was among the 39 best young Sub Saharan African writers under 40 revealed by the anthology Africa39, whose preface was written by Wole Soyinka. He won the Mark Twain Prize in Literature in 2009. Ali writes in French and in Lingala, one of Africa's most prominent languages. His latest novel, *EBAMBA, Kinshasa Makambo*, written entirely in Lingala, has been translated and published in English by *Phoneme Media* as *Mr Fix-It*. For some time now he has been participating in initiatives from various literary platforms, including Jalada, Writivism, Pen – RDC, etc. Founder of La Plume Upcienne and of the association of young writers of the Congo (AJECO), and presenter of a TV literary show B-One, Littératures, he currently works as the Head of the Wallonie-BruxellesLibrary in Kinshasa.

Maliya Mzyece Sililo – Born in Chipata in Zambia, she has published a novel, two short stories with FEMRITE of Uganda, four children's stories and several English textbooks. A teacher of English Language as a Foreign Language at Evelyn Hone College in Lusaka, Sililo, born in 1952 has been involved in script writing for the popular Zambian soap, *Kabanana* and is one of the writers for the television channel, Africa Magic's *Love Games*.

Acknowledgements

This collection, like an earlier one before it – *All the Good Things Around Us* which was also published by Ayebia Clarke Publishing Limited in Oxfordshire in the UK enjoyed tremendous patronage from some of the masters of the short story and younger emerging talent. *The Gods Who Send Us Gifts* is published in two editions – in Europe and United States with distribution in South Africa by Ayebia Clarke Publishing and internationally. The East African edition is to be published by Louise Umutoni at Huze Press.

I would like to thank first, Nana Ayebia Clarke MBE, the Managing Director of Ayebia Clarke Publishing Limited and my regular UK Publishers over the years and her husband David and as always, thanks to their editorial staff especially their regular academic Editor Dr Kwadwo Osei-Nyame Jnr in the preparation of the manuscript for this anthology. I am also thankful to the Director of the Huze Press, Louise Umutoni for the East Africa edition and her recommendation of some of the contributors.

Appreciation is also due to Sarah O Apronti who read through the manuscript and made useful editorial comments.

Currently a Research Associate at the Centre of African Studies of the School of Oriental and African Studies, I will want to extend sincere gratitude to the Centre's Manager, Angelica Baschiera and her assistant, Anna De Mutiis as collaborators of the Conference at which this anthology will be launched at the Brunei Gallery in October 2017.

Ellen Aaku-Banda the award-winning Zambian author, contributor to *All the Good Things Around Us*, was Juror of the

Macmillan Prize for African Writing and Instructor over the years in creative writing. She was very helpful even under difficult circumstances as an Advisor on contributions from southern Africa.

Of all the stories only two have previously been published: Njabulo S Ndebele's *Death of a Son,* first published in 1996 and Monica Arac de Nyeko's *Grasshopper Redness* which was first published in *Seventh Street Alchemy: A Selection of Works from the Caine Prize for African Writing* by Jacana Media, 2006. Kofi Awoonor's poem, *Those Gone Ahead* originally published as part of the collection, *Herding the Lost Lamb* (2013) is re-produced in *The Promise of Hope: New and Selected Poems, 1964–2013* in the inaugural African Poetry Book Series by Amalion Publishing. The Publishers also wish to acknowledge *Chimurenga Chronic* for their kind permission to reproduce the collated photo image of the 1962 Makerere Conference delegates on the front cover of this Anthology. In addition, I would thank the individual Contributors for their interest in agreeing to making their stories part of this memorial anthology.